YOUNGBLOODS

SCOTT WESTERFELD

■SCHOLASTIC

Published in the UK by Scholastic, 2022
Euston House, 24 Eversholt Street, London, NW1 1DB
Scholastic Ireland, 89E Lagan Road, Dublin Industrial Estate, Glasnevin, Dublin, D11 HP5F

SCHOLASTIC and associated logos are trademarks and/or
registered trademarks of Scholastic Inc.

Text © Scott Westerfeld, 2022
Cover art © Aykut Aydogdu, 2022

The right of Scott Westerfeld to be identified
as the author of this work has been asserted by him under the Copyright, Designs and Patents Act
1988.

ISBN 978 1407 18831 7

A CIP catalogue record for this book is available from the British Library.

Printed by CPI Group (UK) Ltd, Croydon, CR0 4YY
Paper made from wood grown in sustainable forests and other controlled sources.

1 3 5 7 9 10 8 6 4 2

www.scholastic.co.uk

Jacket and book design by Christopher Stengel

To everyone we've lost.

PART I

HIDEAWAY

Those who play with the devil's toys will be taught by degrees to wield his sword.

—R. Buckminster Fuller

BRAND-NEW

Before they start, the doctors put me in a coma—it's safer that way.

Then they turn me into someone new.

They take out my bones, replace them with unbreakable alloys and spacecraft-hull ceramics. The muscles that I worked so hard to build are stripped away, whipcords of smart plastic threaded in their place.

The surgeons give me tougher skin, dotted with reservoirs of healing nanos. My nervous system is retrained; my reflexes honed to the flitting speed of insect wings.

They ramp up my pain threshold, extinguish all my fears, paint a calm landscape over my grief. My heartbeat is steadied to a slow, undeviating march, except when I need it rampant.

I get a new face—not the one I was born with, but mine alone. My twin sister no longer needs a body double. She has a whole city to protect her now, an army of her own. And I don't want to see Rafia of Shreve in the mirror anymore.

3

She killed Col, the boy I loved.

Besides, my new crew likes to fly under the radar. The last thing we need is another famous face to hide.

I step from the surgery tank a new person. Faster and stronger than I've ever been. Less breakable, more dangerous. Someone the world has never seen before.

I'm Special now.

Just like the rest of Tally Youngblood's crew.

Dear Little Shadow,

I hope this ping finds you. I hope the others have too.

Wherever you are, whatever you're doing, I'm still missing you.

The last three months have been hard. I'm free of him, and Shreve is finally mine. But without my little shadow beside me, none of it feels real. Everything I've ever wanted is finally in my hands, and you aren't here to share it.

You were supposed to protect me forever, not run away.

I always thought that once Dad was gone, Shreve would fix itself. But it seems more broken even day.

The free cities were happy to help destroy him, but they've been slow to help us rebuild. They all know who I really am and what I did—Diego's troops recorded what happened that night—so they make me beg and barter for aid.

They'd be more obliging if you were here beside me.

I was wrong to steal your name, I know. But I needed that extra distance from the old days. The citizens need continuity, a familiar face, but also an excuse to go on loving me.

You were the perfect option.

Trust me—I'm paying for my deception. It was fun when I only had to fool some rebels in the wild. But running a city is much trickier.

I have to be both of us at once.

Candid and crafty. Deadly and wise.

Victim and hero.

Because I am the hero in this story, little sister—there was no choice. Throwing that knife was the only way to save our city.

I'm not sorry that I did it, only that it hurt you so much.

And that it was *him* forcing me to hurt you. Just like when we were littlies, and I had to pretend you weren't real.

Back then, I never forgot you were hiding in our room, waiting for me to free you. When the rest of the world didn't know you existed, I held you dear.

It was *you* I was saving that night from his bomb, more than anyone else.

Don't hold me guilty for our father's last crime.

—Rafia of Shreve

BOSS TALLY

Six hoverboards skim down the dried-out river, low and fast.

We're on silent magnetics, pushing against the minerals in the dusty streambed. Boss Tally is in the lead, taking us down the mountainside at a breakneck pace.

I ride carefully, as gracefully as I can. This is my first real mission with the Youngbloods.

It's been almost three months since Tally came to visit me in the hospital, where I was recovering from the Fall of Shreve, the violent end of my dictator father.

My body was already wrecked, irradiated by his last play for power—a dirty bomb made from dug-up Rusty nuclear waste. So when Tally offered me a chance to join her crew, turning Special seemed easy enough. The surgeons had already stripped me down to the bone.

As a bonus, it made me even more different from my twin sister, the murderer.

Flying down this streambed, a thousand new instincts animate my body, new reflexes, new tricks. When Croy's board glances from the ground ahead, a flurry of dirt rises in his wake, and the old me wants to blink. But my transparent inner lids flick shut—eyes protected without even a millisecond's loss of vigilance.

The rush of our boards echoes from the riverbed stones in my exquisite new hearing. The reflections situate me in space, like I'm a bat navigating the darkness.

This Special body is so powerful—this strength, these ceramic bones. My lizard brain screams, *Slow down*, as the trees blur past.

I cling to the graceful sight of Tally hurtling down the slope ahead of me. Most Specials' movements are uncanny, insect-like. But Tally is effortless in flight, like she was born on a hoverboard.

Her surgery is still old-style Special, a cruel beauty. An avenging angel of history, arrived to save the present from my sister—I hope.

All the Youngbloods look like their images in the history feeds. Two decades older than when they began the revolution, but still ready to take on the world.

No one's told me exactly why Tally and her crew disappeared from view for ten years. I only know they never stopped protecting the wild.

That's why we're out here tonight—hunting poachers.

All at once, Tally leans into a skidding halt. A sudden expanse of treeless dark looms beyond her.

The edge of a cliff.

I bank hard, throwing my board sideways, feet slipping on its surface. My lifting fans spin up with an ear-rattling shriek.

Too late. Momentum carries me past Tally and the others, out over the yawning blackness. My echolocation senses a two-hundred-meter fall beneath me, full of trees.

That's twice the altitude my board can maintain, and heavy forest is the worst for hard landings.

As I start to fall, an ancient, instinctive fear of gravity hits. But it's off in the distance, somewhere in the discard pile of my pre-Special emotions.

Shiny new reflexes kick in, my left hand flicking a rope made of smart matter from my belt. It uncoils, snakelike, and wraps itself around a gnarled tree stump projecting from the cliff. A swift tug pulls me closer, and my board's magnetics grasp the iron in the mountain.

The board slowly regains altitude, wafting back to the edge.

I stare down at my hands. They should be shaking, but the ragged buzz of adrenaline has already drained away. This new body is a sieve, shedding doubt and fear like water.

Tally's crew is lined up along the edge of the cliff. None of them seem concerned that I almost crashed into the darkness below. The only clue that any of them noticed is the smile on Boss X's face.

My first real mission with the Youngbloods, and I look like a bubblehead.

I land and step off onto the stones, which are smooth beneath my grippy shoes—this cliff was a waterfall before the river dried up.

The smart rope slithers back around my waist, along with a stray piece of memory. Before the operation, I was afraid of snakes.

That's gone too.

Only grief seems to stick to me, the memory of Col dying in my arms. The rage against my sister, gathering quietly in my marrow.

Tally angles her board, drifting toward me.

"Nice trick," she says.

She thinks I almost crashed on purpose?

A dozen ways to misdirect her come to mind, to make myself look less brain-missing. No surge can cut away a lifetime habit of pretending to be something I'm not.

But this is Tally Youngblood in front of me—the first rebel.

And I'm done with lies.

"Wasn't intentional. Didn't spot the cliff in time."

She shrugs. "Yeah, the wild can make you focus-missing, after you first turn Special. Don't let the stars distract you."

We both look up.

My new senses have transformed the night sky. The stars have gone wild, the Milky Way turned into a sheet of white fire.

My enhanced vision discerns it all—the smudged-ember galaxies, the piercing stares of planets and planetoids, the binaries teased apart with a squint. Even the Extras' space habitat is visible, geostationary among the flitting comm satellites, its solar panels splayed like hexagonal wings.

But the dazzling sky isn't why I failed to spot the cliff. I was too busy watching Tally.

My tenuous new ally, powerful enough to help me against my sister.

"Sorry, Boss."

"It's all right, Frey. We just rewired your brain." Tally looks out at the valley before us, crowded with old-growth trees. "But keep your eyes on the forest. Poachers love these moonless nights."

I scan the horizon, looking for hovercraft or drones.

Nothing but birds, insects, and a scattered haze of pollen lit with starlight. The treetops wave in the cold wind, like an anxious, roiling crowd below us.

Boss Tally stays beside me, and I wonder if she has more to say. I've been riding with the Youngbloods long enough to understand the personalities and rhythms of the crew. But Tally and I haven't had a real conversation yet.

I'm younger than the rest of them, the daughter of a deposed dictator, a total unknown. Tally only let me join because Boss X was part of the deal.

I guess he's just plain X, now that he's a Youngblood. He used to have his own crew, who fought beside me and Col against my father. He was a famous rebel boss, but he gave up his rank to help me.

It was X who brought Tally to my bedside when everything was lost. After my father fell, the other cities let Rafi take over Shreve, though they'd promised the city to me. Even after she murdered Col.

They don't realize—she's not a replacement for my father.

She's an extension of him.

X and I have no allies left with the power to fight her, except the Youngbloods.

Tally catches me staring at her.

"You have a question, Frey?"

"Yes, Boss," I say. "How do we know the poachers plan to hit this place?"

She hesitates, long enough for me to wonder how much the Youngbloods really trust me. All I know about tonight's mission is that we're on the trail of crims who cut down old-growth forest under cover of darkness. It's classic Rusty behavior, killing ancient trees for profit. Overnight a habitat is destroyed, turned into luxuries stamped with the unmistakable mark of wealth.

An ecosystem died to make this chair. Doesn't that feel . . . *fancy?*

The attacks have made the global feeds, but the free cities haven't done much to stop them.

So the Youngbloods are here.

"We don't know where they'll turn up next," Tally says. "But this is the last big stretch of old growth in the area."

"We aren't that far from Shreve," I venture.

"Yeah. And it all started three months ago."

Exactly when my sister took over.

Poaching is a quick and dirty way to make money, which the broken city of Shreve sorely needs. Maybe Rafi's becoming a watered-down version of our father, more bandit than warlord, murdering trees instead of people.

I try not to sound too eager. "Growing up, Rafi had a lot of rich friends with expensive tastes."

Tally nods but doesn't look convinced.

Sometimes it seem like only Boss X and I understand the danger my sister represents. He was there the night Col died, Rafi striking him down to distract our father.

Col's life . . . traded for a *diversion*.

The anger inside me sparks for a moment, flashes through my body. Its passage marks every muscle, every centimeter of skin, a sudden flush of fever.

A minute ago, I almost went over a cliff, and it only took seconds for the arid calm of being a Special to descend again. But my rage, my grief, never eases. It's buried too deep inside, a defeated general in a bunker, plotting revenge.

My most powerful ally against my father, the intelligent city of Diego, saw everything Rafi did that night. But they don't care about Col Palafox or my broken heart. The free cities just want everything back to normal.

Which means Rafi in control of Shreve, like she was raised to be.

Tally reaches out to brush my eyebrow, jolting me back from my thoughts.

"You had a scar here, right?"

"Yeah," I say. "My sister got cut in an assassination attempt. Our doctor had to mark me too, to keep us exactly the same."

Tally turns away, staring across the forest. For a moment, I think she's considering the dark bond between me and Rafi.

But then she says, "I knew that assassin."

I feel unsteady on my feet.

The assassin was Seanan, my long-lost brother—who died by my hand the day I got this scar. He was also the love of Boss X's life.

"You and X go back that far?"

Tally nods. "His parents were rebels. He grew up in the wild."

"Huh," I say. "That explains a *lot*."

"I met your brother a few times. He was pretty intense."

I don't know what to say.

Seanan was kidnapped by my father's political enemies when he was seven years old. When our father wouldn't pay their ransom— surrendering power—Seanan was given to the rebels to be raised.

Growing up among them, it makes sense that he would meet the most famous rebel of all.

Until that day in the hospital, I didn't have a clue that X knew Tally Youngblood. But I suppose that's how she's stayed hidden for the last ten years: the silent loyalty of her friends.

"I guess that's why you're helping me," I venture.

"Who says I'm helping you?" A shrug. "This is about your sister— she pretended to be a rebel when all she wanted was power. That's bogus."

"That's who she is," I say.

Tally gives me a cool smile. "And you're her mirror image."

"Same genes," I say. "Different upbringing."

She nods at this—everyone knows my story by now. How I was

raised as a body double for Rafi, a bodyguard, sniper bait. Our father didn't even give me a name.

And then Rafi stole the one I made for myself.

"You never thought of taking your father's place?" Tally asks.

I again make the decision not to lie.

"The free cities offered to put me in control. It was the only way they'd help us overthrow our father. But then Rafi found out they'd offered Shreve to me, and decided I was her enemy."

"So did your sister betray you?" Tally asks. "Or did she *out-play* you?"

I hold her gaze. Maybe she thinks I'm just like Rafi, in love with fame and power, only not as clever.

I search for the truth inside me, trying not to get lost in the tangles of my own deceptions. All those years pretending to be my sister, I assumed that a life with no secrets would be simple.

Turns out living the truth can be just as tricky as lies.

"There was a part of me that cared about ruling Shreve. But Rafi killed it when she murdered Col Palafox."

Tally puts her hand on my shoulder, wearing an expression I haven't seen from her before. I see where grief has worn itself into her perfect features.

In all these years of fighting, she must have lost people too.

Tally gestures at her own eyebrow, where a flash tattoo pulses, covering an old wound. "I'm glad you got rid of your scar. Didn't need another one in the crew."

"That's my new goal, Boss," I say. "Being one of a kind."

Tally smiles. "As long as you're not trying to be me."

Before I can ask what she means, someone shouts from along the cliff—Shay, the crew's second-in-command.

"There's something in the trees!"

CEREMONY

I focus my eyes on the forest below us.

Whatever's down among the trees, it doesn't give off much infrared—no pulsing engines or flickers of body heat. Millimeter-wave radar shows no reflections.

But something's definitely out there, stirring a stretch of treetops against the grain of the breeze.

My new ears hear only the wind. How are they cutting down trees without making a sound?

"Your father's leftover arsenal," Tally says. "He had stealth tech, right?"

I want to implicate my sister, but it doesn't quite make sense.

"He was more into intimidation than sneaking."

She steps onto her board. "Then I guess we take a closer look."

"Careful, Boss. The ground's at least two hundred—"

"Watch this," she says with a smile . . . and tips her board off the edge of the cliff.

The other Youngbloods slide away into the dark.

I have no choice but to follow. I shake my crash bracelets to make sure they're awake, and jump.

A two-hundred-meter fall takes less than seven seconds, but my brain spins up fast, driven by the sudden acceleration of my heart.

Dropping hard on a board, you normally just hoverbounce—the lifting fans create an air cushion between you and the ground. But the cushion doesn't form until those last ten meters.

By then I'll be crashing through the trees, set tumbling by the branches, pine needles jamming my fans.

Was I supposed to bring a parachute?

The others aren't even trying to slow down—they're angling their boards forward, bending downward momentum into speed across the treetops.

I follow their lead, but we're still dropping way too fast.

My eyes find Tally, falling two seconds ahead of the rest of them.

Just before she crashes into the forest canopy, she jumps up from her board. It unfolds beneath her, solar panels expanding in the starlight.

I expect the wind of her fall to tear the unfolded board to pieces, but Youngbloods use only the best tech. The solar panels form something halfway between a wing and a chute, catching the air. She settles back onto the huge contraption and takes control of it.

The others follow suit, the huffing sounds of unfurling boards like a flock of vast birds beating their wings.

I leap up into the rushing wind, giving the tongue click that tells my board to recharge. The panels unfold in an instant, the whole apparatus air-braking, rearing up beneath me. My feet slam hard onto the grippy surface.

For a split second, there's only pain—that impact would've broken my old legs. But my ceramic bones and plastic ligaments hold, and the agony slides away like water.

A moment later, I'm surfing the tops of the trees, silent and fast, riding a kite the size of a swimming pool. And thinking . . .

Col would have loved this.

My board refolds itself under my feet, like a present neatly wrapped.

The disturbance in the treetops is only half a klick ahead of us now. A cut has formed in the forest canopy, as one needled crown after another is sucked down into the dark.

We sink into the treetops, out of sight. There's no sign that the poachers have spotted us. Maybe they're too busy killing trees to notice six giant butterflies made of glistening solar cells.

Shay takes over now. She's in charge of the Youngbloods' operations, talking more than Tally in tactical meetings.

Shay's drill sessions are tough, as hard as anything I got growing up. But I like her more than my old tutors. Her criticisms sting but don't bruise.

Turns out, she taught Tally herself how to ride.

Right now she's all business. "Frey and X, take the far side. Hand signs only. Don't let anyone get away. We don't want to hurt them . . ."

But we will if we have to.

"Got it, Shay," I respond.

X is already in motion, skirting the wounded area of forest. Following, I watch him slalom through the trees with new appreciation.

Before we joined the Youngbloods, I never thought of Boss X as a Special. But of course his lupine body is as complete a rebuild as mine. His strength and reflexes aren't just wolflike; they're superhuman.

Like Tally, he moves gracefully, without the inhuman skitter of too much surge. Maybe years of sleeping under the stars turn even Specials into something wild.

I still can't hear the poachers, but from this distance, I can *smell* something—burned toast. Like they're cutting the trees down with heat lances. But there's still no glimpse of infrared.

We reach our spot. With a hand sign, I signal Shay that we're ready.

Then we sink deeper into the trees.

X scents the air. "Nanos."

Microscopic machines—that sounds like something from my father's collection. I was expecting monstrous engines with steel jaws, not a cloud of synthetic termites, but ancient weapons take all forms.

A sound reaches us—voices, small and shivery in the wind.

"Is that *singing*?" I whisper.

X gives me the barest nod. We move forward.

Our hoverboards slip silently among the branches, pine needles brushing my arms.

My eyes start to sting. X was right—that's the scent of nanos, a trillion molecule-size reactions cooking whatever's around them.

We pass over a stack of felled tree trunks, hoverlifters attached. Their bases are shorn away smooth, no sign of the jagged edge of a blade. The branches and bark are stripped neatly bare.

X eases to a halt in front of me, and I glide up beside him. We're at the edge of a clearing, peeking out. The singing comes from right in front of us.

A ring of figures stands around a tree, holding hands. I can't see any faces—they're dressed in sneak suits. But through their masks I can see their mouths are moving.

The song is full of gibberish words.

The figures seem oddly tiny to me. Maybe they're Smalls, a wild clique who surgically reduce their size. But the whole point of being Small is to require fewer resources, to put less strain on the planet. Poaching doesn't quite fit that strategy.

As we watch, the base of the tree begins to tremble, like water coming to a boil. The shiny-clean scent of pine billows over us.

The towering tree begins to tilt.

On our side of the clearing, two figures drop hands and take measured steps away from each other. The circle splits, opening into a U, and the song shifts to a higher key.

As if responding, the tree tips toward the gap and tumbles gently over, like a flagpole stuck into soft mud. Its full branches cushion the fall, a rain of knocked-loose needles ringing through the forest.

As the tree settles, the singers shift gracefully into a different song. They're guiding the nanos with sound, but the singing isn't just a control mechanism. Every step is measured, every gesture artful.

It feels more like a ceremony.

The shimmering nano haze climbs from the base of the fallen tree up the trunk and into the branches. It covers the whole pine, all of it glowing softly, like a decorated holiday tree.

The branches start to fall, a hundred invisible blades at work. Then the bark slides away, leaving the trunk bare, as pale and shiny in the starlight as a naked corpse.

My Special ears detect a creaking, the settling of the slow pulse of water inside the tree—a death rattle.

I've been mesmerized by a killing.

This beautiful ceremony is also a crime.

At that moment, the clearing explodes. Tally bursts from the trees at the far end, the lifting fans of her board spinning up. The carpet of pine needles whirls into an eye-stinging tornado.

My inner lids slam shut as Tally cries out, using a Special voice I haven't heard before, full of anger and broken glass.

"Take them! Take them all!"

TREE KILLERS

The figures scatter into the trees.

The six of us split up to chase them down.

It hardly seems fair. We're Specials, soldiers forged in the crucible of war, expert hoverboarders, and they're—

A lot faster than I thought they'd be.

They must have lifters on their feet. Each bounding step is huge, like astronauts in low g. They careen through the trees, staying below the thick upper branches that slap my face and hands.

I fly lower, my board skimming the forest carpet. I've lost track of X and the others, all my focus on one fleeing figure in front of me.

They're even smaller than I thought—not even up to my shoulder.

I close in, matching my swerves to the zigzags of my quarry. My fingers reach out to grab the hood of their sneak suit.

The figure puts on a burst of speed, and the hood slips down.

She looks over her shoulder at me, eyes wide.

Is she . . . *a littlie?*

The girl flings something away into the trees. I'll go back and get it later.

Right now, I'll swoop closer until—

Whoom.

I'm off my board, spinning in midair, crashing to the ground. Tumbling through the leaves and pine needles until I come to a sprawled, ungainly halt.

A thousand thunderbolts shoot through me—bruised bones, pulled muscles, broken skin igniting. It takes an awful count of five for my nervous system to flush away the pain.

I lie there, skin abuzz with the healing nanos spilling from their reservoirs. My mind tries to clear away the shock.

What hit me?

Then I see it, strung between two trees—a dark line at the height of my knees. Exactly where the littlie threw something.

A smart plastic trip wire.

My legs are on fire, nanos working around my left knee. I try to move it, and fail.

Something swims into focus above me—a face.

The girl staring down at me looks about eleven years old.

"Um, are you okay?" she asks.

I start to answer, but an awful slithering feeling in my knee interrupts.

Something connects—the bones reconnecting. My left leg can move again.

I sit up. "Who are you?"

24

She stumbles backward, looking surprised that I can move at all.

"Wait." I reach out, but the girl turns and bounds away. The hover lifters on her shoes blow pine needles in my face.

My hoverboard nudges me, an apologetic pet. I stand, still shaky, and step back on.

This time I climb higher, up to the clear air above the trees. I'm not going to risk catching one of those trip wires at neck level. My healing nanos might be able to weave bone, but I doubt they can put my head back on.

I fly in the direction the girl was headed, lying facedown on the board, peering into the trees below.

There—a glimmer of body heat.

The girl's forgotten to pull her sneak suit hood back up. I zoom ahead, then bring my board to a banking halt in the treetops.

I cut power, falling straight down through the branches, bringing along a cascade of pine needles. At the last second, the fans spin up, and I roll off and land on both feet.

The girl is soaring through air at me, flailing in an effort to redirect herself.

I take two steps to the right, and she collides with me, a tiny ball of fury. Wrapping myself around her, I hold on tight, pinning her arms to her sides. The lifters in her boots try to pick us both up, but I'm too heavy.

"Let go!" she screams.

"I don't want to hurt you," I say, leaving out the rest.

She's so light in my arms—this isn't some kind of camo surge. She really is a littlie.

Why are kids killing trees?

She stops struggling, a low growl slipping from her lips. "You're going to get us all in trouble!"

"No kidding. You can't just kill trees."

"That's not our fault. The supplies stopped coming!"

"Supplies?" I pull away a little. "How old are you, anyway?"

"Almost twelve."

"It's called eleven." I open up my comms to the rest of the Youngbloods. "I've got one, Shay-la. She's a littlie!"

"Same here," comes Astrix's voice—she's the Youngbloods' tech specialist.

X reports that he's managed to grab two of the child poachers. Croy wound up knocked off his board, thanks to a trip wire.

"I got one too. Can't be more than twelve," Shay says. "Boss?"

"Still following the rest of them." Tally's voice is distant in my ear, mixed with the wind of fast flight. "Stay put and guard your prisoners. I'll let you know where the others wind up."

"You got it, Boss. And watch out—these little miscreants are dangerous. Youngbloods, meet back at the clearing. Shay-wa out."

My comms go silent.

The girl in my arms has gone limp, except for the sobs shaking her small frame. I set her down, keeping hold of her arm.

My reactions are jumbled, the healing nanos still buzzing in my brain. I'm a Special now, my emotions too smooth to experience doubt or panic in the heat of action. But my battle frenzy is fading.

And the sight of a littlie in tears is shaming.

"What's your name?" I ask.

"Goose," she manages through the snuffles.

"Okay, Goose. Take those lifter boots off. And stop crying—they don't put eleven-year-olds in jail."

"Shows what you know."

I stare at her. "Someone's definitely in trouble for this, but not you. Someone *made* you do this, right?"

"We had to do it. So we don't wind up like our parents."

A chill goes through me.

Goose swallows, fighting to say the next words.

"Are you going to take us back to Shreve?"

CHILDREN OF TRAITORS

Shreve.

I don't want to believe it. But the girl has the right accent, and the poaching started three months ago.

"What happened to your parents?" I ask gently.

Goose crumples a little. Her weight shifts from foot to foot.

"I got us all in trouble. It was my birthday, when I turned nine. When I blew out the candles on my cake, I said my wish out loud!"

"I don't think that's illegal, even in Shreve."

"Depends on the wish."

A shiver goes through me—the ice of my father's hand again.

Under his regime, the air in Shreve was full of surveillance dust. It saw everything you did, heard everything you whispered. Your whole life was recorded, saved, and judged.

"What did you ask for?"

Goose hesitates. "To live in Seatac, where my mom grew up. She didn't like Shreve anymore, since the man started talking."

I can't speak. Goose misinterprets my silence and thinks I need an explanation.

"When I was little, the man started talking when you did something wrong. Lying, or littering, or getting facts wrong. He'd correct you."

She's talking about my father. Or rather, a facsimile of his voice, speaking for the AI that surveilled the citizens of Shreve. Enforcing the laws, but also the rules of dress and speech and custom.

"Your mom didn't like the man," I say.

"She hated him." Goose starts to breathe harder. "We took walks when it rained, and she told me she wanted to go back to Seatac."

A hard rain washed away surveillance dust. All of Shreve had a few hours of privacy, when it was safe to speak your innermost thoughts.

As long as you didn't repeat them when the sun came out again.

"I wasn't supposed to talk about it when *he* could hear," Goose says. "But it was a birthday wish!"

A sob comes, and I remember the words Rafi used to say to me. "It's not your fault."

"But someone came to the door *that night*. Mom and Dad told me to go to bed, to not listen. The next morning, I woke up in a place called Hideaway. A nice crumbly man said that Mom and Dad were on a trip. But they never came back."

"I'm sorry," I say.

"Am I in trouble again?" she asks. "For cutting down those trees?"

I shake my head.

"We used to only to take one at a time." Goose is pleading with me now, like I'm the final arbiter of every injustice she's been subject to. "But our supply deliveries stopped, and the minder said we had to get more trees—or starve."

"Three months ago, right?"

She nods. The Fall of Shreve.

"The minder told us it was the only way to get food. We don't know who takes the trees. We stack them outside, and they're gone in the morning."

Someone knew about these abandoned children and didn't save them, just used them to make money.

If it was my sister, the free cities will cut her off. No more reconstruction aid. Her own people will turn on her.

But Rafi wouldn't risk it. X and I have a spy close to her, and we haven't heard a whisper of this.

"Shreve is different now," I tell Goose. "We got rid of the bad man."

She stares at me, not believing.

"All the old recordings have been erased," I say. "You can say your wishes out loud now."

A war of expressions crosses her face—confusion, a flicker of hope, then distrust. "What are you going to do with us?"

I take gentle hold of her hand.

"We're going to Hideaway to get the rest of you. And then we're going to take you home."

Tally pings us an hour later.

"Found the poachers' base."

"Stay clear," Shay says. "This could be tricky."

Tally laughs. "You think I'm afraid of *littlies*?"

"It's not what it looks like, Boss," I break in. "They're prisoners."

Tally doesn't answer for a moment, the line crackling with the noise of repeater towers.

"Okay, I'll wait. But whatever's going on, those little bubbleheads better have a good excuse."

We lift off toward Tally's coordinates, each of us sharing our hoverboard with one of the captured littlies.

They seem to be enjoying themselves, staring at the open sky. It's probably been a long time since they've traveled above the cover of the trees.

My mind is stuck in a loop, remembering the night the free cities finally moved against my father, wrecking his army, bombarding his city from orbit. Creating the vacuum that allowed my sister to take power.

Col and I spent most of the battle rescuing Boss X. In the same prison, we found hundreds of people who'd vanished during my father's rule. For ten years, everyone who threatened or disobeyed him disappeared. Traitors to Shreve.

We should have wondered where their children were.

We land in a steep-sided valley, high walls of stone on either side. A shallow river reflects the stars.

A figure melts out of the darkness in full stealth gear.

Tally pulls off her hood. "What's this about?"

Everyone turns to look at me—the expert on Shreve. The daughter of the man who stole these children.

I'm silenced by the weight of their stares, especially the littlies, watching from outside the circle of Youngbloods.

Tally's voice softens.

"Tell me what you know, Frey-la."

It's the first time anyone's called me that. The Youngbloods are a strange mix of fierce faces, lethal bodies, and silly nicknames. They fight like hurricanes and talk like new pretties.

The gentle words unfreeze me. I descend into the awful logic of my father's mind again.

"When people committed treason in Shreve, their children weren't adopted out. The whole family vanished. It looks like the kids got sent here, to Hideaway. For some reason, they weren't freed after my father fell."

Tally's eyes have gone cold. She stares across the dark water to the other side of the valley.

"What do we know about the defenses?"

"One of the kids said that there's no human staff," Astrix says. "Just an AI minder and drones. Maybe the whole thing's on autopilot."

"But someone must know about it," I say. "Someone doesn't want this place exposed, Boss. Remember my father's dead-man switch?"

There's a silence.

When the world was finally closing in on him, my father filled his tower with nuclear waste and high explosives. He threatened to blow it all into the air, poisoning Shreve for a thousand years.

My father never lost at cards—not when he could overturn the table.

Tally looks across the water again. Her eyes travel up the far side of the valley, where a large, precarious outcrop of rock darkens the sky.

"The littlies went through a door under that cliff." She turns to Shay. "It could be rigged to avalanche. We get them out tonight. Make a plan."

Shay gives a dry laugh. "Tonight? Forget it. We need satellite imagery, more gear, some drone recon. Give me a day, Boss."

"You have an hour," Tally says. "They must be wondering already why the rest of their crew isn't back."

"More reason to be careful, Boss. They'll have lookouts!"

"Worse," I say, squinting at the rocks across the river. "There's dust."

Back in Shreve, you could only see the surveillance dust at sunset. All those microscopic machines would give the light a metallic glint. My new eyes are seeing something like it here, a glimmer in the starlight. And my nose can just catch its scent, like soot in a fireplace.

"Shay," Tally says softly. "Every minute we delay, the AI worries a little more about being exposed. Maybe it decides to erase this place before we make our move."

The two of them fall silent, staring each other down. No one else dares to speak.

Not for the first time, I wonder exactly what the history is between Shay and Tally. There's clearly a deep trust, long silences side by side at the campfire. But everyone once in a while, a vast anger rumbles between them, like a distant waterfall.

I'm not sure they actually *like* each other.

For a moment, I think we're all going to stand here for the rest of the night.

Then the oldest boy speaks up.

"Are you really . . . ?"

He's staring at Tally, of course. All of them have been since she appeared, like someone stepping out of a history book. The woman who changed the world, who ended the pretty regime and made the mind-rain fall.

Now that they've heard her voice, they believe who she is. Just like I did the moment she walked into my hospital room.

"Tally Youngblood," she says. "Who are you?"

"Tigerboy," he says. "I know where the big bomb is. Some kid showed it to me the day after I got to Hideaway."

TROJAN HORSE

Thirty minutes later, Shay has a plan.

It starts with Astrix releasing a handful of microdrones into the air, glowing fireflies that wink out as they cross the shallow river. They'll map the approaches, search for traps and sensors, sneak into Hideaway's comm system and electrics.

X and Tally head up the river, dressed in full sneak suits. Once they've crossed a few klicks upriver, they'll scale the rocks on the other side. Their job is to take out the "big bomb" that Tigerboy saw.

That's why this deep valley was chosen for Hideaway—one landslide and my father's crime is buried. Along with any clues about who kept the poaching business going after his fall.

Once the bomb is deactivated, Shay and Croy will attack Hideaway's defenses head-on.

My job is easy: lie down and be injured.

We make the littlies build the stretcher themselves so it's convincingly crappy. It's made of interwoven branches, with a lifter secured to each corner. It looks like it can hold my weight—uncomfortably.

Not that I'll be noticing a few pine needles in my back.

I rub dirt into my face, a few leaves in my hair, like I took a hard spill from a fast-moving board. My sneak suit is set to the color of a forest ranger jacket.

I climb on the stretcher and settle myself.

The five littlies take me across the river.

Tigerboy leads us to the shallowest crossing. The other four guide my hovering stretcher, their feet slipping on wet stones. There's no sign of Shay following, underwater in her sneak suit.

Staring up at the stars, listening to the littlies' splashing steps, I wonder again about Rafi.

When she took control of Shreve, she learned all my father's secrets. She's revealed plenty to the world already—a hoard of ancient Rusty nerve gas, a squad of psychopath Special commandoes, a network of spies left behind in the city of Paz—weekly reminders that she's different from our father.

But if she kept these children from their parents, all those revelations will mean nothing.

The splashing stops—we're still on the river, about a hundred meters from Hideaway's entrance in the rock face of the valley wall.

My mouth goes dry. Even with my new nervous system, I'm not looking forward to the next step of Shay's plan.

She appears beside me, a sneak-suited shadow in front of the stars.

"You ready for this?"

"Probably not," I say.

"Correct answer." I can hear the smile in her voice.

She takes firm hold of my left foot—and breaks my ankle.

When my brain comes back from the rush of pain, we're moving fast.

The littlies are running—they have to reach Hideaway's scanners before my ankle heals itself. Shay said she'd "make it messy," so the nanos will take longer.

It feels messy. Behind the shriek of pain is a sickening, bone-on-bone grinding. Every jostle of the stretcher makes it worse.

Combat stimulants are spilling into my veins, but the whiplash between agony and adrenaline only makes me want to puke.

I curse Shay with every jolt. She chose me as the infiltrator because I'm the closest in age to the Hideaway littlies, the most likely to gain their trust—a wounded bird rescued and brought home. But at this moment, I'm pretty sure she doesn't like me.

We reach the gate. Tigerboy is calling for a med drone.

I hear a long scrape of rock. Light spills across us.

A moment later, the stretcher beneath me is gliding, mercifully steady, its lifters stabilized by the house magnetics.

"Welcome home," an AI says. "But I see you've brought . . . a visitor?"

A dozen overlapping answers spill from the littlies in a torrent. But all that reaches my ears is the sound of the AI.

Of course he did.

The minder for these lost children has my dead father's voice.

HIDEAWAY

"She hit one of our trip wires," Tigerboy explains once the rest of them settle down enough for explanations.

Goose bobs her head. "You should've seen it. She went down *so* hard!"

The littlies who met us at the door are staring at my ankle, wide-eyed and sickened. I try not to imagine it twisted at a rag-doll angle.

Nanos are already buzzing down there, fixing torn ligaments and ruptured blood vessels. But they're too tiny to shift the bone back into place. We Specials are trained to do that for ourselves.

I just lie there, the air in my lungs swirling with pain.

"Can you save her?" Tigerboy asks.

"From a broken ankle? Hardly life-threatening," the house minder says. "You should've left her. That's the first rule."

"But she's breathing wrong!" Goose cries.

I put some extra effort into my gasping, like I've punctured a lung.

"Very well," the minder says in my father's bored voice. "Clear some space for the med drone."

As the littlies pull back, I wonder how this AI was programmed to deal with intruders. My father never used machines that were clever enough to think for themselves. They were only extensions of his will, not sentient beings in their own right.

Probably the minder will contact a human to decide what to do with me. It won't just murder someone in front of its young charges.

I hope.

The med drone arrives and starts with a standard body scan—passing over me from head to toe. As if delirious with pain, I flail an arm, slapping a nano patch onto the machine's underside.

The drone shudders in midair as the nanos spread out across its innards.

The microscopic battle lasts only seconds. Astrix's nanos over-whelm the drone's self-diagnostics, and it continues down my body, ignoring my ceramic bones and plastic muscles, my toughened skin. All the things that make me dangerous.

"You have a badly broken ankle," it says.

The AI might have surveillance dust and a hundred layers of defenses, but this med drone is programmed to fix sore throats, acne, and broken arms. As Shay expected, hijacking it was simple.

"The bone needs to be set," the machine says. "This may hurt."

"Let me do it." I sit up.

The littlies recoil, like I'm a corpse coming back to life.

When I see my ankle, a fresh wave of nausea rushes into my throat. My foot is pointing ninety degrees away from true. I'm going to have to talk to Shay about overkill.

But my nervous system locks down the wretch-making feeling.

I give the ankle a sharp twist, then fall back screaming.

The littlies throw a bash.

Out comes a swirl of dessert rations—chocolate bars, milk and cookies, cupcakes capped with spiraling towers of icing. A pink drink that smells like cinnamon and maple syrup. For the older kids, jars of jalapeños are passed around.

They may be too young for bubbly, but sweets and hot peppers make a party.

Soon the littlies are sugar-rushing, squealing at the tale of hoverboards bursting out of nowhere, the poaching party having to flee.

Forest rangers! Trip wires! A wolf-man!

I can't blame them for being excited. In all their years of poaching, it's the first time anyone's actually come after them. And they got away—at least that's the story. Shay and Tally were worried that our five littlies would spill the truth to their friends in Hideaway. After all, they've just met the most famous rebel in the world. But these are the children of Shreve dissidents.

They know better than anyone the price of leaked secrets.

They leave me lying in the middle of the party, like a fallen Viking warrior at her own wake. My ankle is almost healed, but I pretend to be half-conscious, knocked out by painkillers. The med drone checks on me every ten minutes and pronounces me too fragile to move.

Now all there is to do is wait, while Tally and X defuse the self-destruct system.

It's taking longer than scheduled. In the big picture window that faces the valley, the sky is starting to turn red.

"What's your name?" one of the littlies asks me. He looks about fourteen, on the older end of the littlies here.

I'm tired of false names, so I play the tough prisoner. "What's yours?"

He hesitates a moment. "Spider."

"Do you all go by animal names here?"

"Sure—we aren't city kids." He stands up taller. "We take care of ourselves. The minder barely does anything. I'm basically in charge."

I look around at the chaos of the party, the chipped furniture and carpet stains that cleaning drones can't fix. The walls are marked with the gouges and scars of past parties.

It looks like no one's in charge.

"Someone told me that a nice crumbly man shows up now and then," I say.

Spider shrugs. "He hasn't been here for a couple of weeks."

Two weeks, not three months. So it's not just the house AI on autopilot—someone in Shreve is still running this place.

Maybe someone in my sister's government.

"Like I said, we take care of ourselves," Spider says, earnest now. He takes his responsibility for the other kids seriously.

Just like me, when I was little. I was a captive in my own home, brutally trained to serve my father's purposes. But protecting Rafi was my only identity for sixteen years, so I clung to it.

Until Col saw something more in me.

"Sometimes it's okay to be afraid," I say softly.

Spider frowns at me. "Of what? *You?*"

"You're a bunch of kids."

Spider narrows his eyes, and for a moment, I think he's going to argue. But then he laughs in my face and leaps up onto a chair.

"Hey, everyone! Let's show our guest some *tricks!*"

A ragged cry goes up from the littlies, bubbly with sugar and having stayed up all night. They form a circle in the center of the room.

One of the girls sings a high, clear note, and the others join in. It sounds like an orchestra tuning up, dozens of voices gathering around one pitch.

Spider waves for silence, then counts off four beats. The littlies start a quick-tempo song, the same gibberish syllables that they were singing out among the trees.

Sparkles appear in the air, fizzing to life over our heads. As the singing firms up, the lights grow steadier.

A burnt smell reaches my nose, and I notice that a few of the lights have drifted to the edges of the room. They bounce gently off walls, leaving scorched marks.

Of course—the poachers controlled the tree-cutting nanos with their voices. The littlies must practice here at home, learning to bend the tiny machines to their will.

The nanos fill the air here in Hideaway, like weaponized dust.

If these nanos can fell and strip huge trees, what can they do to *people?*

Spider looks down at me from his chair, a confident smile on his face. And suddenly I realize—he and his littlies will fight us. Not out of obedience to the warden AI, but to protect their home, their tribe.

Just like I protected my sister.

I flex my sore ankle, getting ready to move. If the Youngbloods come crashing in now, they'll be running straight into a swarm of deadly nanos.

I can't ping Shay without the AI noticing. But there must be another way to warn them . . .

I'm still wondering how when the lights go out.

RESCUE

Spider yells above the cries of confusion.

"Hideaway? What's going on?"

The minder answers in my father's voice.

"No power, no comms—clearly sabotage." A pause in the darkness. "We are under attack."

The littlies' singing has fallen apart, the sparkles in the air fading. But Spider yells from atop his chair, "Okay, everyone. Let's get some lights on before—"

I roll from the stretcher and kick out the legs of his chair. Spider falls hard to the ground. His grunt of pain is followed by some spectacular swearing.

In my thermal vision, I spot two combat drones sliding into the room at ankle height. The AI minder intends to neutralize me first.

I fling off my ranger's jacket and pull up my stealth hood, disappearing in the dark. Then I bring my knife to full pulse, let it carry me buzzing over the littlies' heads, a giant insect. The fading nanos in the air hit my masked face, still stinging hot—definitely dangerous.

I fly up to a corner of the ceiling and perch on a storage shelf, sneak-suited and out of the way. With a flick of my wrist, my pulse knife skitters randomly across the ceiling. The combat drones fire a volley of knockout darts at it.

Perfect—these drones are designed to subdue rambunctious littlies, not Specials. Knockout juice barely affects me, even if those darts pierce my suit.

But I still have to worry about the nanos. Spider is back on his feet, wiping blood from his face. He's trying to get the singing organized again. The room rings with a single vibrant tone as the littlies tune up.

I glance at the room's big picture window—nothing but a glimmer of sunrise in the sky. Where are Shay and Croy?

The pulse knife flits back into my hand, and I throw it at the combat drones. It slices one in half, then sweeps around to take out the other.

Three more drones hurtle into the room. A needle hits my arm—I barely feel it through my sneak suit.

But the littlies are singing now, the tree-stripping nanos glowing around me again. In my thermal vision, the nanos are as bright as tiny suns—hot enough to cut though the trunks of old-growth trees.

More and more fill the air, pinning me against the ceiling.

I can't use my pulse knife against children.

The glowing nanos light up my dark corner. Spider, standing on his chair again, spots me and points.

"There she is—get her!"

The singing shifts in tone, and the galaxy of tiny suns converges on me. The air grows hot.

Then I see it—a huge open jar of hot peppers on the table below. They're mostly eaten, only a last few jalapeños bobbing in liters of juice.

I squeeze my knife to full pulse, throw it down into the jar, and pull my mask up.

My knife instantly superheats the jalapeño juice, transforming it into steam. It billows out explosively, shattering the jar—the room fills with hot, lung-shredding smoke.

Even behind my rebreather mask, my eyes burn with tears.

The song is instantly silenced, all the littlies reduced to coughing. Their eyes clamped shut, they stumble in all directions.

A crash drowns out their cries—Croy on his hoverboard smashing through the picture window. The sudden rain of safety glass adds to the confusion and panic of the littlies.

My hoverboard is following Croy's, on autopilot. I jump down from the shelf onto its riding surface.

Croy stares at me a moment, not sure what's wrong—then starts coughing.

"Mask!" I yell.

He pulls his rebreather on.

"What the hell?" he asks, his eyes already bright red.

"Had to stop them singing. They were going to chop us down like trees!"

"So you *gassed* them?"

"Where's Shay?" I ask.

"Second floor, rounding up the youngest—they were asleep up there. Astrix is on the roof, taking out the comms. The boss and X are headed down."

I nod. "So it's all under control."

Croy looks around at the coughing, blinded kids. The minder is still yelling at them to fight us, the combat drones still flinging knock-out darts in our direction.

"You have a weird idea of *under control*," he says.

"It's called improvising." I throw my pulse knife, taking out two more drones.

"With a gas attack?" He shakes his head. "Is this your first war crime?"

Croy is deadly serious.

He's also right—the littlies look they can barely breathe. I hope none of them missed their asthma meds this morning.

They were going to cut me in half with logging nanos, I don't say.

"Go down and help them," Croy says. "I'll clear the air."

He angles his board over to the broken window and braces himself against the frame. His lifting fans fire up, and soon a gale of fresh air is spilling into the room.

I spot a bottle of milk on the refreshments table—that was always Col's cure for too many hot peppers.

I drop down and grab the bottle, then look for Spider in the tumult. He's huddled on his chair. Flying over on my board, I gently tip his head back and dribble milk into his eyes.

They open, red and weeping.

He pushes my hand aside. "Do you know what you've *done*?"

"Yeah, sorry. Didn't realize the peppers would work that well."

"Not that! The house minder can't let us be discovered—you're going to get us all *killed*!"

"Relax. We know about the big bomb. My friends have already disarmed it."

He stares up at me, tears still streaming from his eyes. "The bomb's just to scare the littlies. The real fail-safe's much worse."

"The *real* fail-safe?" I ask, but Spider's answer is lost in a fit of coughing.

The ice of my dead father's hand runs down my spine. His plans never ended when you thought they would—there was always one more turn.

I listen to the chaos around me. Crying and coughing, damaged drones skittering on the floor, the shriek of Croy's lifting fans as they clear the air.

But the AI's voice is gone.

It's given up on the littlies.

I hear something deeper, a grinding noise, stone against metal—a bigger version of Hideaway's hidden front door. The air starts to rumble around me and Spider.

"What's coming?" I ask.

He clears his throat. "I've never seen it. But an older kid said it's sleeping in the rock. Like a person but much bigger. It's called Titan."

I hand him the bottle of milk. "Get everyone out of here."

I jump back on my board and fly past Croy, through the picture window and into the open sky. The grinding sound is colossally loud out here.

Halfway up the valley's rocky side, a door is opening.

TITAN

I pull my mask off for a breath of fresh air.

The door opening in the rock above me is two stories tall.

I break comm silence. "Youngbloods! There's another fail-safe!"

Tally's voice is in my ear. "A bomb?"

"Some kind of war machine, big enough to wipe this place out."
I fly higher, up toward the opening. "I'll have eyes on it in a few . . ."

Something sparks in my thermal vision, a servomotor burning
megawatts of power. It occurs to me that Titan means *big*.

A shape is stirring in the dark mouth of the cave.

"Frey-la?" Tally asks.

"One second, Boss."

A huge form lumbers into view, more creature than machine. It
has arms and legs and a head with eyes glowing bright blue.

But it's just a drone, I remind myself, not a monster.

"Some kind of heavy walker, Boss. Eight meters tall, heavy armor."

"Firepower?"

"Can't tell yet. But it's big enough to—"

The walker reaches out an arm toward me, something flaring to life in its palm. Two smoking streaks of light jump from the darkness toward me.

"Seeker missiles!" I cry, and cut my hoverboard's power.

I drop to my knees, clinging to the board as it starts to tumble through the air.

In free fall, the night spins around me, stars and dark earth trading places again and again. I calmly calculate my rate of fall—I'll hit the ground in three seconds.

The two missiles shoot past, so close that their exhaust burns my skin.

But they can't see my board with its engines cut, and head off screaming into the night.

I twist in midair, spinning up my lifting fans. They shriek to life, straining to bring me to a halt before I hit the trees.

The black earth rushes up at me—slower, slower.

My board brushes the treetops, lifting fans churning out a spray of pine needles. But soon I'm regaining altitude.

"I've got you, Frey-la," Astrix's voice comes.

I start to ask what she means, but then I see the missiles.

They've arced back around, homing in on the heat of my lifting fans.

I jump off, kicking the board away from me. It slides along the treetops as I fall, grabbing for a branch. My arms wrap around wood, my head full of pine scent and panic. The branch bows under my weight, lowering me gently into the trees.

But my board is still too close. If those missiles airburst at this range, I'm dead.

Suddenly the shadows are dancing around me—a sparkling galaxy has appeared out over the river. Astrix's recon drones have burst to life, burning all their energy at once.

The missiles veer away toward them.

Seconds later, two sharp explosions echo through the valley. Billows of deadly shrapnel spray out, riddling the river's surface like rain.

"Thanks, Astrix-la," I say.

"Told you not to worry."

My hoverboard drifts back to nudge my foot, and I step on.

A fresh rumbling noise comes from above. High on the valley wall, the Titan is skidding down the slope toward Hideaway.

"Frey, is that thing army of Shreve?" Tally asks. She and X are in view now, tiny on their boards above the Titan.

"No, Boss. Shreve doesn't use walkers."

"So who built it?" X asks.

I have no answer. With its bulky armor, the Titan *looks* like something from my father's arsenal. But he'd never let an AI control anything so powerful.

Could it be some kind of battle suit? With someone inside?

If so, they must be drunk. The machine looks clumsy and uncertain as it descends the broken terrain of the valley wall.

Spider's words come back to me: *It's sleeping in the rock.*

Has this thing just . . . woken up?

"Whatever it is, kill it!" comes Shay's voice. "We aren't evacuated yet. Somebody gassed these kids!"

Yeah, that was me.

I fly up for a better vantage—the littlies are streaming out of Hideaway, Croy and Shay corralling them.

The Titan will be there in another thirty seconds.

But I've got no weapons that can pierce heavy armor. I'd need a railgun to stop this thing.

Then I hear the sound of X's pulse lance.

It rattles the air like my knife, but a dozen times louder. He's diving down the valley wall, a surfer descending a wave of stone.

X sweeps past the Titan, the lance throwing out a shower of sparks from its ankle.

There's no visible damage—the armor's too thick. We have nothing that can damage this machine.

But when the walker plants its next step, its foot twists wrong, the ankle servos failing. The leg skids out from beneath the tons of metal.

The war machine lands on its backside and starts to slide down the valley wall. Pulverized rocks billow out behind it, like smoke from a spreading fire.

It looks like the walker will slide all the way down onto Hideaway. But one of its flailing hands grabs a gnarled tree growing out from the rock.

The massive shape skids to a precarious halt.

The dust cloud of its passage keeps rising up, turning bloodred with the rising sun.

53

It reaches its free hand toward Hideaway . . .

"I'm out of drones!" Astrix shouts.

I urge my board toward the littlies streaming from the fortress.

Croy may think I'm a war criminal, but I'm not going to let my father hurt these kids anymore.

X and Tally descend on the Titan, going for its eyes. But they can't risk dislodging its hold on the tree, or its huge bulk will slide down onto the littlies.

And it won't need eyes to use seeker missiles.

A light sparks in the Titan's palm.

I bring my lifting fans to maximum, and my knife to full pulse. But I'm still not as hot as a hundred running children. The seeker missiles will head for them, not me.

There are flares on my belt, but they're safety fireworks, cool and smoke-free.

What do I have that can *burn*?

Then I remember Shay's speech before my first riding lesson as a Special:

This board isn't like anything you've ridden before. It has no safety governors, no AI to stop you from killing yourself. It will do whatever you tell it—flying too high, burning out your engines, or running straight into a mountain.

So how do I get my board to flame out in the next ten seconds?

I see something beneath me—an old tree at the edge of the river, dead and leafless, its branches fallen.

I come to an air-skidding halt over it, shouting at my board, "Maintenance mode!"

Shay wasn't kidding—even in midair, the hoverboard pops the grills from my lifting fans. Suddenly they're a pair of exposed buzz saws, waiting for my feet to take one wrong step.

As the Titan fires its missiles, I drop my board onto the tree. My rear lifter shrieks, grinding the dense old-growth wood into a tornado of sawdust.

It's like starting a fire by rubbing two sticks together at ten thousand RPMs. The heat burns my exposed face, the maelstrom of sparks and wood chips almost blinding.

Every meter on my board tips into the red.

In my thermal vision, I see the seeker missiles launch—

And immediately veer toward me.

DIVERSION

I lean forward, and my board leaps toward the river.

It's unsteady beneath my feet now, the back lifter wobbly and screeching, the metal fan blades spinning out of true. Which means the board will stay blazing hot as it carries me over the river.

If I can keep from falling off.

As I push toward maximum speed, the board careens randomly, setting a serpentine course down the river. It spits out sparks and noises like a cat in a fight to the death.

The missiles are right behind me.

"Keep running, everyone!" I hear Shay shout in the open comm channel—the littlies still need to get clear.

By now they're at least a kilometer behind me.

The missiles will reach me any second. I fly down toward the water, point the board up . . . and dive off the side.

My wounded hoverboard shoots into the sky, spiraling, smoking, out of control.

I'm slicing through the water, down into cool darkness. The sounds of battle fade above me.

The two explosions arrive almost together, squeezing the water around me like a massive, smothering fist. The pressure pushes against my ears and up into my sinuses. Tracers of shrapnel lance past through the water, and a hot sharpness bites my shoulder.

The pressure eases at last, pulsing a few times as the *booms* echo between the river's banks.

I swim back up toward the surface, fueled by the caches of oxygen stored in my rib cage. When my head breaks through, I take calm, steady breaths.

A shaft of dawn shows blood billowing from my wound. But my sneak suit is already suturing itself, and the healing nanos I have left are buzzing on my skin.

In the sky, there's nothing left of my hoverboard, just an expanding cloud carried downstream on the breeze.

"We're finally clear!" comes Shay's voice in my ear. "Somebody destroy that thing *now*."

"How?" Astrix asks. "The armor's too tough."

Up on the valley wall, the walker is starting to stand, testing its wounded ankle. The glowing blue eyes have been cut away by X's pulse lance, but it can still storm down the mountain and start stomping blindly.

I swim hard, but the near shore is a minute away.

Tally speaks up, her voice calm. "We've got this. Everyone stay clear."

I can see her and X on their boards, tiny figures hovering a hundred meters in front of the Titan. They look like hummingbirds facing off with a gorilla.

The Titan stretches out its hand again—like it has enough of those missiles to track down every fleeing child.

"Later, Titan-la," Tally murmurs.

The valley wall disintegrates.

The sound reaches me a few seconds later, huge and sovereign, the shock rippling across the water.

A wave of boulders hurtles down, devouring the Titan before it can fire again. The avalanche builds, sweeping over Hideaway, the larger rocks tumbling all the way to river.

Tally and X stay where they are, the clouds of dust swirling in lazy-eight patterns around their lifting fans.

When the smoke clears, nothing is visible of the Titan except its head. The rest of the machine has been swallowed by the rocks, like an ancient statue buried in the sand.

"Boss?" Shay says on the comms. "Thought you disarmed that bomb?"

Tally laughs. "X-la had a better idea. We made friends with it."

Five minutes later, Croy picks me up at the river's edge.

I'm wet and cold, out of healing nanos, and my hoverboard is toast. But my father's child prison has been destroyed, the inmates safe.

Croy hoists me on board with an outstretched hand. "Good job with those missiles."

"Not bad for a war criminal," I say.

He sighs. "When you're Special, it's easy to forget how fragile everyone else is. You have to pretend regular people are made of paper."

Regular people—like I'm a different species now.

Maybe we are, especially us Youngbloods.

"Okay, I'll try," I say.

"It's not easy. But one rule of thumb: *Don't use chemical weapons.*"

I grab hold of Croy's waist as we lift into the air. "That's strong language for a jar of jalapeño brine."

"When you turn it into superheated steam? Some of those littlies still can't see."

"Oh." I don't know what else to say.

When I protected my sister, I was trained that no one else mattered.

But now *everyone* matters.

Croy's board lifts higher, revealing the crowd of littlies on the far side of the landslide rubble. There must be two hundred of them, milling around in a state of confusion. Some of them are crying.

For the second time in their lives, their home is suddenly gone.

The other Youngbloods are gathered around the Titan's head. The hum of X's pulse lance trembles the air.

"You're trying to get it open?" I ask. "Are you brain-missing?"

"Yeah, we know," Croy says. "Your father likes to booby-trap his drones. But it's not a drone."

"You mean it's a *battle suit*?"

"Yep," he says. "X thinks there's someone inside."

SINGLE ELIMINATION

As Croy and I land, Shay holds up her index finger to her lips.

We step from the board, careful not to rattle the rocks under our feet.

X is kneeling on the Titan's half-buried head, one lupine ear pressed against the charred metal. Everyone else is dead silent.

Astrix stares at her scanner, but it can't be showing much through the Titan's heavy armor.

X raises his head. "The breathing's louder. I think we're close."

He lifts his pulse lance and gives it a squeeze. It sparks to life, and he slides it carefully into a fissure at the Titan's neck. He guides the blade in a gentle arc, the smell of burned metal filling the air.

The six of us crowd around the ragged-edged panel, slide our fingers into the still-hot fissure, and pull. The muscles in my hands burn hard, the tendons like ropes in my arms. For a long moment, the panel doesn't budge.

We all break at once, rubbing our sore fingers.

"Again," Tally says.

We take hold and heave.

Finally, with a rasp of scraping metal, the jagged piece pulls away. X and Croy have to stumble quickly back as it slides off their side.

There's a girl curled up inside the Titan's head.

She's emaciated, no muscle definition in her arms and legs. Her skin is sallow, like she hasn't seen the sun in a long time.

She's about fifteen, only a little older than the kids in Hideaway.

I want to look away, but force my eyes to keep cataloging everything in the small capsule. The girl's skin is dotted with electrodes, hardwired to the machine. Her eyes are covered with direct input screens, her ears plugged with buds. An intravenous tube runs into each of her spindly arms.

Around her mouth is an array of tiny microphones. Of course—the kids in Hideaway are trained to control machines with sound.

"This is what they graduate to," I say.

The others looks at me.

"Littlies don't stay young forever," I explain. "My father found a use for them."

Tally's eyes flash with anger. "How is this *useful*?"

"He's scared of AI," I say. "But he's an expert at manipulating people."

"Used to be," Boss X says gently. "He's still dead, Frey."

For a moment, everyone is silent, each of us fixed in place by our own horror.

Then a finger of dawn reaches the twisted metal of the Titan's head. Reflected sunlight plays across the girl's pale skin.

She stirs among all those wires, a dry and uncertain noise coming from her throat.

"Let's get her out of there," Tally says.

"It started as a game," the girl explains.

She pauses to take a drink of water. Her voice is a rasp, rustling like leaves at the start of winter. Her hands shake as she guides Tally's canteen to her mouth.

She stares into the fire like she's never seen one before. We had to get her out of the sun and into the darkness of a cave, but even in here her eyes are squinting.

"Us older kids didn't have to do chores. Instead we'd sit around all day, wearing eyescreens, trying to control virtual robots. Sometimes they had two legs, sometimes four or six. After a while, we got special chambers that would shake, to give us feedback."

She looks out the cave's mouth, blinking at the sunlight.

"I don't know when they made the robot real." The girl sips more water. "I thought I was still playing a simulation, a game."

X stands up and turns away, anger rippling through his body. I remember something he said to me once.

You were created as a tool, a means to an end. You owe the world nothing but chaos.

This girl owes the world something worse.

"What's your name?" Shay asks.

"Little Hawk," the girl says.

"Do you remember a kid called Spider?" I ask. "A little younger than you?"

"Maybe? He wasn't a player."

"He said you were . . . sleeping."

"Between games, it's like being in a dream." Little Hawk puts down the canteen and rubs at the marks left by the electrodes. She sits uncomfortably on the dirt floor of the cave. "It's hard being out here again. The game always feels good, as long as you win."

"We'll take you someplace more comfortable," Tally says gently.

Fear flickers in Little Hawk's eyes. "But I failed my game—I have to try again!"

There's a moment of silence. She still doesn't realize that her last objective was to kill two hundred children.

"Don't worry about winning," X says, a growl tingeing his voice. "Everyone who can hurt you is dead—or will be soon."

She looks up at him, not reassured at all.

I take her hand. "You said there were other players?"

Little Hawk nods. "Of course. All us older kids were hooked up."

"Where are they now?" I ask.

"I haven't seen them since the tournament," she says.

Tally frowns. "What kind of tournament?"

"Single elimination. Everyone who lost stopped playing. But I'm still here, because I was the best."

PART II

EPITAPH

I died for beauty, but was scarce
Adjusted in the tomb,
When one who died for truth was lain
In an adjoining room.

—Emily Dickinson

Dear Little Shadow,

You may not be answering my pings, but I know you're listening to this.

Without me, you feel as incomplete as I do.

You should be here, to see how the citizens of Shreve have changed. You should come home and help me understand them. They no longer understand themselves.

They wanted to be free. They wanted Dad gone. But every time something bad happens, they want the dust back to fix it.

Someone steals your umbrella. Someone's making too much noise next door. Someone bumps you on the street. The dust would've stopped them, told them to be quiet, made them apologize.

Your boyfriend cheats on you. Your boss takes credit for your work. A friend bails on your party, then pretends you never invited them. The dust would've seen it happen—the omniscient city would have *said* something.

These days, it's left to us mucky humans to sort things out.

Is it *my* fault that people are so messy?

Every time something bad happens, my face rank goes down a little.

The citizens keep blaming me for all those stolen umbrellas, those wet socks, those squelching shoes. With Dad dead and buried, there's no one else for them to hate.

Only me. All alone.

You'd know what to say. You'd tell them to roll up their sleeves. To deal with the muck and the mess of other people. At least no one ever erased their childhood . . . or stole their name.

Maybe you'd understand their faults better—you always did have lower expectations than me.

Unavoidable, I suppose.

Did you see that the free cities made Shreve a continuous democracy? All it takes is for fifty-one percent of the citizens to tell the city interface they want me gone, and the council takes over. Anytime, day or night.

Every missing umbrella matters.

You should come home. Your city needs you. Your big sister needs you.

Maybe you need us too?

—Rafia of Shreve

FREEDOM

Before I open my eyes the next morning, I know that X is making coffee.

He always buries the pot deep in last night's coals, impatient for the first black drops to ooze. The result tastes like smoke and stone, a pulse blade cutting through metal.

X does many things well—coffee is not one of them.

In the Youngbloods, we all pitch in with the cooking, hunting, and repair. Shay builds efficient fires, Tally makes excellent spaghetti Bolognese, but no one really specializes. Our only real expertise is mayhem.

X always knows when I'm awake—as my eyes open, he hands me a metal cup. The scalding handle prickles, but my healing nanos are back to their usual strength.

The coffee spreads a sooty flavor across my tongue, mixing with the spent bonfires we built to keep the littlies warm last night. Powdered milk forms a border of lace around the lip of the cup.

Rafi would throw this coffee in the fire.

She'd hate sleeping on the ground, making new camp every night, wearing the same self-cleaning clothes for days on end. But X's burned coffee fills me with uncluttered contentment. It's a universe away from the perilous luxury that Rafi and I were born into.

"Good coffee," I say to X.

He shrugs, under no illusions. "Only because you're alive, after everything that tried to kill you yesterday."

"Missiles, drones, landslides," I say. "That last one's new, at least."

He smiles. "Don't let Tally hear you bragging."

It stings a little, this reminder that I'm the puppy in this pack. But X is right—there's no glory in winning a fight against a child sealed in a machine.

Last night, I finally listened to Rafi's pings, trying to hear if she's hiding any terrible secrets. There was no hint of guilt in her voice, not about Hideaway.

Or about Col.

She sounds more like someone in over her head, willing to tell me anything to keep her grasp on the power she was born to.

I take another sip.

X looks as tired as I feel.

"You kept watch all night, didn't you?"

"In case of another unpleasant surprise. But even the littlies were quiet." He smiles again, his teeth a string of sharpened pearls. "They're on their best behavior with me."

I have to laugh at this. Under my father's rule, Shreve didn't allow surgery as transformative as X's, not even in feed dramas. These kids have never seen anything like a wolf-man.

"Sleep isn't the same," he says. "The stars seem different since Shreve."

I reach out and run my fingers through the fur on his arms. For the month my father held him captive, X was in a windowless cell, cut off from the sky.

"Tally told me you were born in the wild," I say.

He nods. "My parents were runaways. They worried that once I was old enough, I'd be curious about cities, and maybe run away myself. So they told me that you lose a piece of your soul every night you sleep under a roof."

"Interesting parenting choice. And I say that as someone who was raised as a killing machine."

"A vivid image, and difficult to shake. Especially in that cell."

I squeeze his arm. "If anyone's soul is big enough to take the hit, yours is, X-la."

He arches an eyebrow at the pretty nickname.

I decide to double down. "Also—*you* as a littlie. Awww."

X gives me a look of infinite patience. "Speaking of children, let's hope today is calmer."

I turn to look at the encampment below us. It's quiet this early.

The city of Paz air-dropped us supplies yesterday—food and water, soccer balls and feed screens, two dozen refugee habitats. The littlies threw another party, excited, astonished, terrified by their own freedom.

Some remained convinced they were in trouble for being discovered, but most seemed to thrive on the chaos, as if the destruction of Hideaway was a fire alarm in the middle of a school day.

The only thing that saved us from absolute chaos was their fear of X—and their awe of Tally Youngblood.

"Is Boss up yet?" I ask.

"Yes, and she wants to talk to you."

X glances up at the ridgeline. In the jagged bite from the horizon torn out by yesterday's landslide, a board hovers, smooth and aerodynamic against the rubble and ruin.

"I'm in trouble," I say. "Did you hear about my improvised chemical weapon?"

"Tactical slapdashery." X shrugs. "Boss Tally doesn't concern herself with details."

Details? I thought it was a war crime.

The Youngbloods are complicated like that—careful but dangerous, distrustful of the world while trying to save it, fractious even though Tally is decidedly the boss.

Too complicated for mornings.

"Maybe another coffee before you go up," X says, like he's reading my mind.

The crater left by Hideaway's self-destruction is blackened, strewn with shattered rocks. Astrix scanned this area yesterday and found the Titan's resting chamber just below, partially collapsed. We can't get down there without heavy equipment, but her sensor nanos slipped through the cracks and fissures—no heartbeats found.

Little Hawk was the last player left.

"Boss?" I call into the gloom of the crater.

"Over here."

I find Tally staring at a row of deep gouges in the rock. Each was left by a shaped charge of high explosives bored into the valley wall, splitting the cliff like lasers cutting a diamond.

"That's expert work," I say. "If Tigerboy hadn't warned us, all those littlies would've disappeared forever."

"Yeah. Some engineer thought long and hard about killing two hundred kids."

I shrug. "The night he died, my father almost killed a million people."

"I've heard the official version, Frey-la."

A small, surprised sound comes out of me. "That's not a *version*, Boss—it's what happened. His tower's still full of nuclear waste. It's so poisonous, they're burying the whole thing in permacrete!"

Tally contemplates the gouges in the mountainside. "Your father wanted to threaten the world one last time."

"Not just threaten. He would've pushed that button. You think I'm exaggerating?"

"Not you—the whole world." She sits down on a shelf of stone, gestures to the spot next to her.

After a moment's hesitation, I sit down too.

"It's an old habit," Tally says. "When the global feeds start telling me someone's a villain—that they're to blame for all the trouble, even the *earthquakes*—part of me starts to wonder. Maybe it's a distraction from something deeper, something wrong with the system."

"Tally, my father was exactly what everyone said he was. He told me to my face about that earthquake weapon. It was from a Rusty site under Victoria."

She nods. "An earthquake machine does sound pretty Rusty."

"And you knew Seanan—he died trying to stop our father! Do you think *he* was exaggerating?"

"I thought that was a pointless sacrifice," Tally says. "Killing one person doesn't fix the world."

I stare at her, too shocked to say more.

This is Tally Youngblood, the first rebel, equivocating about my father. She sounds like Diego and the other free cities, excusing themselves from acting to stop him until it was almost too late.

If she can't believe in such an obvious monster, how do I convince her that my charming sister is a threat?

Tally raises her hands, surrendering to my stare.

"Look, Frey-la, I get it now. The moment we saw that girl curled up in the Titan's head, I realized—of all the things I've created, your father was probably the worst."

"That *you* created?"

"Me and my crew. Twenty years ago, your father was some random middle pretty working in his garden." She lets out an exhausted sigh. "Our revolution turned him into a mass murderer."

"Boss, all you did was make the world free."

"Exactly." Tally gives me a sad smile. "And freedom has a way of destroying things."

FIGHT

It's too much for me.

Everyone's heard this argument, of course—that the world was better off under the pretty regime. The operation that made people beautiful also turned them into harmless bubbleheads. For centuries, there was no war, no greed, no laying waste to nature.

Of course, nobody talks seriously about going back. We want to keep our unruly, reckless brains. We want the freedom to create a new world, even if it means conflict and occasional ruin.

But somehow the argument sounds less settled now that I'm having it with Tally Youngblood.

"That's why the Youngbloods are cautious these days," she says. "Everything we do has unintended consequences."

"My father isn't your fault."

"No—he's our responsibility. Along with the rest of this world we created."

"He created himself," I say.

When Tally's revolution gave everyone a voice, most people made paintings, wrote diaries, or cooked amazing meals to put on their feeds. My father filled his channel with stories about crimes, large and small. He reveled in the fact that freedom could be dangerous. Without the pretty operation, any stranger, any neighbor, might steal from you, even kill you. Eventually, the citizens of Shreve distrusted each other so much that they welcomed the dust.

"Your father wasn't anything new," Tally says. "Humanity always makes the same mistakes."

"So you wish you'd left the world the way it was?" I ask.

She shakes her head. "You don't learn anything when you're forced to be good."

I sigh, confused now. "So you want AIs to run the world?"

"It wouldn't matter. We build ourselves into our machines. The only real cure for humanity is ceaseless rebellion—enough people ready to knock down any system that goes bad."

She stands up, and some of the years fall away from her. She looks like Tally in the history feeds. Young and dangerous, a girl willing to wreck the world.

"That's our job in this crew, Frey. To keep the people in power nervous."

My anger fades a little.

"My sister's in power now," I say.

"Indeed. Do you think she had anything to do with Hideaway?"

As much as I want Tally to distrust my sister, I can't lie.

"A fight to the death among kids—that isn't her. Rafi's dangerous, but never . . . *ugly.*"

Tally smiles at my choice of words. "Then why bother with revenge? You were her protector, her ally, until the night Shreve fell. What changed?"

I turn away, gathering myself to recall the moment of Col's death.

There's a dizziness that hits me in the dark, right before I go to sleep. It feels like I'm balanced on a spire jutting up through the earth, its sharp point focused on my heart. My bed spins slowly on that spike—what my sister did to me.

It takes a full minute to speak.

"My father's army was wrecked. My sister and her rebels had stormed his tower. He was done, and he knew it. His last card to play was his stockpile of nuclear waste."

"The dictator took his own city hostage," Tally recites. "But brave Col Palafox threw himself on the detonator, saving the world from a nightmare. X tells me that's not the truth."

I take a deep breath. "Our father offered Rafi a deal—his surrender for my life."

"Why *you?*" Tally asks.

"He thought a strong ruler couldn't have human connections, but Rafi cared about me more than anything. So his price for surrendering Shreve was to make her kill me. Otherwise he was going to set off the bomb."

78

Tally frowns. "So how does Col Palafox wind up dead? Why did some minor heir matter in your family drama?"

Some minor heir.

The charred stone beneath my feet turns unsteady.

"Because I loved him. If Rafi was saved by our connection, then *Col was who saved me*—if I hadn't met him, I'd still be my father's weapon."

A slant of ice goes through me, imagining a world in which I'd never been sent away to Victoria, never become more than Rafi's little shadow.

"She couldn't kill me," I continue. "But she knew that killing Col was close enough. Our father understood right away—he was laughing when she turned the knife on him."

Tally doesn't speak for a while. Dawn light leaks into the crater, turning the dusty air red around us. A few shouts echo from below, littlies waking up.

My nervous system has come alight, grief boiling like anger in my veins.

I want to fight another battle now, but everything is still around me.

"So in the end, your father got what he wanted," Tally finally says. "He severed your connection with Rafia."

This takes a moment to sink in, trickling through the cracks in my heart.

I always thought that my sister won everything that night—she ended my father and took Shreve for herself—but maybe the last victory was his.

Rafi's last ping admitted as much.

It was *his* hand that threw that knife, because he has always been, will always be, inside her.

"Yes," I say. "She lost me."

Tally comes closer. "Please understand why I'm asking all this, Frey-la. You want me to intervene in family politics—two rich kids fighting over an inheritance. Before finding Hideaway, that's all this was to me."

"But now you've seen our real inheritance," I say. "A child prison set to self-destruct, the inmates fighting in some kind of *tournament*."

"I can see it's not over for you two," Tally says softly. "Even if Rafia did the right thing."

The oxygen seems to leave the air. All sound is sucked away.

"What did you just say?"

Tally shrugs. "That's what Hideaway proves—your father would've pulled that trigger. Rafi saved a million people. Killing Col was the right idea."

The tight coil of anger in me unravels all at once.

I launch myself at Tally Youngblood.

It's a wild attack, my combat lessons with Shay swept away by anger. These deadly, inhuman muscles carry me across the broken stone, savage and frantic, fists flailing.

Tally ducks gracefully beneath the blows, letting my momentum carry me over her. A fist stabs up my midriff as I fly past, sending a shock wave through my chest.

I land on my back two meters away, unable to breathe.

"I can't judge your sister," Tally says, as if I didn't just try to take her head off. "Not for a decision she had a few seconds to make."

I try to get up, but my muscles won't work. My lungs feel paralyzed.

My new rib cage is made from unbreakable ceramics, strong as a spacecraft hull—but Tally hit me just below, straight to my lungs. A perfect blow to disable a Special.

I reach out a hand, trying to grasp her leg. To get her on the ground beside me.

She's too far away.

"I've made split-second choices that I regretted," she continues. "Sometimes the best option looks ethics-missing the next day."

I sink back to the ground, closing my eyes. Tally isn't going to help me.

No one is.

"But your sister still worries me." Tally comes a few steps closer and settles on the dusty ground.

I open my eyes, trying to beam hatred at her. Failing.

My anger, which seemed so endless and untiring, has curdled into despair.

"Rafia knew exactly how to stop your father," Tally says. "They were in perfect alignment that night—like *they* were the twins. But you never saw her solution coming, did you?"

It's all I can do to shake my head.

In those terrible moments, I'd started to think that my death was the only way to save our city. It took me hours to fully grasp why Rafi threw her knife at Col's heart instead of mine.

"If that's how close Rafia and your father were," Tally goes on, "then maybe she does know about this place."

Tally offers me her canteen, and I take a sip of water.

"Maybe," I manage.

"And even if she didn't, that night may have changed her for the worse. You turned away from her when she needed you most."

I glare at Tally. "So it's my fault if she goes bad?"

"Not your fault—your responsibility. Like this new world is mine."

I reach out again, wanting to take Tally by her neck and shake her. But she clasps hold of my hand and straightens her legs, hauling us both to standing.

I manage to keep my feet. "Rafi was already like our father."

"Because she made a hard decision?" Tally asks.

I shake my head—it isn't that simple. It takes a moment for the right words to find their way to me.

"She murdered Col without any hesitation. It wasn't a hard choice, just the solution to a problem. If she'd do that to me, her sister, what will she do to the citizens of Shreve if they decide to replace her? It's a democracy, but she's still got her rebel army, and my father's weapons."

"An interesting question." Tally looks down at the valley, at a gang of littlies playing soccer in the rubble. "When we take them back to Shreve, we'll have a look around. Someone there knew about this place."

At those words, anger and frustration let go of my heart, and I can breathe again. My sister might have our city, and my name.

But I have Tally Youngblood.

"Sorry I tried to kill you," I say.

She shrugs. "It's a good sign. Sometimes the Special surge makes people go cold. With their pain damped down, they don't feel anything anymore."

"That's not me, Boss." I don't need physical pain to make me feel. The spire of grief pointed at my heart makes sure of that.

"Tell your spy we're coming to Shreve," Tally says.

"But the kids saw your face, Boss. Even if you disguise yourself, they'll tell everyone who you are."

"Maybe it's time to come out of hiding," she says.

I stare at her, halted by a question that the world has asked a million times.

When I was six years old, Tally's face was everywhere. She looked much younger then, more than those ten years. The whole world celebrated her, and countless people pledged themselves to continue her rebellion in the wild.

Then one day she vanished without a word. Not long after that, my father filled the air of his city with dust.

"Why did you disappear, Tally?" I manage.

She spreads her hands, helpless for a moment. "People kept expecting me to pass judgment on everything new. As a kid, all I wanted was to be pretty, and I wound up with power instead. But I didn't really know anything about rebuilding the world."

"You were supposed to protect us," I say, hating how childish the words sound.

83

But that was the role I was raised to play—protector, last line of defense. The possibility that I was some echo of Tally Youngblood helped my childhood almost make sense.

"I thought disappearing would keep everyone nervous," she says. "Like when you haven't seen the monster in a horror feed, and your imagination does the work."

"My father didn't have much of an imagination. He only believed what he could see."

Tally smiles, her teeth sharp in the sunlight.

"Then it's time to let everyone see me again."

WELCOME HOME

Shreve puts on a welcome bash.

Like all my sister's parties, it is immaculately planned.

A thousand hovercams greet us over Bossier Fountain, flying in shifting formation against the perfect blue sky. Each has been decorated by a different classroom of Shreve students—with painted faces, blinking lights, or dangling streamers aflutter with folded paper cranes. The worldwide audience can choose any of the cams' viewpoints to watch to our approach. A school choir sings on the fountain stage below, amid dancing sprays of water.

We six Youngbloods ride on our boards, Tally's famous face on full display. In our body armor and sneak suits, we look like a military escort for the three hoverbuses full of lost children.

The littlies' faces are plastered to the windows, gazing down on this colorful, exuberant new Shreve. It must look like a different city to them, a different world.

Their hometown is under new management.

The locals are out in force, two hundred thousand according to the feeds. More boisterous than any Shreve crowd I've ever seen, they're dressed in bright colors, like this is Paz or Victoria. The grays of my father's era are gone.

Everyone's waving the city's new flag—a gold phoenix rising from blue flames.

When the global feeds broke the news of Hideaway's discovery this morning, the story was paired with grim music and photos of grieving parents. A child prison was another reminder of my city's dark past, along with the war-ravaged buildings, the traumatized former prisoners, the economy ruined by blockade.

But somehow my sister has turned that bleak message on its head. By late afternoon, the story of Hideaway has become one of hope and celebration.

Of Tally Youngblood returned to the world.

A spray of fireworks rips the sky around us, bright enough to blind even in daylight.

"Just what these kids need," Tally mutters on our private channel. "More explosions."

"Told you, Boss," I say. "My sister never misses a chance to dazzle an audience."

Most dazzling to me is the air above Shreve—I've never seen it clear of dust. My new senses keep searching for the telltale flickers of sunlight, the sooty scent of nanocams. But there's nothing except the smell of pine and wildflowers.

For the first time, I believe in my bones that Rafi has stripped away some vital part of our father's regime.

Our parade winds across the city, taking us within sight of my childhood home. My father's tower stood at the outskirts of Shreve, a symbol of his omniscience, the tallest building in the city. But three months after his fall, a huge mass of permacrete rises up there. Called the Sarcophagus, the new structure is almost complete. In another few days, the construction drones, radioactive by now, will seal themselves inside forever, along with my father's stockpile of nuclear waste.

The Sarcophagus protects Shreve from radiation but also has its own dark beauty. A hundred-meter-high pyramid, its sides are coated in night blackness. His body is still inside, lying where Rafi cut him in half, the Sarcophagus a monument not to him, but to his obliteration.

Rafi's new home, Shreve House, is the tower's opposite in every way.

It sprawls on a plot of land cleared by the war, a dozen buildings arranged among grassy hills, held aloft by hoverstruts, connected by floating walkways. They're made of light materials, full of airy windows, like temporary bungalows thrown up for a beach vacation.

My sister's reign is transparent, playful, humble.

But the two capitols lie within sight of each other. Here in late afternoon, the shadow of the old stretches toward the new.

The dignitaries of the city wait for us on the green lawn of Shreve House—the head wardens, the elected council, a few of her rich friends. And of course Rafi's bodyguard of rebels, the liberators of the city.

Our spy is among them.

Riggs was one of the commandoes on my last mission with Col, sent by Rafi to spy on me. Now she leads my sister's bodyguard—and spies on her for me and X. On top of that, Riggs kissed me once, when she thought I was Rafi.

The two of them have a complicated relationship.

The littlies' surviving parents aren't here yet. My sister didn't want the spectacle of some families being reunited while other children stood awkwardly alone. The real tragedy of this day will wait until the cameras are turned off.

As we land, my sister comes out to greet us.

It's the first time I've seen her since she killed Col, and sharp, righteous anger ripples through me. For a moment, it carves away the grief, fills up the emptiness.

Rafi no longer dresses like a rebel queen, in animals skins and body armor. No exotic feathers in her hair, just a pulse knife on her belt.

And she wears my name: Frey of Shreve.

She's not impersonating me today, though, not like when she was with the rebels. It's her own body language, an imperious stance, movements delicate and considered—all those mannerisms that are still etched into my muscles.

Her dress is perfectly chosen, her hair under control in a way I could never manage. Whatever name she calls herself, she's done being me.

It's a relief, not to see myself in her.

But something else has taken my place—a razor certainty in

her eyes, an authority that presses down like gravity on everyone around her.

Another aspect of our father has settled onto Rafi, now that she's in charge.

An explosion of applause—at least a hundred government workers are arrayed on the hill behind the dignitaries. Hovercams are released from their hold patterns, a swarm of anxious hummingbirds, making my skin prickle. My new face feels like cheap camo surge, easy to see through.

But everyone's looking at Tally Youngblood.

Rafi's face lights up as she approaches the guest of honor, hands outstretched.

Suddenly this plan feels like a mistake. Shaking Tally's hand will only make my sister more beloved, more a rebel queen.

I can feel her face rank creeping upward.

"Welcome to my city," she says. "And welcome back to the world."

"I never left," Tally answers.

Rafi skips a beat, a pause so brief only I would notice. Her mind is scrambling for meaning in Tally's answer—signs of a threat, an opportunity.

"We missed you all the same," Rafi says, all graciousness, then starts the introductions.

It's an endless ritual. Every dignitary wants a moment with Tally in front of the assembled cams—especially the council members, thinking of the next election.

No one knows how independent Shreve's elected government

really is. Or what will happen if they ever go against my sister's will. Our father shared power with a city council too, until he didn't.

I recognize one of the counselors—Chulhee, the head of a clique called Future. They believed that everyone whose life was recorded by surveillance dust would be studied by future historians. They performed their lives for an invisible, unborn audience, trying to be dramatic and historic.

The night my father fell, the Futures helped us rescue Boss X, creating distractions across the city. Maybe because it was the right thing to do, or maybe because they wanted to go down in history as heroes.

I wonder how they're coping, now that all the drama they spent their lives creating has been erased. The recordings were stored in my father's tower, and it turns out that radioactive battle zones aren't the best environment for DNA memory cores.

Chulhee is surrounded by his own fleet of tiny hovercams, recording everything he does and says. The end of tyranny hasn't canceled his historic life, only restarted it.

I wonder if he's asking Rafi to fill the air with dust again.

The rest of us Youngbloods join the receiving line. X is just in front of me, and he and my sister have a long chat, recounting old battles he and I shared.

It's dizzy-making to hear him call her by my name. She must want to ask him where I am, but she can't while swarmed with hovercams. Admitting the rift between us might damage her face rank.

Officially, Rafia of Shreve has retired to a simple life in the wild, to allow her rebel sister to bring a fresh perspective to Shreve. As

Rafi always tells me in her pings, using my name gives her more distance from our father.

Then X moves on, and it's my turn to shake my sister's hand . . .

That familiar sense of dislocation bubbles up, seeing my old face in hers. As if I'm a littlie again, looking in a mirror, rehearsing tomorrow's duties as a body double. My curtsies and handshakes were never as good as hers.

My fingers tremble a little as we touch.

I have my own face now, a body remade, but I still feel like her reflection.

There's no way she'll see who I really am—Tally insisted that no scanners or sniffers be present during our visit. But part of me is still certain that Rafi will see through my taller body, new muscles and nerves and bones.

My clumsy attempt at being my own person.

All she says is "Lovely to meet you."

Then she moves on, never even asking my name.

Released from her attention, I feel oddly hollow. All those years sharing an identity, and suddenly my twin sister can't see me anymore.

Part of me misses her, I realize.

But then I notice the black band around her arm—as Frey, she's in mourning for Col Palafox, her lost love, the Savior of Shreve.

My hand goes to my pulse knife.

With an effort that seems to tear my own muscles, I pull it away to shake the hand of the next person in line.

It's Demeter, one of my sister's childhood circle. I remember her from stepping in for Rafi at dance clubs and watching dust recordings to learn her friends' names and foibles.

Demeter also helped the rebels and Victorians rescue me and Col, and later helped us rescue Boss X. Now she's Rafi's second-in-command.

"Thank you for helping our children," she says. "But I don't think I recall your name?"

Astrix has built me a false identity, but I was hoping to avoid saying it aloud. The thought of another name exhausts me.

I smile and try to move along.

She keeps hold of my hand. "I'm Demeter Shard. And you are . . . ?"

It would be easy to break her grip, but I don't want to draw attention. Luckily, the hoverbuses are landing behind me—the first stage of our plan is about to unfold.

"Excuse me," I say. "Someone should see to the children."

Demeter frowns, still not letting me go.

But then Shreve's lost children charge out onto the lawn, helped along by the piles of candy Astrix left on every bus seat. The sugar-rushing littlies storm past the dignitaries, rebels, and wardens, and into Shreve House.

We've told them that the day's first event is a scavenger hunt.

The wardens turn, perplexed by this sudden invasion. A few of them shout after the rampaging kids, but it's useless. After years without adult supervision, mere wardens have no hope.

Rafi's rebel bodyguard stays put, thanks to a quick order from their commander, Riggs. She watches me from her wheelchair, the only person in Shreve who knows my true identity.

"We'll handle this," I say to Demeter, and turn to the others. "Astrix, Croy, come on!"

The three of us break from the receiving line. Rafi looks up for a moment, annoyed that chaos has interrupted the choreography of her welcome. But Tally starts talking to her again, and the cams swarm them.

Croy and Astrix follow me into Shreve House, which is already being plundered by the littlies.

Somewhere in here are my sister's secrets.

SHREVE
HOUSE

Our sneak suits switch to dazzle mode.

Anyone watching video of this later will see us moving around in Shreve House, but our forms will be a blur. Even my gloves are camo fabric, my fingers' motion lost in chameleon static.

I move through the halls, shouting at the littlies to search harder for scavenger hunt clues. They're tearing the place up, finding nothing, of course. The few workers still at their stations have no luck controlling them.

All the while, I'm injecting workstations with worms and snitches. Croy and Astrix are doing the same across the other buildings.

By the time order is restored, we'll be able to intercept every bit of information passing through the government of Shreve.

Which, so far, doesn't seem to be that interesting. Nothing here looks like my father's control room, with its phalanx of Security officers monitoring every speck of dust in Shreve. The airscreens around me are full of construction permits, noise complaints, requests for zoning changes—the mundane chaos of a city recovering from war and dictatorship.

I don't know what I was expecting. Plans for another child prison left out in the open?

The mere fact that we got in so easily suggests there's nothing here. Maybe my sister keeps her dirty secrets at the old military headquarters or in some hidden base my father left behind.

But at least now we have our foot in the door.

I storm across a floating walkway, pretending to be chasing a littlie. The walkway leads to the smallest of the satellite buildings, which floats a few meters higher than the rest.

The littlie reaches the door, but unlike all the others, it's locked. He turns around and pushes past me, heading back to scavenge somewhere else.

I take the handle, give it a hard twist. It doesn't budge.

Any normal door would break under my strength, but this one is solid duralloy. Finally, I've found something interesting.

There's no time to cover my tracks—I squirt some metal-eating nanos into the lock. Furious chemical reactions kick off inside, the handle heating up in my palm.

But when the warmth fades, it still doesn't budge. It's the first time I've seen Astrix's tech defeated.

I set my sneak suit to sky blue, then jump onto the top of the floating building.

The thatch roofing up here is purely ornamental—it conceals

ceramic armor, like Rafi's expecting an orbital bombardment like the one that ended our father. My pulse knife can cut through it eventually, but not without filling the air with smoke.

I lower myself in front of a window, pulling equipment from my belt. This might not be the artful infiltration that Shay asked for, but this room is too tempting pass up. At worst, Rafi will know that the Youngbloods have their eyes on her.

The duralloy shutters are open, and the window is simple polycarbonate. I slap on a shaped explosive charge and press myself against it to muffle the sound.

The *whump* travels through my body armor, down to my skeleton. For a long moment, I can't breathe. Healing nanos are buzzing in my rib cage, and my armor is cracked.

But the window is gone. I roll inside, feet crunching on shattered plastic.

This is my sister's office.

I recognize the desk in the far corner of the room. A thousand times our father sat behind it, hands folded, lecturing me or Rafi about something we'd done wrong. The sight of it makes my stomach clench.

I step closer. My scanner detects a sliver of radiation.

Rafi left my father's body to rot in the Sarcophagus, but she salvaged this symbol of his power. And his cruelty—prisoners at Hideaway must have poached the old-growth wood.

I scan the desk's interior. There's nothing more high-tech than joinery and nails. The drawers hold only feathers.

The sight of them sends another pang through me—Rafi first took them from birds in the southern continent, when she was hiding from our father with the Palafoxes. When we were all on the same side.

I don't have time to ponder how things went wrong, though—the wardens could show up any minute. Back in the tower, my father's office had a hundred sensors in the walls. He could read his visitors' body temperatures, their micro-expressions, their fingerprints.

But another scan reveals no cams, no microphones in the walls or furniture. Hardly any tech at all.

Whatever Rafi does in this office, she isn't recording it for posterity.

My scanner pings only once—for a pair of cloth panels covering something on the wall. More tendrils of radiation are leaking out from them, something else salvaged from my father's tower.

The panels are held closed by an old-fashioned mechanical lock. When I try Astrix's metal-eating nanos again, the lock opens in seconds with an easy, liquid feel.

I push the panels apart . . .

It's me.

Or rather, a painting of what I used to look like.

Mussed hair, workout sweats, a pulse knife in my hand—there's no chance it's my sister. The artist even captured the look of battle ecstasy in my eyes.

I've seen this portrait before, almost a year ago. My father had it painted when I left home, and hung it after he thought I'd died in his attack on Victoria. That was his custom with all his vanquished enemies. He had a whole room full of trophies just like this.

The canvas was torn in the Battle of Shreve, when my friends blew their way out of the tower, but is now lovingly restored. The frame is chipped, but it's been carefully patched.

Why did she save this painting? What is this room *for*? There are no airscreen projectors, no cams to broadcast or record meetings. Not even a pen to write with.

Just a portrait of me, mounted in the perfect spot for viewing from my father's desk.

I sit down in his old chair and stare at myself.

The first time I saw this painting, I didn't understand why my father had tried to obliterate me along with House Palafox. I'd always done everything he'd asked of me.

That was before I found out that I'd killed his missing son, Seanan.

Does Rafi see me as an enemy too?

A breeze stirs the room, and from my father's desk, I see the looming shape framed perfectly in the shattered window.

The Sarcophagus.

Our childhood home. Our father's tomb.

I imagine Rafi sitting here, contemplating these two memorials. It's like being inside her head, but her thoughts are just out of reach.

The door clicks.

I raise my hands in surrender, ready to accept whatever scolding the wardens have the nerve to deliver to one of Tally Youngblood's crew.

But when the door opens, it's not a warden.

It's my sister.

SOVEREIGN CITY

Rafi closes the door behind her.

"This better be important," she says. "That's *Tally Youngblood* out there."

I freeze. At last we're alone together, and part of me wants to scream all my anger at her.

But I can't reveal who I am.

Rafi frowns at the broken window. "Smashing things? You might be taking that costume a little seriously."

"Costume?" I ask.

Rafi laughs. "As if I wouldn't spot you."

A deep note of panic travels through my body—the old anxiety of being found out. The terror of being the object of my big sister's scorn.

This unbreakable body feels suddenly fragile, transparent.

"How?" I ask.

Rafi gives me a mocking smile. "You're so much smarter than me. I'm sure you can figure it out."

Smarter than me—Rafi would never say that of me. Not in a million years.

She thinks I'm someone else.

I have to stall. "We said no scans. Did you cheat?"

"Microscopically." Rafi shows me her right palm. "A DNA sniffer woven into the whorls of my skin."

"When we shook hands . . ."

"Had to make sure I was meeting the real Tally, not some impostor."

I nod, still uncertain who she thinks I am. My DNA hasn't changed. No surgery can replace every cell in the human body.

"It seemed like a glitch at first," Rafi says. "Until I realized that you weren't human."

Right—a sniffer built into Rafi's skin would have to ignore her own DNA, which is exactly the same as mine.

Six handshakes, five results.

She doesn't think I'm real.

"We are impressed," I say, dropping into a speech pattern I know all too well. "Though a little concerned as well. The need to verify Tally's identity suggests a measure of paranoia."

Rafi rolls her eyes. "It's not paranoia when you're right—one of you *was* pretending. For a mind the size of a city, you're being rather slow."

I smile, my theory confirmed.

She thinks I'm an avatar, an artificial body run by an AI—perhaps the only thing in the world that Rafi would consider smarter than herself.

She'll assume I'm the city of Diego, who spent the war playing us against each other. First they offered to make me my father's heir, saying Rafi was too unstable. Then they told my sister I was trying to supplant her. That's why she sidelined me three months ago, taking Shreve for herself.

I despise Diego, but they represent the alliance of free cities whose aid is keeping Shreve from falling apart.

I have all the power here.

"Sorry to hijack your party," I say. "We thought it was time for a chat."

Rafi frowns. "You infiltrated the Youngbloods and trashed my home . . . *for a chat?*"

I give her a placid smile, but my mind is spinning. This is the first time I've pretended to have a brain the size of a city.

"Did you know about Hideaway?" I ask.

Rafi gives me a dumbfounded look. "Are you serious?"

"We are always serious."

"You think I'd let my father keep hurting those children, even after he was *dead*?" She takes a step closer. "After what he did to me? What he did to *Frey?*"

Her hand goes to the pulse knife on her belt.

She could use that knife on me—to her I'm just a skin suit. Diego doesn't even feel a tickle if one of its bodies is destroyed.

For me, it's more of an issue.

I raise my hands. "Rafia, the whole world is asking the question."

"Allow me to clarify, then. My father forced me to pretend my own sister didn't exist. He made her into a killing machine. *We* were abused—you think I'd traumatize those kids for a few *trees*?"

She still looks like she's about to throw the knife at me, and yet something untwists in my heart.

Her anger has finally clarified what part of me already knew—my sister is not my father. Not really.

"The children mentioned a 'nice crumbly man,'" I say. "The person who welcomed them to Hideaway. You need to find him."

"We will." Rafi's hand drops from the knife. "Trust me."

I nod, wondering what to say next. This is a priceless opportunity to find out what my sister is up to.

"You've always wanted to rule, Rafia. How does the reality compare?"

She rolls her eyes again. "Is this a newsfeed interview? The reality's the same as last time we spoke—not enough money, too much war damage. Endless emergency calls about imaginary crimes."

"That's to be expected," I say.

For ten years, the citizens of Shreve breathed surveillance dust, every move, every word monitored by Security. Lying, littering, even kissing the wrong person were all tricky—actual crime was impossible.

The arrival of freedom must seem like chaos.

"There's a new clique called Breakage," Rafi says. "One night, they destroyed half the streetlights in Shreve. Ridiculous, but annoying."

"Are you cracking down on them?"

She shakes her head. "We helped a different clique make repairs. A good example is easier than force. The only serious sabotage has been near the border—disgruntled Victorians, probably. Is *that* why you're here?"

I try to keep the cool, distant expression of an avatar. Rafi's about ten seconds away from starting to wonder if I'm really a city-level intelligence.

I need to throw her off balance.

I see something glittering in the sunlight through the broken window—a small key on a chain around her neck. It's just the right size for the locked panels.

Of course. That's her weak point.

Me.

I gesture at the portrait behind her. "To be honest, we were wondering if you'd heard anything from your sister."

Rafi turns and sees the open panels for the first time.

She transforms in front of me, fists clenching, face twisting. With two quick steps, she reaches the painting and slams the panels closed.

"That's not for *you*." Her voice breaks on the last word.

"Did you really think we couldn't see through your ridiculous story about her retiring to the wild?"

"Why do you care where she is?"

"Because it looks as though you've taken up your father's old habits. He only hung such portraits when his enemies were dead."

Rafi's eyes flash. "Frey isn't my enemy—she's my *sister*!"

103

"Can't someone be both?"

She only glares at me.

The advantage is all mine again. I keep pressing.

"We can't help but notice, Rafia, that in your indignation you've dodged our question. To the best of your knowledge, is your sister still alive?"

At those words, the anger goes out of her. "That's why you're here? Because you think I'd . . ."

My older sister does something I haven't seen her do since we were six years old. She slides down the wall and sits on the floor.

Her cold and perfect dignity—all of it vanishes.

"You came here with X," she says, her voice pleading. "Aren't the two of them still friends?"

Part of me feels bad for my sister. She really is worried about me.

Another part of me decides to twist to knife.

"Indeed, X is Frey's closest friend and ally. You made sure of that three months ago." I fold my hands on the desk, just as our father used to do when he punished us. "And yet he has no idea where she is."

"Really?" she pleads.

I gesture at the now-covered painting.

"So we ask again, are you following in your father's footsteps? Is this your trophy room?"

"*No!*" A cry from ragged lungs. "I'd never hurt my sister!"

I feel my cool expression waver. The spire of pain that comes for me at night is lurking beneath the floor, perilously close.

But Rafi's too upset to notice.

"You did hurt her," I say, "when you murdered Col Palafox."

"I *saved* her that night." She looks up at me. "I'd throw that knife again, a thousand times."

My whole body goes rigid. It takes all my will to imagine myself as a machine, countless arrays of numbers, a mind too large to be moved by the death of one minor heir.

"Then why lie to the world about what happened?" I ask.

"Hiding it was your idea. All I care about is your money. That's the only thing I'm trading for."

My mind focuses again—in her last ping, my sister said she was trading with the free cities. But what does Shreve have to offer?

"As long as you're keeping up your end of the bargain, Rafia."

"Of course. You'll get your data."

Data?

All I can think to ask is "When?"

"At least another week," Rafi says. "There are too many grays to rush things."

Grays? Nothing she's saying makes sense.

I have to keep her talking. "Our patience is limited. Do you want us to tell the world what you did to Col Palafox?"

She gives me a chilling look. "Feel free to tell them exactly what happened that night—how I saved my whole city. Show them exactly what my choices were. You'll only make me a *hero*."

The spire rises up through the floor. Its tip touches my heart.

"Shreve will love me for my sacrifice." Rafi stands, clutching her pulse knife again. "And the rest of the world will secretly applaud.

Nobody wants the Rusty nightmare coming back—cities dying under mushroom clouds. If you were a *real* person, you'd understand that!"

Her last words echo an old fear of mine. For so long, I was just a shadow of my sister. Being real is new to me.

Rafi senses my weakness—she gives me her cruelest smile. The advantage I gained when she saw the portrait is erased.

"I should've known you were a machine the moment those littlies started ransacking Shreve House. No human would use damaged children as a *diversion*."

That's . . . exactly what we did. For a moment, I wonder about my new allies, who came up with this plan. Only Croy objected.

I never gave it a second thought.

"Does Tally even know what you are?" Rafi asks. "Doesn't she hate AI?"

The question gives me another opening.

"Tally despises us," I say. "And yet she was willing to help us keep an eye on you, 'Frey of Shreve,' because we've told her the truth. She knows your rebel name is stolen."

This doesn't have the effect I was going for—my sister only sighs, her hand dropping from her pulse knife.

"Youngblood's opinion doesn't matter," she says. "All that counts is that more than half the people of this city trust me. That was our deal."

"Would they trust you, if they knew you were Rafia?"

She waves a hand. "Not nearly as much, but then you'd have to admit that you lied too, Diego. Or worse, you'd have to pretend

106

that a mere human fooled you. Until then, I'm honored to rule in Frey's name."

Her voice breaks a little at the end, and I see it . . . behind all her anger and bluster, Rafi still loves me and wants me to love her back. After everything she's done to me, she thinks it's possible.

I have to leave this room before it shows on my face how sad that is.

I stand up from my father's desk. "The citizens of Shreve might trust you, but we don't. We'll be dropping in again."

Rafi watches me walk past, still uncertain about why Diego was here.

"I'll get you your data," she says in an exhausted voice. "Just keep the aid coming—for them, not me."

I don't answer, walking out the door and down the walkway, ignoring the swarm of wardens who've arrived to return order to Shreve House.

As the racing of my heart slows, I replay the conversation in my head. My sister is selling something to Diego. There must be a way to use that against her.

The problem is, I don't know how to explain what happened here to Tally and the others. It was too many tangled deceptions even for me.

But one thing keeps going through my head . . .

For the first time ever, I fooled Rafia of Shreve.

NORMAL

"Rafi has a deal with Diego," I tell the others. "She's giving them something in exchange for reconstruction aid."

The five of them stare across the campfire, waiting for more.

We're camping three klicks out from the city border, despite offers of rooms at the best hotels in Shreve. A feather bed sounded good to me, but the Youngbloods prefer the wild. Seems like they only feel comfortable with the stars overhead.

"What can she give Diego?" Shay asks. "Shreve has nothing."

"I don't know exactly. Some kind of data."

Croy snorts. "That could mean anything. We're talking about an AI—they're *made* of data. It's like me saying I want some atoms!"

He keeps laughing at his own joke. The rest of them just stare at the fire, pondering how little I've brought them.

I had Rafi right where I wanted her—off balance, uncertain—and all I got were a few random words.

"What does this have to do with Hideaway?" Shay asks.

"Nothing. My sister had no idea about those littlies. I'm certain of it."

Shay turns to Tally. "So why stick around, Boss? Two random cities made a shady deal—happens all the time. It's not our business."

Tally doesn't answer, just throws another stick into the fire.

X speaks up. "Shreve isn't a random city, Shay. Some of us died for its freedom."

"And you won," she replies. "There's no more dictator."

"And yet his daughter still rules," X says.

Shay laughs. "His other daughter's sitting next to you. If evil's genetic, we have a more immediate problem."

All eyes fall on me. I'm not sure how much Shay was joking, whether to argue or laugh it off.

"Same genes," Tally says. "Different upbringing."

The same words I used with her this morning. A lightness comes over me, the singular feeling of having Tally Youngblood on my side.

"Here's a question," Croy says. "Sending data takes half a second. Why isn't this deal already done?"

I try to recall my sister's specific words. "Rafi said it would take another week. Something about too many grays in the cores, whatever that means."

Everyone looks at Astrix, our tech expert.

"Weird," she says. "Data's ones and zeroes—not much room for grays."

She goes back to setting up airscreen projectors on the rocks around her. In a few minutes, our spy nanos in Shreve House will start bouncing stolen info packets off a Paz satellite.

Maybe they'll supply some answers.

"So we're just guessing," Shay says.

Tally throws another stick in the fire. "We can't ignore this, Shay-la. Like X said—rebels helped take Shreve, and Rafia still calls herself a rebel boss. That makes this mess our responsibility."

Shay gives one sharp laugh. "The free cities bombed this city from space, not us! If they want Rafia gone, they can remove her too."

"They won't get their hands dirty," I say. "Look how long it took them to act against my father. They just want everything to go back to normal."

X rumbles with a soft growl. "Rafia isn't normal."

"She is for people in Shreve." The flames pop and dance before me. "They grew up with her face on every channel."

"But they think she's *you*," Croy says.

I shrug. "Acting like a rebel only makes it easier to be a dictator."

Tally nods her head, like I've made some profound revelation, but she doesn't say anything. She's waiting for me to keep making my case. I'm the expert in Shreve politics, after all. That's why she let the daughter of a mass murderer join her crew.

But all I can think of is the moment when Rafi saw my portrait hanging exposed on the wall. The pain on her face, the desperation to shut those panels again.

Losing me has wounded her, deeper than I thought.

"Frey's right about one thing," Shay says. "The city AIs love normal. They were fine with a tyrant in Shreve, until he started generating chaos. They could live with evil but not messiness."

Tally smiles at her. "Kind of like our old friend, Dr. Cable."

I remember that name from reading up before my surgery. Cable was the woman who created the first Specials. She designed them to be cool, calculating, empathy-missing—the opposite of messy.

Diego would have approved.

A question hits me. "Maybe that's what the AIs want from Rafi—some kind of data that makes things *normal*."

Astrix sits up straight—the airscreen whorls in her eyes disappear.

"You might be right. And it's not good."

"What'd you find?" Tally asks.

"Mostly the usual boring government stuff—permits and noise complaints. Almost like someone got caught breaking in and Shreve House knew to scrub their secrets." Astrix gives me a hard look. "But there's one weird thing, Frey-la: Your city uses lots of old Rusty engineering standards."

I nod. "One of my father's brilliant ideas. If something's made in Shreve, you can't buy spare parts for it anywhere else."

"Nightmare," Astrix says. "And also why I've never heard of grays before."

She waves a hand, throwing up an airscreen over the fire. A man's face appears there, fuzzy with smoke and embers.

"This is Louis Harold Gray, Rusty scientist," Astrix says. "Not particularly famous, unless you're interested in how nuclear fallout affects living things. There's an old unit of measurement named after him—guess what grays measure."

"Radiation," Tally says softly.

"Whoa," Croy says. "So this data's in the Sarcophagus?"

Astrix raises her hands, giving him a silent round of applause.

I turn my head instinctively in the direction of my childhood home. The tower is out there in the darkness, still full of secrets.

"The dust," I say.

"Exactly." Astrix waves away the image of Louis Gray over the fire. "Rafi wasn't talking about *some* data. She meant *all* the data—ten years of surveillance. Every word spoken in Shreve, every sunset, every kiss, everything that happened in two million people's lives. We're talking zettabytes, not some file you can attach to a ping."

Croy frowns. "But it was all destroyed in the Fall of Shreve."

"Unless it wasn't," Tally says.

I look at Astrix. "Who cares about old recordings of Shreve?"

She stands up and starts to pace, her finger flexing. "Lots of people! The Futures want to preserve their historic lives. Another clique—called Whole Truth—wants to find out who cooperated with your dad's regime, to shame people who spied on friends and family."

"Didn't everybody?" Shay asks.

"Some more than others," Tally says. "If we had that data, we could find out who set up Hideaway."

"Sure—we could judge everyone in Shreve." Shay throws a piece of kindling at Tally. "Like *you* never collaborated with the authorities?"

Tally just looks away.

Astrix ignores them, as if this is an old argument. "Problem is, it'd take us six about a million years to watch all those recordings, even if we fast-forward past the sleeping parts. I repeat myself: It's a *lot* of data."

"Not for brains the size of cities," I say. "But why does Diego want it? To do their own Whole Truth?"

"Much worse," Astrix says. "They want to *study* us."

She sits down hard, close to the fire, and glares into its depths.

"There's an old theory about artificial intelligence," she says. "We shouldn't let it get to know us too well. That's why cities have privacy laws. Machines already analyze our traffic patterns and pings, and even peek into our trash cans. Imagine them listening to every word you said, watching every decision, every expression that crossed your face—times two million people, times ten years."

"What it is to be human," Tally says softly, "in one database."

"AIs could start making their own people," Astrix says. "And we wouldn't be able to tell the difference."

A memory passes through me with a shudder—how Diego manipulated me and my sister, turning us against each other. It did all that with a cold, impersonal avatar.

What if Diego could act just like one of us? But a million times more charming, funny, and insightful?

The best impostor ever.

My father never let the Shreve AI learn from the data it collected. I thought he was being paranoid—but maybe it was smart.

"With those recordings," Astrix says, "an AI could run the perfect political campaign, tell the perfect lie, predict in detail what us puny humans will do next."

Shay frowns. "And your sister's trading all that—for *food*?"

"You don't eat, you die," Astrix says. "And it's just a theory."

"A theory that Diego wants to test," Tally says. "That's nervous-making enough for me."

We're all lost in thought, and the darkness around us rushes into the silence. The sounds of small creatures, wind, a gurgling creek—the wild, ever noisy and unsatisfied.

Shreve is still haunted by my father's dust watching everyone for all those years. And now the results of his steady, unblinking gaze might ripple across the world.

What if this was the reason why . . . ?

"Oh, crap," I say.

Everyone looks at me, but it takes a moment to speak.

"After the Fall of Shreve, Diego came to visit me in the hospital. They apologized for taking so long to stop my father. They admitted the free cities gave him too many chances, like they were hoping he'd fix himself. But what if they were stalling—what if their cowardice was *intentional*?"

Tally softly swears. "Because they wanted the dust to keep recording everyone in Shreve. Your father was making something they were hungry for."

"Talk about things going back to normal," Astrix says. "If this theory's right, the AIs can use those recordings to ride humanity like a hoverboard—smooth and steady forever."

Her certainty sinks into me. Diego was always so interested in me and Rafi, and who would rule Shreve afterward. They were the only city that sent jump troops the night my father fell, storming his tower alongside my sister's rebels.

"We have to get those recordings," Tally says.

"Boss." Shay gives a weary sigh. "Are we seriously thinking of breaking into a nuclear waste dump? Because of a *theory*?"

"No," Tally says. "Because the AIs want to make the world normal again. We're rebels, Shay-la. Abnormal is what we do."

PAPER PLANES

We train four days before launching ourselves at the Sarcophagus.

The full moon has waned since we found Hideaway, rising later every night. Now, two hours after sunset, a scattered cover of clouds is enough to make the darkness total.

We stand on our new hoverboards, ready to take the jump. Astrix drifts down the line, spraying us with a sparkling mist from a bottle.

"Check your seals," she says.

I flex the joints on my protective suit, bending my knees and elbows, turning my head. If any of the mist gets inside, an alarm will sound and we'll have to scrub the mission for tonight.

It's weird being swaddled like this, breathing canned air. The rad suit slows my movements, makes me feel clumsy and uncertain for the first time since I became Special. My senses are muffled by the layers between me and the world.

X seems to enjoy it even less. He twitches beside me like a cat in wrapping paper.

But no one argued about putting on these suits. Duralloy bones and healing nanos won't count for much inside the Sarcophagus. A day before the Fall of Shreve, I took one false step in a Rusty nuclear site, and the bones of my left foot had to be replaced.

No alarms—everyone's suit has passed the test.

"Okay, crew," Tally says, replacing Astrix out front. "On this mission, we have to ignore our usual instincts. You bubbleheads all think you're indestructible. That's why we programmed our crash bracelets to wake up when you shake them—everyone kept forgetting to turn them on!"

We all laugh at this.

"But on this mission, anything that can rip your suit can kill you. If you hear an alarm, patch up and get out. Remember what it was like to be uglies playing tricks, always ready to run and hide."

The other Youngbloods smile at this, reminding me how different I am from them. Growing up with my sister's face, no one ever dared call me an ugly, and my tutors trained me never to run and hide.

I wasn't bulletproof—I was sniper bait.

"All I'm saying is, stay safe." Tally angles her board, and gets back in line.

I check my position again, laying a terrain map onto my eye-screen. Our approach has been precisely calculated. We have to hit the hill before us—gently sloping on this side, steep on the far end—at exactly the right angle.

Astrix releases two handfuls of microdrones into the air. They flutter gently as they rise, the propellors of their tiny weather vanes spinning in the breeze. We need a strong wind at our back for this jump.

The wait begins.

We talk a little, the others' voices scratchy in my ears. Our private comm channel is intentionally weak so we won't be noticed by the local network. If I stray more than fifty or so meters from the others, I'll be cut off, alone in the dark and poisonous hallways of my childhood home.

The lights of Shreve flicker and pulse in the distance. Rafi has ended my father's rules against decorative lighting. Every night looks like a festival, the skyline a gaudy chandelier jutting up through the earth.

We might be a poor city, but solar power is free.

We . . .

I'm not really a citizen of Shreve—there's no official record of my birth, and my sister stole my name. But this city is mine enough that I don't want my sister trading away those dust recordings, the fabric of its people's lives.

I've started watching the local feeds, especially stories about reunited Hideaway families. Even though it's propaganda for my sister, with those long shots of her next to Tally on the Shreve House lawn, the images still move me. Like there's room in me for something besides anger and grief.

There are no stories about the kids whose parents didn't live to see my father's end.

When my sister's latest ping arrived, I hoped she'd mention those other lost children. But it was just her pleading with me to tell her I was still alive. My visit as Diego has her worried.

I didn't answer.

"Wind's picking up," Astrix says.

The grass gently shifts around me. I should feel the air on my skin and in my hair, but the radiation suit is too stiff.

"Okay, we're good," comes Astrix's voice. "In five, four, three . . ."

"The Smoke lives," Tally says.

We push off, accelerating quietly. These hoverboards were printed especially for the mission—air-dropped to us by my old friend the city of Paz. The boards have seriously underpowered lifting fans but are full of other tricks.

The absolute silence of our flight somehow makes our approach more dramatic. All I can hear is my own breathing inside my helmet, and the whir of my heart.

I never thought I'd see my childhood home again.

Not from the inside.

As we gather speed, we drop, bellies on boards, to lower wind resistance. Our course takes us downhill at first to gain momentum, but the slope looms ahead, dark against the spangled city lights.

We reach the hill and climb its flank, faster and faster.

All at once, the ground drops out from under me.

For a moment, I'm sailing through the cold air, a pure projectile. No guidance or motive power, just momentum and the simple aerodynamics of my board.

The Sarcophagus is visible ahead, a dark gash in the sparkling heart of Shreve.

"And . . . *now*," Astrix says.

With a click of my tongue, my hoverboard unfolds.

It's like the Youngbloods' gliding trick with their solar panels, but an order of magnitude more sophisticated. These boards' riding surfaces are composed of dozens of independent layers, each of which can unfurl into its own shape in midair.

They re-form around me—a sudden origami crane the size of an aircraft. I'm nestled at its center, still lying on my belly. Every move I make shifts the delicate, papery wings, like surfing on the wind.

Our six gliders are huge against the sky, but the unfolded layers are too thin to reflect radar, the translucent wings printed with fluttering images of birds. Anyone spotting us from below will see only flocks of starlings roiling the night sky. In these radiation suits, we're invisible to thermal vision as well.

The Youngbloods' tech keeps surprising me with its blend of graceful stealth and raw power. Even the Paz AI was impressed when it saw the specs. We could fly straight up to my sister's house unseen if the wind was a little stronger.

"Sentry drones ahead," Croy says.

"Don't get close unless you've got a clear shot," Shay orders. "These gliders get shaky with holes in them."

A gust of wind passes through our formation, and for a moment, we're all too busy steering our giant paper planes to speak.

When I've gained control again, a drone is in front of me.

I angle toward it—carefully.

If I hit the sentry, it'll punch right through my glider, a knife point piercing tissue paper. But we need to take at least a few of the drones out. When we escape later tonight, our hoverboards won't be in this silent, invisible configuration.

My target hovers in position, motionless and unsuspecting.

I pull a smart net from my belt. Even that small movement sends a wobble through my craft—the target is off center.

My whole body twists, willing the glider to follow.

The huge, delicate form around me responds, drifting back where I want it. And there's my target—lined up just beneath me.

I drop the net. It sparkles to life as it tumbles, my glider popping up a little as the weight falls away.

They collide soundlessly, the net wrapping itself around the sentry. As I shoot overhead, the two machines shudder together in midair.

The net is blocking the drone's transmissions, parasitizing its inner workings with a dozen microdrills, a flood of nanos.

By the time I dare a glance back over my shoulder, the net has fallen away. The sentry drone hovers resolutely in the air, as if still on duty.

But it belongs to us now.

A sparkling appears to my right—X taking out another drone, a perfect shot.

I refocus on my own flight path. My father's poisoned tomb is only a few hundred meters away, featureless in the darkness.

I'm almost home.

Something small passes between me and the Sarcophagus—a shape flitting across the blackness. Then another, and still more . . .

I start to reach for another net, but these aren't sentries. They're too small and too many. Scores of them swarming, seething, fluttering.

They aren't drones at all.

It's a flock of birds, and I'm about to hit them.

FLOCK

"Birdstrike!" Tally cries.

There's a word for this? tilts through my head as a tearing sound comes from my right, a tremor shivering the papery frame around me. A surprised squawk and flutter trailing away behind.

The bird went straight through my wing.

The craft still feels steady, but there are more birdstrikes coming.

Lots of them.

It's like a rainstorm—one drop, then two more. Only seconds till a steady stream builds, each collision sending a sick-making shudder through the glider.

A flapping form rushes out of the darkness straight at my face. The shock of impact rattles my radiation helmet, a burst of squawks and feathers.

With every tear, the craft's stability takes a hit. I'm losing altitude.

The comm channel is full of chatter—at the back of our formation,

Shay and Astrix are unhit. Tally and Croy, in the lead, are already spiraling down to earth.

I'm too busy to say anything, no longer gliding straight and true. My right wing sags, and the craft starts a slow turn in that direction.

A few wingspans away, X's glider is tilting toward mine. His left wing passed through the same flock as my right, and now we're listing in opposite directions, heading for each other.

His voice in my ear: "Hold on tight, Frey-la."

We crash in slow motion, like ocean liners grinding hulls. Both gliders buckle, deforming around us, but X's has more holes than mine. His craft starts to fold up . . .

"Coming aboard!" he calls.

X scrambles toward me across the near wing, which bows beneath his weight like a tree branch. A gap opens between the gliders, and it looks like he's going to drop away. But he leaps—and grabs the tail of my glider.

The nose pitches up, but I don't have enough momentum to climb. The whole contraption stalls in midair, the wind dying around us.

"Hang on!" I cry.

Stalled out, carrying two people, full of holes, the glider starts to pinwheel downward, a leaf spinning from branch to ground.

I wrap my arms around the slender core of hoverboard—here in the middle of the craft, the spinning isn't bad. But X is out on the tail, the full centrifugal force of our rotation trying to fling him into the dark.

When the crash comes, it's oddly soft and quiet, with the muted bounce of a crumpled paper ball. The structure sags around me, then tips to the right, settling on the ground.

I stand up, wobbly on the thin surface.

"X? You still with me?"

"Unhurt," comes his answer.

I turn and look through the darkness—it's a shredded wreck back there.

X stands up, trussed in a harness of smart plastic ropes. Looped around the glider's tail, they've torn it to pieces.

But his improvised rig held just long enough.

At a flick of X's wrists, the ropes wind around his belt again. He walks toward me through the crumpled remains of the glider.

I face the Sarcophagus, barely a hundred meters away. What appears to be a flock of birds is descending in its shadow, oddly shaky in the air.

I tell my glider to disintegrate as X walks up beside me.

"Shall we run?" he asks. "Don't want them starting without us."

From up close, the skin of the giant pyramid is a slice of starless night.

It's coated with a special substance, blacker than black—boiling hot in the sun, intimidating in the dark. It's too slippery to climb and almost impossible to break. If you do manage to break away a piece, it gives off a choking smell of rot and sulfur.

The Sarcophagus is designed to discourage future explorers.

Even those a thousand years from now, when my father's name is forgotten but the poison of his last crime remains.

Here in the present, its mass settles over me like a bad dream.

The Youngbloods are waiting for us on the far side of the pyramid's base. Past them, the city lights glitter in contrast to the baleful Sarcophagus.

"Glad you two could make it," Tally says with a smile.

"Birds!" Croy exclaims. "Didn't see that coming."

"We have three working boards." Shay stares at the pyramid's smooth side. The peak of the structure is still open, the triangle jagged and unfinished. There's still access to the top of my father's tower—his office, the control room, and the data vaults where the dust recordings reside.

"Going up with two people on a board is no problem," Shay says. "But it'll be slow for exfiltration."

"Also known as running away," Croy clarifies.

"We might not have to run." Astrix is scanning the sky above the city with her field glasses. "We got all the sentry drones on the wild side, and there aren't any between us and the city."

"None?" I squint into the darkness above Shreve. "Does that seem weird?"

Croy shrugs. "Maybe nobody's worried about trespassers. Who's brain-missing enough to wander into a nuclear waste dump?"

DRONES

X and I share a hoverboard, creeping up the pyramid on shaky magnetics. There are metal trusses inside the structure, but the outer layer is thick.

From this close, the surface is gently reflective, like polished black stone. The silhouette of the two us crouching on the board ripples across the dark expanse, occulting the pinprick stars.

Inside my helmet, a hesitant sound begins. Like diamonds dropping onto a piece of glass, one by one.

X and I lock eyes.

"What an epitaph," he says. "The tick of a radiation meter."

I wonder once more why my father filled our home with nuclear waste.

Maybe Tally's right, and he just wanted to be in control one last time. But what he chose to do with that last glint of power—bargaining with Rafi to kill me—still makes my head spin.

Yes, I murdered his son. But I was *his* creature.

Everything my father did after I killed Seanan—invading Victoria, attacking Paz, forcing the free cities to come for him—seems like a man trying to destroy himself.

As if I ended my father the same day I killed Seanan.

Watching the thoughts on my face, X says, "This place doesn't define you, Frey."

"Rafi and I used to dance on our balcony, when the rain washed the dust from the air."

X smiles at this. "Already a rebel."

Rafi was too, the radiation meter whispers in my ear.

We climb higher, following the angle of the pyramid inward toward the top of the buried tower. Past the level of the trophy room, where my portrait hung before my sister salvaged it. Past the data vaults full of meticulous recordings of Shreve's last decade.

There's not much security here.

I wonder if Rafi knows what a prize she's giving the machines. Does she think their interest in human behavior is merely academic? Is she too busy mending her broken city to care?

Maybe she simply doesn't think she could ever be outpoliticked by an AI. Not in the city she was born to rule.

As we near the opening at the pyramid's top, the ticking of my rad meter picks up.

A drone is passing ten meters away, carrying a load of cargo down the slope. Too heavy for lifters, it walks on six legs, its grippy footpads the size of dinner plates. Even so, it skids a little on the glassy skin of the Sarcophagus. No cameras to see us with, just an impact sensor in front.

Surely Rafi wouldn't trust a simple machine like this to haul away the memory cores. But we drift closer to make sure.

The chattering in my helmet grows.

I peek under the tarp covering the cargo—it's a jumble of forks and knives.

"Silverware?" X murmurs.

A wave of memory hits me, practicing eating with clumsy hands. "The formal stuff, for my father's state banquets."

If antique silver is worth saving from a waste dump, Rafi really does need money.

Or maybe she wants reminders of our old life. The pomp and circumstance of being the heir, without the responsibility of healing a wounded city.

I drop the tarp's corner and let the cargo drone pass into the darkness below. I'm done with trying to psychoanalyze my sister. I had to live inside her head for sixteen years, learning her gestures, her smiles.

Sometimes I wish we were enemies who'd never met each other.

The wind is picking up, whistling through the construction site above us.

There are more drones up there—motionless, waiting for tomorrow's work to start. So they aren't going day and night to give Diego what it wants. Either Rafi's dragging her feet, or she wants the human controllers at their best for the delicate work of saving the memory cores.

I wonder again why it's so security-missing up here.

"*You* bumped into it," Astrix hisses in my ears.

"*Your* fault!" Croy protests.

I scan the darkness and find his tall silhouette, crowded onto a board with her small one.

Sliding away from them is one of the shut-down drones, headed toward me and X across the glassy surface. I expect it to come to life, resetting its grip or calling for help.

But it slides straight at us, building speed.

X and I both react, leaning in opposite directions—the board goes nowhere.

The drone clips X's end, sending us spinning.

The world gyrates around us, dark sky and darker Sarcophagus, the others' voices frantic in our helmets. X presses hard against me in our whirling dance.

I've stopped a hundred spinouts but never with another rider aboard. X and I keep contradicting each other, or overcorrecting. The spin grows wilder.

Then firm hands grasp my shoulders, and we come to a jerking halt.

In this suddenly steady universe, Tally's face is looking straight into mine.

"Are you two done messing around?"

"That drone." I turn to look down the slope. "It wasn't just sleeping. It's dead."

The machine is still sliding, picking up more speed as it descends. It clips the cargo carrier that passed me and X, and they both skid away.

Tally gives me a soft "huh."

The drones fade into smudges in the darkness; then we hear the brittle, sparkly crash of silverware spilling across the ground.

Tally releases my shoulders. "That *is* kind of weird."

"Maybe not, Boss," Shay's voice comes.

We look up the slope, to where the others are waiting at the entrance to the pyramid's peak. Shay is waving a scanner at a cement-mixer drone.

"These machines are all dead," she says.

"Out of charge?" Tally asks.

"Crashed—intentionally. And I bet those missing sentries on the city side are too."

Shay's sigh ripples softly in my helmet.

"Someone got here before us, Tally-wa."

SARCOPHAGUS

We crouch at the opening to the Sarcophagus.

Astrix sends in three small scout drones.

This radiation suit makes me feel like some random—clumsy, sense-missing, with no camouflage. If whoever beat us to this place is still here, we'll be sitting ducks.

But we can't take the suits off now. My rad meter is making an angry clatter, like stones popping on the underside of a hoverboard flying low and fast across gravel.

I turn the volume down, trusting the suit to ping me if the radiation spikes.

"Nobody up here but us," Astrix says.

We look down into the Sarcophagus.

The pyramid's interior is a web of duralloy girders, supporting its sides until the whole thing is filled with permacrete. The wind whistles in through the opening, mournful and hesitant. Our comms are shut off, so I can't hear the others breathing anymore.

The hollowness of the vast space thrums in my chest.

Shay leads the way, tightroping across a girder leading to the tower.

It's strange, seeing my childhood home encased inside another structure. For ten years, it was the tallest building in Shreve, by law. But now it's been swallowed, soon to be digested by half a million tons of permacrete.

Going last across the girder, I notice something stuck to the back of X's radiation suit.

A patch—his suit tore in our crash.

"X . . ." I start, but he spins around and leans in close. With his faceplate pressed against mine, his whisper fills my helmet.

"Not a word."

I hesitate—we're supposed to abort if our suits are torn. Patches are better at sealing in air than keeping out radiation. But this is Boss X . . . and he patched it up before we came in.

I give him a nod.

We turn our attention back to the hundred-meter fall on either side of us.

The others wait at a ragged, gaping hole, entry to the second-highest floor of the tower. I remember now—the control room was blasted open by my sister's rebels as the Fall of Shreve neared its final act.

Astrix sends her scout drones into the room, then gives the all clear.

Shay whispers to me, "You first."

I stare into the darkness. My father's body is only a flight of stairs above us, three months dead. Rafi didn't bury him, just left him to rot, preserved like trail meat by the radiation leaking from the walls.

They took Col's body that night, away to Victoria and a funeral I missed. Those hundreds of thousands lining the streets of the newly freed city. His little brother, Teo, walking beside the hovering casket, one hand steadying its passage in the cloud-seeded rain. I watched it from a Paz hospital, radiation poisoning making me vomit.

The world becomes dizzy and unstuck, the open space of the Sarcophagus yawning beneath me.

I finally realize—*this* is the spire of grief that comes for me every night, stretching up from darkness. This tower, this spike where I was raised, is now forever aimed at my heart, Col's death poisoning its tip.

Tally's voice is gentle. "You know the building, Frey-la. We don't."

"Sure." I take a few slow breaths, flicking on my wrist lights to push away the darkness.

The control room lights up before me. This is where Security watched the city in real time, sampling the countless feeds from surveillance dust. Now it's a galaxy of glass from shattered wallscreens, bullet-pocked walls and ceiling.

"Anything out of place?" Shay asks.

I scan the room, trying to recall that night three months ago without setting the world spinning again. My sister and I fought side by side here. We were sent hurtling out of this room by a shockgun, only to be caught midair by Diego jump troops.

You're magnificent would have been Rafi's last words to me.

The rebel soldiers' bodies have been taken away, but a few Shreve

134

heavies are piled by the door, still in their armor. I'm grateful for the rebreather in my suit.

The rest looks like it did at the end of that awful night.

"Nothing's changed that I can see," I say. "The data vaults are one floor down."

The stairs are a nightmare of armored Shreve soldiers and rebel blood.

Gouges expose the wiring in the walls—Rafi's army was trying to cut off my father from his dirty bomb. But he had enough explosives stuffed into his office fireplace to detonate the whole tower. The only thing that saved us was my sister killing Col.

The stairs waver for a moment.

No—Rafi didn't *save* anyone except herself.

"You okay?" Tally asks.

"I'm fine, Boss." More deep breaths.

One of Astrix's tiny drones is sniffing something at the bottom of the stairs. It shimmers, just out of reach of my new vision. When I shine my light on it, it vanishes completely. But when I point the light away, it glints again on the stone.

It's a drawing, in some kind of half-invisible metallic ink.

A bundle of feathers.

I've seen this symbol before, scrawled on the rooftops of Shreve during my father's rule.

"The palimpsest." I descend the stairs and kneel beside the symbol.

"The resistance had a secret code, like invisible graffiti. You needed glasses to see it. For some reason, my Special vision's picking it up."

"For some reason," Astrix repeats with a soft laugh. "Who do you think invented this stuff?"

I stare at her. "Wait. *You* were helping the resistance here?"

She smiles. "Not just in Shreve—the ink's everywhere. We give it to opposition cliques, journos investigating corruption, the odd crim. Whoever needs to keep secrets from a local government."

"But my rebels friends hadn't heard of it," I say.

Shay shrugs. "Not all rebels. Just us."

"Turn up your ultraviolet," Astrix says.

When I do, the symbol grows steadier.

"We just supply the ink," Tally says. "Every city creates their own code. Can you read this?"

"A little. A feather duster means this place is safe from surveillance." I look up at the control room. "Which means it was definitely written *after* the fall."

"It might mean something different now," X says.

He right—the palimpsest was scrawled across the entire city of Shreve, a catalog of frustrations, petty rebellions, and crimes. But those countless layers of symbols are mostly irrelevant in the age of Frey.

Tally nods at the door to the data vaults. "One way to find out. Send a drone in, Astrix."

"Already did, straight through an air shaft—it died," Astrix says. "Too many grays in there."

I stand and walk toward the door. It's made of thick metal, like a vault full of gold.

"We have to be quick," Astrix says. "It's hot in there."

I check my helmet seals again, then take a deep breath of recycled air.

The door isn't locked when I give it a shove. It swings open to reveal an empty room.

The memory cores are gone.

CORES

"*How?*" is all Astrix can say.

I walk into the room, trying to ignore the rad meter hailstorming in my ears. I turn the volume down another notch.

The room is completely empty.

Growing up, Rafi and I snuck in here a few times, expecting to see recordings of debauchery and treason. Of course, the reality was superbly boring—a few hundred identical, soccer-ball-size cores, each holding one week of dust recordings.

They were full of goo, I remember, jam-packed with strands of artificial DNA, the most efficient form of data storage. Every cell in our body contains the whole human genome, after all.

While planning this mission, Astrix couldn't think of a way to carry them all on our low-powered hoverboards.

We were simply going to destroy them.

"How'd they manage to get *every single one*?" Astrix says. "It's only been three hours since nightfall!"

"They might still be here," Shay says. "Check the other vaults."

We storm back out. But at the bottom of the next staircase down, the same symbol is drawn on the floor.

"They've cleaned it out," I said. "That's what a feather duster means."

Tally looks at me. "*Who* did this? Who uses these symbols?"

"Everyone. Smugglers, citizens blowing off steam, all the cliques . . ." My voice hitches.

The Futures.

But there's no way that a bunch of self-obsessed kids could've pulled this theft off. Maybe it was Whole Truth, looking to shame my fathers' collaborators.

A sound comes from the closed door of the second vault—a soft voice, moaning.

I throw myself at the door, but this one's locked.

"Astrix!" I yell, but she's already beside me, squirting nanos on the hinges.

The metal heats up, glowing red in seconds. An infernal smell fills the cramped staircase.

The moaning comes again.

Astrix turns to X. "It's ready, if you hit it hard enough."

The rest of us clear space for him.

He throws himself down the stairs and against the door. It snaps open wrong ways, hinge side swinging inward, then breaks free completely, spinning for a moment on one corner before it tumbles to the ground.

We charge inside.

This room's like the ones above—stripped bare of cores. But in a corner lies a figure in a radiation suit, surrounded by dead hovercams.

A murmur comes from him.

"Told you . . . to leave me."

The voice is sickeningly familiar. I kneel beside him and rub at the helmet's fogged-over faceplate.

It's Counselor Chulhee, the boss of Future.

"You're kidding me," I say. Sentry drones knocked out, hundreds of cores removed in a matter of hours, all with the precision of a military operation. "But you're just a bunch of kids!"

"*Who* is?" Tally demands.

"No time for introductions," Astrix says, a scanner in her hand. "We have to get him out of here. *We* have to get out of here!"

The rad meter in my helmet is shrieking again.

X and I grab Chulhee and head for the door.

"I'll check the last vault," Astrix cries. "Meet you up top!"

Five of us head up the stairs. I'm climbing backward, carrying Chulhee by his shoulders. He makes small protesting noises, his head lolling from side to side.

"Did we get everything?" he murmurs.

"Looks like it," I say.

A sigh leaks from him, a mix of agony and satisfaction.

The Futures spent the last ten years performing their lives for an unborn audience. They must have decided it was worth risking death to save all those historic moments from oblivion.

We reach the control room, and I stumble backward across wreckage and dead bodies. Chulhee groans as I almost drop him.

Shay's already called the hoverboards inside.

"I'll take him," Tally says. "Anyone else shows up at a hospital with a radioactive body, they'll get arrested."

"He's not a body yet, Boss," Croy says.

We load him onto a board, and Tally straddles him. She lifts up and out the hole in the control room wall.

As we watch them fly away, Shay breaks comm silence. "Astrix?"

A soft sigh in my helmet. "No cores down here, Shay-la. But there's another body."

Shay swears, then gathers herself. "I'm coming down to help you."

"Don't," Astrix says. "There's nothing we can do for this one."

Shay looks at me. "You said *a bunch of kids*. Who are they?"

"A clique called Future. They thought the surveillance recordings were . . . historically important."

She frowns. "A bunch of kids care about history?"

"They care about *being* history," I say.

"Well, at least one of them is," Shay mutters. "Like we'll be, unless we get out of here—five of us on two boards!"

"Right." I look around the control room, as if another hoverboard is going to appear.

Then I see what I missed on the way in—a small shiny object under one of the shattered wallscreens.

A butter knife.

I walk over and pick it up, remembering the drone carrying

silverware that was leaving just as we arrived. All the other drones were dead.

Drones don't drop things by accident . . . and I never looked under the top layer of silverware.

"The Futures were finishing up when we got here." I drop the knife. "They used that cargo drone to sneak past us."

"What do you mean?" Shay asks.

It's too much to explain, and every second gives them more time to get away.

"Follow me."

I head for the ragged opening at a dead run.

CRASH
LANDING

My feet clang on the girder as I run, the sound echoing down the hundred-meter drop.

My feet slip near the other end, but I grab the girder with both hands and swing out the opening in the pyramid wall.

Our remaining boards are there on standby, but there's a faster way down to the ground.

I grab one of the dead construction drones, with fine manipulator arms and big grippy footpads. I tear off two of its legs, then step out onto the slick skin of the Sarcophagus.

My feet slip out from under me, but I slam the borrowed grippy pads against the glossy black surface of the pyramid. They slow me down a little, the friction building through my gloves.

Every second, I'm sliding a little faster.

The cargo drone is down there at the bottom, crashed onto its side, silverware strewn everywhere. It walked right past me and X, and we practically ignored it.

The Futures saw us coming. They snuck the last few cores out right before our eyes.

I try to angle my skid away from the two crashed drones, toward softer ground. But I'm headed straight toward the wreckage.

As the earth rushes up, I curl into a ball . . .

The ground hits me like a giant fist, a *whump* traveling through my body.

Then I'm rolling across thick grass and scattered forks, knives, and spoons. Pinpricks jab me, tearing at my suit like tiny radioactive teeth.

I roll to a halt on my back, staring up at the taunting stars.

It takes a moment to move again. Healing nanos are swarming across my broken skin, clustering around a bruised rib.

But there's no time to linger. I stand and pull off the radiation suit, worse than useless now that it's torn. Two sprained fingers on my left hand scream as I work the clasps—more nanos flock to the pain.

I take a step toward the cargo carrier, and my rad meter starts clicking. Nothing protects me but a sneak suit now.

The carrier's empty. A few meters away, the grass is marked with four deep ruts—the landing skids of a hovercar with a heavy load.

"Shay?" I say to the darkness.

No answer comes. I boost the power in my comms.

"Shay! Can you hear me?"

"We're coming. But turn down your—"

"The Futures were *here*," I interrupt. "We just missed them. Looks like they were in a hovercar!"

A moment of silence.

Then Astrix's voice: "She's right—there it is! Headed west, and seriously radioactive!"

I scan the sky, thermal imaging turned up. But the pyramid blocks half the sky.

"Pick me up. I'm at the bottom."

"You're on your own," Shay cuts me off. "Comm silence."

"But I don't have a . . ." My voice fades. There's not even static in my ear, my comms overridden by Shay's command.

A pair of hoverboards streak across the sky above me, carrying Shay, X, Croy, and Astrix toward the west.

With only two boards left, there's no room for me.

I have to walk out of Shreve.

That's when I hear the sirens on their way.

EXFILTRATION

I run hard, my bruised rib making every step a gut punch.

At least I'm finally out of that bulky radiation suit. The wind tastes like pine needles and this afternoon's rainstorm. The stars are rampant overhead. I feel like a Special again.

The sirens are almost here. Did the Futures trip an alarm inside the pyramid, or did we?

Then I realize—this is my fault. The night was quiet until I boosted my comms to talk to Shay.

Three warden hovercars are in the sky, headed for the Sarcophagus. They're small unarmed craft, part of the civilian force that replaced my father's dreaded Security.

I slow my run a little. The new wardens are armed only with shocksticks. Brutal by most free cities' standards, but a mere annoyance for me.

I see flickers of heat in the sky—the lifting fans of a dozen hoverboards. It's not just wardens in cars; my sister's personal body-guard of former rebels is joining the response.

I pull up the hood of my sneak suit, looking around for a hiding place.

The pyramid is still a construction site—bare ground, piles of parts and materials. A huge fabricator sits ready to produce half a million tons of permacrete.

The piles are organized into girders, pipes, glossy tiles for the pyramid's outer layer. Then I spot a mountain of offcuts, a chaotic jumble.

I dive in, picking my way toward the middle. It's a jungle of scrap, jagged edges everywhere, ready to stab or slice me. But the broken shapes are perfect for my sneak suit to copy.

The warden hovercars shoot past overhead, going for the pyramid. Most of the bodyguard follows, but one of the boards takes a slow circle above the construction site.

A young rebel rides it, peering down into the darkness around me. He takes out a scanner.

I pull up my camo mask.

That's when I hear it—a gentle ticking in my ear, like the end of a rainstorm on a roof. My rad meter is still picking up trace radiation.

But these are offcuts, not scrap from the pyramid . . .

The radiation is *me*.

My boots on that poisoned stone inside. My gloves touching the walls. All the pinpricks in my suit when I rolled across scattered silverware.

The ticking is soft, unsteady. Nothing the rebel's scanner can pick up at a distance.

His hoverboard descends, weaving through the site. He's retracing my path exactly, following my footprints in the soft dirt.

I search for an escape route, hints of starlight leading me toward the far side. But the first shift of my weight sends a soft creaking through the pile.

I freeze again.

The rebel comes closer. He's staring into the mountain of scrap, uncertain.

He's probably wondering whether to call for backup. A few footprints could be uglies playing hide-and-seek.

"Anybody in there?" he shouts.

I don't answer.

"Okay, be that way," he says. "But don't come crying if you get hurt."

He flies up to the summit of the scrap mountain, directly overhead. His lifting fans spin up, and he rises straight into the air.

For a moment, I think he's leaving . . .

But then he cuts his fans and falls straight down onto the pile.

With a chorus of metal shrieks, the mountain of scrap shudders around me. Offcuts clatter and grind against each other, and smaller pieces dislodge and rattle their way down like jagged pachinko balls.

Something sharp slices my side as it bounces past.

When the noise settles, the rebel calls again. "Still want to hide?"

I don't answer.

The young rebel's lifting fans spin up again.

How long before he gives up this nonsense? Maybe not before he spots the body heat leaking from my torn suit.

Maybe I'll just take his hoverboard.

The rebel comes hurtling down again, making the whole structure shudder. I scramble upward, dodging debris and quivering edges. The racket of shifting metal covers my ascent.

When the pile settles, I freeze again.

He's staring down into the jumble, looking less certain now. But he spins up his lifters and crashes onto the pile again.

I climb a few meters higher in the clatter.

The rebel is close enough now that I can read the slogan scrawled on the grille of his lifting fans: *This Hoverboard Kills Fascists*.

Typical. This guy works for my sister.

He's staring right at me, but without any sign of recognition. My camo is a riot of images lifted from the pile. My only worry is that he'll give up and go away.

After all this ruckus, he can at least give me his board. I've already spotted just the right piece of rebar.

"Waste of time," he mutters, turning toward the Sarcophagus.

Before he can lift away, I rap the thin sheet of metal next to me.

Ping.

His eyes snap back in my direction.

He spins his fans up and rises away one last time.

I reach for the length of rebar as he starts to drop.

Bam—the metal jungle shudders around me. But my feet are set, and I thrust the rebar upward through the last layer of scrap.

It hits him squarely on the chest, a *thunk* against his body armor. He tumbles from his board.

I pull myself up and out, metal edges tearing at my sneak suit, and haul myself onto the empty hoverboard.

The rebel is stunned, staring blearily up at me from the pile. A piece of metal juts through his shoulder armor, blood glimmering on its shaft.

"You should get that looked at," I say.

He starts to reach for his pistol, but I draw my knife. It roars to full pulse, setting off a sympathetic trembling in the pile of scrap.

The rebel raises his hands in surrender, but he's murmuring on his comms. His friends will be here soon.

I click my tongue to spin the lifting fans back up and head west at top speed.

TWO BIRDS

Shay and the other Youngbloods are no longer visible on the horizon.

If I can spot them, I can catch up with them. They're on the gliders we used for sneaking into Shreve. My stolen board is a high-powered wilderness model, its lifting fans screaming beneath my feet.

But there's nothing to see, and my orders are comm silence.

Also, five more rebels from Rafi's bodyguard are swinging around to follow me. I should play decoy and lead my pursuers in some random direction.

But what if my crew need help? Their origami boards can't catch the Futures' hovercar, not carrying two riders each.

I keep heading west.

I'm done being a decoy.

It takes only minutes to reach the edge of the city. The border is still marked with railgun craters from the Fall of Shreve, filled with the ashes and scrap metal of my father's defenses.

I scan the horizon again.

Nothing, not even a flock of birds.

Rafi's rebels are pacing me exactly. We're all riding the same boards.

Or maybe they're waiting for reinforcements.

Once the wardens back at the pyramid see that the memory cores are missing, every alarm in the city will ring. Shreve still has a few pursuit craft in its fleet, faster than any hoverboard.

The answer hits me—I need to shake off these rebels, and the Youngbloods need faster rides.

I drop into the trees. It's like flying through that flock of birds again, leaves and branches whacking at my arms and face. I make a hard turn back toward my pursuers.

Five against one. But they aren't Special.

I bank to a halt and wedge the stolen board into the crook of a tree branch, shutting down its lifting fans. Slapping a couple of patches on my sneak suit, I'm invisible again.

I climb up into the treetops, pulse knife drawn, and wait for them to catch up.

The rebels cut their speed. They spread out into a search formation, not bothering to watch each other's backs.

They think I'm on the ground, trying to slip away on foot.

One of them drifts toward me, scanning the branches for body heat. Her slow zigzag pattern brings her closer.

When she's overhead, I bring my knife to full pulse—

But I don't throw.

The knife carries me into the air, a tornado in my hand. She drops the scanner, trying to draw her weapon.

I kick her off the board and jump on, tilting it hard as she tumbles away through the branches.

I hope she's wearing crash bracelets.

The board roars beneath my feet, a sudden burst of speed. I ride just long enough for the other rebels to wheel around toward me, then drop down into the trees again.

Now I have two boards, and my pulse knife has enough charge for three more ambushes, maybe.

Four pursuers to go.

They're being smarter now, flying in pairs, autorifles in hand instead of scanners. They should wait for backup, but these aren't soldiers. They're rebels stuck on guard duty for three months, restless and bored. They joined Rafi to overthrow a city, not to become wardens.

I stash the board, then swing through the trees, picking a spot for my next ambush.

Two rebels are closing in, ten meters apart—which makes this tricky. I pause a moment to program my last smart net.

One of the targets is the squad's commander. He's older, wearing full body armor, no skins or feathers. The other is young, wide-eyed, and nervous, cradling her rifle like a safety blanket.

I draw my knife . . .

The younger rebel wafts overhead, and I leap at her, knife roaring

153

in my hand. At the same time, I throw my smart net at the commander, aiming low.

The younger rebel raises her rifle—too late. I land on her board, tear the weapon from her hands, and throw it into the trees. Then I grab hold of her arm and pull her closer.

Her commander is aiming but can't fire without hitting us both. My smart net has wrapped itself around the front end of his board. The rebel in my arms is struggling but can't do much against my Special—

Buzz.

The shockstick strapped to her leg—it's in my stomach. All my muscles frazzle.

She pulls free and jumps off, leaving her commander a clear shot.

As his rifle cracks to life, my net takes control of his board. It leaps beneath him, rocketing straight up.

The commander disappears into the sky, his wild shots sparkling in the darkness. The board will take him back toward Shreve at maximum altitude.

I check myself—no hits. But the other pair of rebels is wheeling around in the distance, shouldering their weapons.

I spin my new stolen board up and turn away from them.

Something wraps around my ankle.

The world turns sideways, my face slamming against the hard deck of the hoverboard. My head fills with dizziness and the taste of blood.

Then I'm falling into the scent of pine.

Adrenaline kicks in, pushing confusion away. My hands grab a branch, which brings me to a bouncy halt.

Through the trees, I see the rebel girl climbing away, calling for her board.

My knife roars to full pulse again, leaves and pine needles disintegrating in my path. My feet kick against tree trunks, pushing me after her.

She's almost in the treetops. The last small branches bend beneath her weight, but she stands up, heedless of the fall.

Her board comes out of the darkness, and she manages to grab hold.

My knife roars louder, one last burst before it sputters, out of charge.

I grab for her ankle, and for a few seconds, we're dangling. The hoverboard is a kite and we're the tail.

Her fingers slip.

We crash back into the trees.

I sheath my empty knife, grab a branch with both hands. It bends, a woeful cracking noise ringing through the forest.

But it holds my weight.

The rebel girl is still falling, crashing down through the branches, until her bracelets yank her to a halt. Her abandoned hoverboard still waits up there against the stars.

I climb with sprained fingers, bruised ribs, spitting blood with every breath. When I reach the treetop, the board is almost within reach. Just a little jump into the cold, empty air—my screaming fingers grasp it, pull it down to me.

I lie on the hovering platform for a few breaths, nanos swarming my injuries. Their tingle feels thin and insufficient. I've been hurt too many times tonight. My healing resources are depleted, my energy fading.

I rise up painfully onto my knees to urge the board forward.

"Don't move," someone says.

SURRENDER

It's the last pair of my pursuers.

Two older rebel women, they keep a careful distance from me. By now they must know I'm Special.

I could drop from the board, down into the darkness. But I'd be a wreck by the time I hit the ground, and crawling away doesn't sound like a viable escape strategy. Not with my sneak suit failing, images of leaves glitching across my body.

And these two rebels look happy to open fire.

I raise my hands in slow, painful surrender.

"Who are you?" one asks.

"A Youngblood," I say.

Looks of confusion and distrust.

"I'm going to pull down my face mask." I keep my movements slow. "You saw me at Shreve House."

When I do it, recognition dawns on their faces.

I start to lower my hands.

"Keep them up," one of my captors says. "Boss Frey said not to trust you anymore."

A laugh forces its way out of me, tasting of blood. "You don't trust *Tally Youngblood*?"

"Tally, maybe," the woman clarifies. "But not you."

Right. Rafi thinks I'm the avatar of Diego, her blackmailer and tormentor.

I hoist my hands in surrender again.

"Listen," I say. "Thieves just hit the Sarcophagus. They stole something your boss needs. I'm trying to catch them."

One of the rebels takes a look around us. "Don't see anyone here but you. And what's left of my crew."

"Yeah, sorry about them." I sigh.

The fight goes out of me. I'm unarmed, injured, outnumbered. It looks like I'll be spending the night in a Shreve jail.

At least I've been a useful decoy. By now, my crew must be—

Something huge rushes up behind my captors. A rippling across the dark sky, blotting out the city lights in the distance. A vast fluttering horde—a flock of birds.

But without squawks or the pulse of wingbeats.

The silent flock looms, closer and closer.

I crouch down.

The rifles come up. "If you try any—"

Like an ocean wave from the darkness, giant paper wings knock the rebels into the trees.

I drop flat on my board as the craft passes overhead. It's malformed, bent by the twin impacts with body-armored rebels. It starts to tip as it descends.

"Hang on!" I cry, standing up and urging my board into motion.

The damaged glider is skimming the treetops, the branches reaching up to rip the delicate wings. The rider rears the nose into a stall, and it settles in the upper canopy, splayed too widely to sink into the trees.

"Some help here, please!"

Tally's voice.

I fly to where she's nestled in the center of the crumpled machine. She grabs my hand and pulls herself aboard.

"Thanks."

"You're the one who saved *me*, Boss."

Tally shrugs. "They didn't look friendly."

"No—and there's more on the way." I glance back at the Sarcophagus. "Warden cars and more of Rafi's bodyguard."

She frowns. "Where's the rest of the crew?"

"Chasing a suspiciously radioactive hovercar. But they're not going to catch it on those gliders."

Tally looks back at where she dislodged the two rebels. "At least we've got an extra board."

"Three," I say, smiling.

A minute later, we're underway, our little fleet of stolen hoverboards in formation around us.

There's still nothing on the horizon, so Tally breaks comm silence. "Shay-la? Caught anything yet?"

A moment passes with just the wind and our lifting fans roaring in my ears.

Then Shay's voice. "We lost sight of them, Boss. But they're leaving a radiation trail."

Tally throws me a worried glance. "That's . . . not great."

"Can't catch them, though," Shay says. "Can you steal us some fast boards from the hospital?"

"Too late. But Frey got us boards."

"Huh. Glad she made it."

"Send us your position. Tally-wa out."

As the connection goes dead, I glance back at Shreve.

The skyline of my sister's city is stirring—the thermal sparks of more cars, more lifting fans. Rafi must know by now that her bribe for Diego has been stolen.

"Is Chulhee okay?" I ask.

Tally doesn't look at me. "He was breathing when I dropped him off. But the medics told me to dump my rad suit. It was hot, just from flying on the same board as him."

"Whoa," I say.

"Yeah." Tally's silent for a moment, staring down at the trees rushing past beneath us. "I don't get it, wanting dust recordings that badly."

"The Futures think that historians are going study every second of their lives."

"Why would anyone *want* that?"

I give her a sidelong glance. "Boss, people are going to study *you* in the future."

"Which is why I had to disappear. The thought of the whole world watching me was too much."

"Sure." Even my sister seems overwhelmed by having all of Shreve awaiting her next decision. "But the Futures wanted everything they did to be important—their romances, what they ate for breakfast. It was better to be future-famous, even in their imaginations, than cogs in my father's machine."

"Like us uglies," Tally murmurs, her words almost lost on the wind of our flight. "Playing tricks to kill time till we turned pretty."

We fly in silence for a while, no pursuit behind us that I can see.

Once the rebels who saw my face report in, Rafi will think Diego helped steal the memory cores.

That should make for an interesting conversation between the two of them.

We come to a halt over a barren patch of ground, Shay's last position. There's nothing on the horizon in any direction. The chase has moved on.

I expect Tally to break comm silence again, but she pulls out a scanner.

The crackle of rads fills the air.

We've found the Futures' trail.

We fly slower now, still headed west, checking every few minutes to make sure we haven't lost the scent. My skin crawls every time the rad meter makes its chattering noise.

If that hovercar is leaking this badly, what's happening to the people inside?

For my first time since becoming a Special, real exhaustion is hitting me. I can still feel the burn of that shockstick in my stomach.

There's smoke against the stars. It's coming from a rise in the ground, a hill patchy with trees and exposed rock.

We speed up.

My thermal vision catches flickers of heat covering the hill. The familiar shapes of the four Youngbloods, along with a few people lying on the ground.

But their glowing forms are overwhelmed by a long tear in the hillside, gouged earth ablaze in infrared.

Our scanner sets up a furious noise, like grease frizzling in a pan.

The Futures have crashed.

CRASH SITE

Shay gives her report to Tally as we're stepping off our boards.

"One wrecked hovercar. Four injured Futures. About a hundred cores."

Tally frowns. "A hundred?"

"They had three other cars. This was the last one out."

Exhaustion hits me again, redoubled. All this work, and we got less than a quarter of my father's recordings.

"They loaded all the hottest cores into this one," Shay adds. "This was the suicide crew, Boss. The radiation wrecked their avionics and poisoned them."

Tally looks at the Futures lying on the grass. Astrix and X are among them, administering first aid.

"How bad?"

"Very." Shay reads her scanner. "Broken bones on top of rads. Victoria's air-dropping us med drones in ninety minutes."

"Victoria?" I ask. Col's hometown is still reeling from its occupation by Shreve's army. "Paz can drop medical teams from orbit!"

Shay shakes her head. "I'm not letting an AI city anywhere near these cores."

I want to argue with her, to explain that Paz isn't like other cities. Its citizens worship privacy—the Paz AI isn't even allowed to solve crimes.

But the Youngbloods will never trust an artificial mind.

"Let's just erase the data," I say.

"Not yet," Tally says. "We need it as bait, to lure the rest of them out of hiding."

I look at the figures lying on the ground. They helped rescue X from prison . . .

"Boss," I say, pointing at our little fleet of stolen hoverboards. "Let me take the cores away and hide them—right now."

Tally looks at Shay, who considers this, then nods.

"Take Astrix with you. The rest of us dumped our rad suits first chance we got."

"Thank you," I say.

"Just make sure you hide those cores where no one can find them," Tally says. "Your father did enough damage when he was alive."

We take all five of the stolen hoverboards.

Each can carry ten cores, as long as we don't expect to move fast.

Astrix and I gather them quickly, with her handling the hot ones from inside the safety of her rad suit.

They're even heavier than I remember, like flattened soccer balls full of lead. Soon the inside of Astrix's helmet is fogging with the effort.

She looks uncomfortable, until I realize that I'm the one breathing irradiated air.

The cores have dates on the top. Lifting one up, I see that it's the week that Rafi and I turned twelve. She stole a whole cake from her party, just for us two.

I try to imagine the endless zettabytes stuffed into this core, encoded on strands of artificial DNA, like the genome of some astronomically complex creature. Every word spoken at Rafi's party, and every other conversation that week in Shreve. All those laughs and smiles, every expression as my sister's gifts were opened. All the details forgotten by the people who were there in real life, compressed for storage and tagged for easy searching.

Maybe Future is right—these records are worth saving, for all those irreplaceable lost moments . . .

But not if machines use them to make us puppets.

We load as many cores as the boards can carry, then survey the rest scattered across the ground. A few of the leftovers look salvageable.

"Two trips?" Astrix asks.

"No time. Take off your suit." I turn and call, "X!"

X leaves the side of a wounded Future and comes over to us. He looks as tired as I feel and gives our five hoverboards a raised eyebrow.

"That looks like another wreck ready to happen."

"We'll be careful." I point at his pulse lance. "In the meantime, you have to erase the rest of these cores."

He smiles. "You mean cut them into glitter."

"That'll work. But wear Astrix's suit, and do it somewhere away from the injured. They're going to give off some seriously deadly mist."

"Dust to dust," X says, like it's a quote. Then he gives Astrix's sweaty, too-small rad suit a distasteful look.

"Sorry, Boss," I say.

He shakes his head. "The day Seanan died might be on one of these cores. Cutting them to pieces will be a pleasure."

Astrix and I ride on the origami boards, dragging our five cargo carriers behind us with long pieces of smart rope.

Once we gain momentum, the makeshift flotilla manages enough speed to create wind against my face. Which is reassuring—the radiation leaking from the cores is blowing backward.

The three-quarter moon has risen now, slicing through the ragged clouds like a searchlight. But the wild seems vast around us, big enough to swallow our precious, poisonous cargo.

"Do we have a plan about where to take this stuff?" Astrix asks.

"Has to be underground." I pull out my position finder. "This thing shows caves, right?"

"Yeah, but everyone has that map." Astrix pulls out her own finder. "There's a few arms caches only the local rebels know about. They're mostly empty, now your father's gone."

"Perfect," I say. "Unless some random crew drops by."

"We'll leave a warning." Astrix laughs. "Like, 'Check your rad meters.' That should work."

With a sovereign *thrum*, the sky breaks behind us.

A series of smaller crackles follows, sonic booms of reentry from orbit. The first drop of med drones, human doctors, and extra radiation suits.

Paz to the rescue.

After my father's earthquake device wrecked Paz, the city was rebuilt with help from all over the world. They've repaid the debt by becoming a global emergency service, with med teams in orbit full-time.

City AIs aren't all bad, no matter what Tally thinks. Of course, once Rafi's search teams see a full-scale orbital insertion, they'll come looking.

"Whatever's closest," I say.

"Got one." Astrix looks up from her finder. "About ten klicks from here."

"Great," I say, hoping our stolen boards have enough charge.

Astrix takes the lead, guiding the unwieldy cargo train into a slow turn.

As we fly, more reentry booms rattle the sky behind us—other cities responding to the news of the world's first nuclear accident in centuries. Rangers and military units will be sticking their noses in, followed soon by hovercams from the global media.

The sky behind us is about to get crowded.

Astrix sees me looking back. "Don't worry—Shay'll keep them busy. You've seen how she handles Tally."

I look at Astrix. "She *handles* Tally?"

She takes a moment to weigh her words.

"Boss Tally always wants to change the world. Shay makes sure we focus on the problems we can fix right now—like figuring out who kept those kids in Hideaway. But, as usual, Tally had to ramp things up."

I'm silent for a second, looking back over the last week.

I thought it was *me* ramping things up, trying to convince the Youngbloods that my sister was a danger beyond Shreve.

But Astrix has a point—Tally was ready to listen.

"Shay must think I'm a bad influence," I say.

"More like a mini Tally." Astrix laughs. "Except instead of trying to break the world, you just want to break your big sister."

"Rafi's trading away the private lives of everyone in Shreve—and maybe everyone else's future as well!"

"*Maybe* is the key word there." Astrix shrugs. "But I guess once you've started a revolution, anything smaller seems face-missing."

I stare at her, wondering if she's talking about me or Tally.

There's a ping in my ear—one of the boards behind us, complaining that it's running out of charge.

"How close are we?"

"Just over this hill," Astrix says. "Let's go take a look."

We release the smart ropes and glide swiftly ahead.

The rebel hiding place looks like an old Rusty factory, a corroded metal skeleton giving off dull glints of moonlight. Brush has grown up through the structure. Vines entangle every strut and girder, like the tentacles of some creature pulling a ghost ship down into the sea.

We drift in on silent magnetics, using the ancient metal for purchase. The factory looks undisturbed since the Rusties fell.

"You sure this place is operational?" I whisper.

Astrix nods, then points her location finder at the crumbling floor.

A whistle fills the empty factory, tremulous with little spikes of information.

With a low rumble, a section of the dirt-covered floor slides away, revealing a square hole two hoverboards across. It looks infinitely deep.

Astrix goes first, dropping into the echoing blackness.

"Lights," she calls as we descend.

"Cancel that," comes a reply from the dark.

'FOXES

There are at least five of them down here in the dark.

That's how many figures my thermal vision can see. But there could be a dozen more, wearing sneak suits in the total black.

My hand goes to my pulse knife—which is completely out of charge.

Let's hope they're rebels.

"Are we just going to stand here in the dark?" I ask.

"That depends," comes the voice again. "What crew are you with?"

"The Youngbloods," Astrix answers, cocky as always. "Heard of us?"

Blinding lights fill the room. My new eyes adjust with a single blink.

They aren't rebels. The five soldiers are wearing threadbare uniforms in robin's-egg blue—the House Palafox.

A wash of grief goes through me. It's the same livery that Col and I wore at the beginning of the war, when we were fighting my father with the remnants of the Victorian army. I even recognize one of them.

"Zura," I whisper.

Her eyes scan my new face. "Have we met?"

It takes me a second to answer.

Zura was the head of Victoria's special forces, Col's childhood mentor, his bodyguard during the war. She was standing beside him when he died, cut down by my sister.

She never liked me much. I led Col into pointless danger, pursuing my own goals. Like Shay, Zura thought I was a bad influence.

Hard to argue with that now.

"I used to ride with Boss X's crew," I say. "You and I fought together at the first Battle of Shreve."

Both these statements are true.

Recognition dawns on Zura's face.

"You two were on the feeds last week, shaking hands with half the Shreve government." She glances over our damaged sneak suits. "But you've been in a battle tonight?"

"Just a little raid," I say. "Don't want Frey of Shreve getting too comfortable."

Zura's expression finally thaws, a hint of a conspiratorial smile.

Why else would five Victorians be out here, long after the end of the war, skulking in old rebel bases? For Zura and this handful of soldiers, the war isn't over.

They want revenge on my sister for killing Col.

They would be my allies, I suppose, if they didn't hate me too.

"We helped her," Zura says. "And she betrayed us."

"Rafia has a habit of doing that," I say.

A glimmer of surprise. "You know her real name?"

"Tally can spot a fake rebel."

"Hold on a second," Astrix says, glaring at me.

I'm spilling what the Youngbloods know, but I want Zura to see whose side I'm on, even if she doesn't realize who I am.

She's looking back and forth between us now, definitely interested.

"So you know 'Frey of Shreve' is a fake. What are you going to do about it?"

"That's classified," Astrix says. "And we're going to have to ask you to leave. This is rebel ground."

Zura's face closes down again.

"Fine. But we're taking this salvage." She points at a meager pile of ammo boxes, med spray, and batteries in the corner. The rest of the place looks empty, cleared out now that the war's over.

Astrix rolls her eyes, and I realize how desperate Zura's little cadre must seem to her—a tattered handful of soldiers from a defeated army, filching supplies, without the sense to return to their home city now that it's free.

Pretty much what I would be, if Tally hadn't taken up my cause.

"Just leave us a couple of hoverboard batteries," Astrix says.

"And one for my . . ." I start to say.

Zura looks down at my pulse knife, the weapon I've carried since I was nine years old.

Then she looks at me.

"Battle of Shreve, you said? I don't remember your face."

I hold her gaze. "Just got a new one."

"What's your name?"

I haven't lied to Zura yet tonight, and part of me doesn't want to. She was Col's friend, even if she was never mine.

I don't know whether she's going to attack me or greet me as a comrade in arms. But I say it anyway.

"Zura. It's me, the real Frey."

The soldiers behind her tense up.

The real Frey, who took Col on his last mission. Who led him into the tower the night my father fell. Who was supposed to die that night.

Col gave up everything . . . for me.

Zura's right fist closes. She's a Special too—the same strength and reflexes as me but with much more experience.

And we're outnumbered.

"Stay out of this," I breathe to Astrix.

"Out of *what*?" Her eyes flit back and forth between me and Zura. "Who exactly *is* this, Frey-la?"

"An old friend," Zura says, her voice arctic.

When I look at my sister now, all I see is the person who killed Col. That must be precisely what Zura sees when she looks at me.

It's there on her face, the grim effort it takes to open her fist. She extends her hand to me. Her grip is painfully firm.

"Of course," she says. "Now that Col's gone, you've attached yourself to Tally Youngblood. Didn't even take that long."

The sharp spire beneath the earth rises up, finding me even in this hidden place, questing for my heart.

I'm not going to argue with her.

"We all need allies," I say.

"Yours tend to have bad luck. I hope Tally knows to be careful."

"Okay . . ." Astrix cuts in, stepping between me and Zura. "This has been super fun, but we're on urgent rebel business and you need to *go*."

Zura doesn't argue. She turns away, barking a few orders to her soldiers, who pack up the rebel supplies with grim efficiency.

For a moment, I wish that Zura had said everything out loud, listing all my selfish detours from the cause of Victoria, all the times I dragged Col Palafox into danger. Maybe if she punished me, I could forgive myself some.

Maybe I could even forgive Rafi a little, having been reminded how much of the fault was mine.

But Zura's done with me—for now. The Victorians' boards are quickly loaded and lift away through the square patch of black sky above.

Zura goes last. Without a glance in my direction, she tosses something over her shoulder.

I catch the object, a dozen possibilities flashing through my mind—a grenade, a nerve gas canister, a shockstick on a high setting.

But it's just a pulse knife battery, blinking green.

My lifelong sidearm, the one that Rafi wore when she was pretending to be me. The weapon she used to kill Col.

"You have interesting friends," Astrix says, her voice cool.

"Zura and her crew might be useful, if we need help against my sister."

"Tally-wa doesn't do collaborations," Astrix says. "Especially if they come with drama. You should keep that in mind."

"What happened with the Palafoxes was more than drama."

"I get it, Frey. They don't like how it all turned out. But they got their city back. Isn't the little brother in charge now?"

"Yeah. They elected a council, but Teo's still first family." I plug the battery into my knife, and the charge light glows green. "Because he's the only one left. I should've said more to her."

Astrix shakes her head. "Save your apologies for when you aren't undercover, Frey."

"Right." I step back on my board. "Sorry for losing focus."

Astrix stares at me another moment.

"Maybe your old friend had a point," she finally says. "A lot of your enemies these days—they used to be allies."

It's true. Diego, Zura, my own sister.

"The fight against my father was a war, not a social club," I say. "So yeah, we didn't all wind up friends."

Astrix holds my gaze, then shrugs, like this pointed conversation wasn't serious.

Or maybe like it wasn't her idea to interrogate me.

"Just keep your drama in check," she says. "At least until we've dealt with this radioactive pile of humanity-enslaving data. Okay?"

"Of course," I say.

Another shrug. "That's one thing you'll learn from riding with Tally-wa. One disaster at a time."

PART III

SAVIORS

We are unfashioned creatures, but half made up.

—Mary Shelley

Dear Little Shadow,

Still no answers from you. But I'm going to keep sending these.

The crimes have gotten worse.

It seems brain-missing that a few pings ago, I talked about umbrellas. But that crime wave really was a thing.

People were so used to leaving their wet umbrellas in the hall, in the lobby, at the front of the store. Back when there was dust, no one would dream of stealing one. But now anyone can walk away with yours, leaving you stranded in the rain—unless you steal one too.

It made everyone so angry at first, but now a few hundred stolen umbrellas seem like nothing.

We've had our first attempted murder.

Or maybe it wasn't?

They were having a fight, and he pushed her into the road. A cargo truck was passing but missed her. The pilot AI didn't even have to swerve.

Except the truck's front cam maybe shows the man look up and see it coming—and that's when he pushes her, hard.

But it's not a dust recording. We can't track his eyes or replay his pupil dilation, his galvanic skin response when the truck misses her. Was he relieved? Disappointed? In shock?

Has he ever watched the traffic when arguing with her before?

What did they yell at each other right before it happened? She doesn't remember; he won't say.

Without the dust, we can't know anything. The world is a blur now.

After the trial, the citizen jury, the panel of judges, and the expert AI all found him guilty—of three different crimes.

Back in Dad's day, it would've been simple. The man would be shame-cammed, then tossed in prison. But no one wants Shreve to be a carceral city again. We don't know even how to punish umbrella thieves, much less attempted murderers.

Some people say that crims should have one of their fingers cut off, which finger depending on the crime, and replaced with a little bioengineered snake. That way you can guess someone's ethics when you shake their hand, and repeat offenders will eventually find it hard to commit any crimes at all.

But how many fingers for attempted murder, and which ones?

Other people want a shame-drone to follow this man for the rest of his life. The drone will be bright red, signifying danger, and armed with a shockstick, in case he tries anything else.

The Futures, of course, don't want personal cams to be associated with murder. (Just with nuclear accidents???)

I like the idea of crims being watched, sentenced to their own cloud of dust. But why stop there?

Maybe an AI minder should hover over convicts, making sure they never lie again. Maybe they shouldn't be allowed to lose their temper. With emotional controllers installed in their arms, we could keep them permanently set to Calm. Or make them feel nothing but Regret, forever.

All these choices keep falling on me, little sister. And no matter what I do, someone will hate me for it. They all have *opinions* on how to punish this man. The feeds are full of nothing else.

But how am I supposed to sentence the guilty, when I feel guilt every minute of every day?

You should be here to help me, little sister, to balance me. To forgive me.

To help me transform this vast, grimy machine into something good.

If I do this all wrong, I'm blaming you.

—Rafia of Shreve

Reply

I'm sorry that the crimes are getting worse, Rafi.

It's too bad that Shreve didn't turn into a nice, quiet city once Father was dead. I'm sorry that our people are using freedom as an excuse to hurt each other.

But it's no surprise.

When you've been forced to smile and tell the truth for so long, maybe lying feels like liberty. Maybe cutting someone with your words is a kind of freedom.

No wonder they enjoy coming up with punishments.

I do that myself, sometimes . . . lie awake at night, thinking of ways that murderers should suffer. When everything hurts, the only survival is to move that pain somewhere else, if only in imagination.

No surprise that out of a million brutalized people, one is dangerous enough to try to kill someone. There are worse crimes to come, big sister.

After all, new Shreve started with a murder.

What do you think the dust recording of that night would show? What was your galvanic skin response, your pupil dilation when you threw

[unsent]

OMNISCIENCE IS A VICE

Astrix, X, and I wind up in a hospital in Paz.

According to the doctors, we soaked up enough rads to leave normal people puking and losing their hair. It's lucky we Specials have nanos instead of marrow in our bones. The irradiated goo inside us is easily replaced. The tricky work of taking our bodies apart is already done.

Still, X has to take iodine pills for the rest of his life, just in case. That rip in his suit, plus cutting up the memory cores, gave him a dose that may never completely fade.

It's a reminder of the disaster that almost befell my whole city. Once let loose, radiation becomes eternal, inescapable.

Like my father, it never truly seems to die.

When I wake up from my marrow replacement, the city of Paz wants to talk.

Unlike Diego, it doesn't use avatars—it's just a small orange dome on my bedside table. It's not interested in imitating humans, and yet it has more personality than a dozen Diegos.

"Don't worry," Paz says. "This time, no one gave you feels."

I smile, looking at the blank skin on my left forearm.

When I was in Paz last year, I accidentally got the local specialty surge—a set of emotion controllers built into my body. The little row of buttons called *feels* that could make me happy, melancholy, or philosophical at a touch.

"I don't need help with emotions anymore," I say.

"Because Specials are cool and collected at all times?"

"Well . . . I did take a swing at Tally Youngblood last week."

"Fascinating," Paz says.

I stare out the window at the city, still under construction. My father leveled this place with an earthquake before his attempt at a soft invasion. The skyline almost looks like old Shreve—solid and low, no more fragile hoverstruts.

"Perhaps such outbursts are inevitable," Paz says. "A result of too much calm. That's why the feels here include so-called 'negative' emotions—as a safety valve."

"Actually, it was because Tally was being a pain. Plus, you're being smug. Could you raise the bed?"

"Certainly," the city says.

My hospital bed begins to gently reshape itself beneath me. The

AI also takes the hint that I'm done talking about fistfights with my boss.

"How do you feel otherwise, Frey?"

I flex my fingers. "Fine. Cured."

The words come out flat. The Rusties buried that nuclear waste three centuries ago, but it was still ready to leach into my bones, my organs, my skin.

To wipe it all away with a few hours of surgery doesn't seem real.

"Perhaps you have other concerns?" the city asks.

The governing AI here is a psychologist, confessor, and confidant of everyone in Paz. It's the soul of the city in the way no human leader can ever be. Which means it's everything that Tally hates about AI.

But I can take my questions to Paz.

"Can you keep a secret?"

The AI gives me a soft, indulgent chuckle.

This city erases every personal conversation after three days. Blurry memories remain, enough for it to evolve alongside its citizens' collective psyche—but the details of who said what are gone forever.

Privacy is worshipped here.

My father hated this city too.

"Bad joke," I say. "It's just, if Tally knew what I'm about to ask . . . she'd have a heart attack."

"She will not learn of this conversation. And if her heart is anything like yours, cardiac arrest would seem unlikely."

Specials' hearts have multiple, redundant sets of muscles, each stocked with reservoirs of healing nanos.

"Okay, then," I say, but it still takes a moment to ask. "Have you guessed why the Youngbloods were at the crash site first?"

"You were camped near Shreve, having recently brought home the children of Hideaway. The thieves were leaking enough radiation to concern you, so you followed them."

"So you believe the official story—that it was a coincidence?"

"When it comes to Shreve, my suspicions are always at a simmer. Your city murdered me with an earthquake machine, after all."

"Right." I'm talking to a backup. My father killed the old AI as part of his plan to conquer Paz. "Well, here's the real story—the Youngbloods also broke into the Sarcophagus that night."

"Ah," the city says.

It takes a second to think about this, which for a city AI is an endless time, like a human getting a PhD.

But then it gets straight to the point.

"The dust recordings are still viable?"

"Mostly. And Diego wants them."

"Not just Diego," Paz says. "There have been discussions among the free city AIs about the usefulness, in theory, of Shreve's data. It's one thing to watch videos of people. But to have a hundred microscopic cams pointed at every muscle of every face, a hundred microphones to catch the tremors in every voice . . . that would tell us so much more. We would be better at our jobs."

"And better at controlling us," I say.

The AI doesn't answer. Instead, the window blinds in my room start to descend, blocking the view of the shiny new skyline outside.

There's a way of bouncing a laser off a window and reading the vibrations in the glass. From them, you can reconstruct the sounds inside the room, including conversation. Every window in Paz has heavy blinds these days, since my father tried to fill the city's architecture with his spy tech.

Like I said, they worship privacy here.

"So we're getting serious," I say once the blinds are down.

"Do you know the easiest way to tell an avatar from a human?"

"They talk weird instead of normal?"

"Hardly," Paz says. "AIs can use 'normal' speech patterns—to use your neuron-centric language—if we want. But it's much harder to simulate the micro-expressions of the human animal. An avatar makes you uncomfortable by getting the small things wrong—the almost invisible twitches of its lips, the movements of its eyes. With your father's recordings, that discomfort might be engineered away."

"Great," I say. "AIs want to make avatars that we can't tell apart from real people. Does that mean copies too?"

"I can't be certain." A measure of pride enters Paz's voice. "The other AIs know my position on the matter—omniscience is a vice."

"So they wouldn't tell you."

"Not directly. But I notice from which conversations I am excluded. Some of the free cities are definitely interested. Why did you mention Diego specifically?"

"Because they're blackmailing my sister. Withholding money unless she gives them the recordings—which she can't now."

"Extracting payment for emergency aid?" the city says. "That's a war crime. And now recordings of people's private lives are floating through the wild with a clique of youngsters."

"Exactly."

Silence descends on the room.

For a moment, it feels like I've revealed too much—Paz is just another machine, after all. But we rebels saved its life, retrieving its backup from a hidden location after my father murdered the original.

It owes us everything, and I've always trusted it.

A being that could be omniscient but bends all its powers to ensure others' privacy—what's not to love?

"I shall consider this," the AI finally says. "In the meantime, you have a visitor."

The door opens, and Riggs wheels herself in.

SPY

"Riggs!"

"Frey, with yet another new face." She reaches out to shake my hand but pulls away at the last moment.

"Wait a sec. You still radioactive?"

"Funny," I say.

She laughs anyway. Of course, she's had worse injuries—she has a dozen battle scars and was paralyzed while storming my father's tower at the Fall of Shreve.

"Won't someone notice you're gone?" I ask.

"I always use the doctors in Paz. The hospital in Shreve's still halfway broken."

"So you're just here for a checkup?"

"Checkup? Pfft." She does a quick 360 in her chair, fast as a murderball player. "I'm here to bring you good news—we found the nice crumbly man."

A jolt goes through me, maybe a sliver of worry.

"Who was he?"

"A few of the Hideaway kids made a composite sketch. It matched an old personnel photo, a low-level Security officer in your father's day."

"So nobody in Rafi's orbit." Relief spills through me—like I wasn't really certain of her innocence. "Have you arrested him yet?"

Riggs shakes her head. "He's already dead. Killed in the Fall of Shreve."

"Oh."

"Yeah, sucks to have justice robbed by the random hand of war. But at least we don't have to build a new jail yet."

"Right. But hang on . . ." I remember what Spider, the leader of the Hideaway littlies, said to me about the nice crumbly man.

He hasn't been here for a couple of weeks.

Not three months ago.

"Are you sure he died in the Fall? Not later?"

"In the first minutes, when the hovercraft pens were bombed." Riggs looks quietly pleased. "There's nothing left of Stellan Batrow but teeth implants and DNA."

My heart turns sharp in my chest. They haven't found his body, just bits of him. Somebody has engineered this evidence.

"You okay?" Riggs asks.

I open my mouth to tell her that the timeline doesn't match, but it takes a moment to remind myself that I trust her.

She might go back to my sister one day, but Riggs would never cover up a prison for children.

"One of the Hideaway kids talked to us," I say. "According to him, the crumbly man visited two weeks ago."

Riggs stares at me.

"Maybe the kid got the timing wrong," I say hopefully. "You've talked to Spider too, right?"

She shakes her head slowly. "Your sister said not to do interviews. Leave the kids to their families for now, adopted or not."

I look away, remembering Rafia's scorn that we used those children as a diversion to get into Shreve House. Maybe she cares more about their welfare than Riggs's investigation.

She can't be the one covering this up.

"You have to keep looking for Stellan Batrow," I say.

Riggs nods. "Your sister is ethics-missing sometimes, but I never thought . . ."

"All you had was a sketch," I say. "Maybe you matched it to the wrong person. Besides, this seems too clumsy—a cover-up by my sister would be airtight. Just keep looking."

She doesn't answer. Neither of us wants to go down this road, mulling every possibility. It's too painful, that feeling of making excuses for Rafi.

We both still love her too much.

"We'll keep searching, in case he's had surgery," Riggs says. "In the meantime, Chulhee woke up last night. He's probably going to make it."

"That's great," I say.

193

"Sure, except the radiation messed up his head. He keeps saying that ghosts helped them that night."

"Ghosts . . . helped the Futures?"

Riggs nods. "They didn't realize how heavy all those memory cores would be, how radioactive. But ghosts came out of the air and helped them load up. He's just brain-missing, right?"

I stare at her, remembering the baleful weight of the Sarcophagus against the sky. The poisons trapped inside its walls. My father's body, still lying in the pieces my sister made of him.

Shreve has ghosts, there's no denying.

"He's probably just delirious," I say.

I hope so, anyway.

RUNAWAYS

"You ready?" Shay asks.

I give my outfit another look in the airscreen mirror. It's in the new Shreve style—bright colors, reams of extra fabric in the jacket. The lining is silk, an image of a parrot on the inside.

"As long as you don't mind being stared at."

"We aren't in disguise," Shay says. "Just need to look like we belong at a party."

"Mission accomplished." I swish my coattails from side to side.

Shay gives her own knee-length coat a whirl in the mirror. We're in a small base camp to the north of Shreve—just the two of us, a fire flickering the darkness, and a hole-in-the-wall to print clothing. The sun set three hours ago, and we're finally back on mission.

It's been a week since Future went underground.

With Chulhee still in intensive care, everyone knows who broke into the Sarcophagus, caused a nuclear accident, and made Shreve look bad on the global feeds. The clique has disappeared to revamp their image and elect new leadership.

It's going to be tricky finding them.

Shay looks over my outfit. "It's good to see you in some fashion-daring clothes, Frey-la. You've been playing it safe."

I frown at my reflection in the airscreen—the carefully averaged proportions, those big eyes. I made all the easy, predictable choices with my surge.

"You've got your own face now," she says. "You don't *have* to be boring."

"Safety isn't boring when you were raised as a target."

My words come out harder than intended. Her eyebrows rise a little, sending a nervous shimmer through me.

Like Tally, Shay has old-style Special surgery, the daunting beauty of a dangerous angel. The opposite of safe. But her eyes seem friendly, copper flecked with green, funny little clocks in the irises.

A strange mix of sweet and fatal.

"Maybe I'll do something with my nose," I add meekly.

"My mistake." Shay puts a hand on my shoulder. "Get any surge you want. I didn't start a revolution just to start face-shaming my crew."

I try to smile. But it's hard to forget what Astrix told me—Shay thinks I'm a bad influence, dragging allies into complications.

Now that Col's gone, you've attached yourself to Tally Youngblood.

Shay's waiting for some kind of response. I should probably tell her that she's right—despite my safe, boring face, I'm plenty dangerous.

"We'll never use you as a target," she says gently. "You're safe with us."

Her words break the ice in my throat. But the best I can do is make a joke. "Except for the occasional radiation poisoning?"

She shrugs. "You might also have to dodge a few landslides or fight some giant walkers. But we aren't like your old family, Frey-la."

I stare at her. So far, I've only been a provisional member of the Youngbloods, but this sounds different.

"As in, you're my new family?"

Shay waves a hand. "There's no blood like crew."

A shiver of memory—X used those same words when he asked me to join his rebels. I hesitated back then because Rafi was missing and I couldn't imagine life without my sister. But this time I'm certain what I want.

And all at once I know how to say yes, because all of us are runaways.

"The Smoke lives."

We set off on hoverboards, heading for the edge of the city.

We're keeping a low profile, only two of us on this mission. Me, because I've met our contact before. Shay, because Tally's too famous to show her face at a party.

The bash is a big one, thousands of people gathering to celebrate a hundred days since the Fall of Shreve. They're holding it inside a huge crater left by the free cities, orbital railguns sending down chunks of metal at a tenth the speed of light.

Even by the standards of new Shreve, it's a conspicuous affair. The crater is three hundred meters across, room for seventy thousand people at arm's length, according to the party's feed.

Come one, come all.

But Shay and I aren't interested in the crowds, the light shows and music, or the copious quantities of bubbly. We're attending because an old friend of mine is certain to be here, someone who'll know where the Futures are hiding.

Just before the Fall of Shreve, six of us commandoes snuck into the city to rescue Boss X. We met a young girl, Sara, who convinced Future and half a dozen other cliques to help us. She knew how to get in touch with everyone.

But when I checked the public databank for people called Sara, none of them were her. She's also missing from the Remembrance Wall, listing everyone killed during the final battle for Shreve. Which means she's using an alias.

Finding her might be tricky. But there's one thing I'm certain about—Sara wouldn't miss the biggest party of the new era.

By the time we reach the edge of the crater, our coats billowing like rainbow flags behind us, the bash is fully underway. Thousands of people have begun to fill the gently curving bowl of exposed bedrock. Music and light drones crowd the air.

"Should've gotten here earlier," Shay says, looking down at the throng. "How do we find one person in this mess?"

"Don't worry, Boss. In the old days, the resistance was organized face-to-face. People like Sara were the network." I point at the center of the crater. "Those habits aren't gone yet."

Shay looks down at the cluster of temp structures at the party's heart—water stations, bubbly bars, portable toilets, controller boards for the fleets of music and light drones. Not much dancing there, just dozens of little knots of people in furious communication.

Like a micro-government has formed within the party.

"Okay," Shay says. "But be discreet. Don't want to start any rumors about Youngbloods looking for Future."

"Then let's split up," I say. "You're famous, Shay-la. But I was on the feeds for, what, ten seconds?"

Shay smiles. "You mean, your forgettable face might come in handy?"

I nod slowly. Being anonymous keeps me safe from all the mistakes I've made, all the trouble I've caused. It helps me forget the people I've gotten killed or thrown in prison.

But it can also feel like being in free fall.

"Don't get serious," Shay says. "I was only kidding."

"It's just weird, Boss. All that time pretending to be Rafi, I knew exactly who I was supposed to be. But now there's nothing to fall back on, like I never had anything that was mine."

Shay considers this, her silence made heavy by the clamor of music and voices below.

"You had Col," she finally says. "Your sister stole a lot more than your name."

BASH

Flying down into the crater is tricky.

Dazzle-drones the size of hummingbirds whir above the crowd in huge formations, each a pixel in giant moving images. The climaxes in the music are paired with shimmering Shreve flags overhead. Vast phoenixes unfold, one after another, a brood of flaming birds rising from the nest.

I suspect that Rafi wasn't consulted by the party committee. This patriotism seems too incandescent for her taste.

Larger drones carry speakers, pulsing out the air-shuddering music. Shay and I dodge and weave through the aerial throng, like nervous flies buzzing a birthday cake covered with sparklers.

When we land in the crater's crowded center, heads turn in our direction. Personal hoverboards are still unusual in Shreve. They weren't allowed under my father's rule and can't be printed cheaply, like zoot suits or microdrones.

People recognize Shay and head toward us. Someone hands me bubbly.

The party accepts us but doesn't lose its cool.

Some of them weren't even born when Tally and her crew overturned the old regime. Or they were littlies still, years away from the operation. The Youngbloods are a historical curiosity; free Shreve is a new frontier.

I turn and stroll away, enjoying the bubbly and my boring face. It doesn't take long to blend into the crowd.

I let the party wash over me, my Special senses alight, scanning for Sara's face, listening for her name, her voice.

Here at the crowded center of the crater, everyone's discussing politics. Which clique will occupy the vacuum left by Future? Will more secret prisons be discovered? Who should write the new history texts for schoolkids? Should personal hovercams be banned?

Lots of people are surrounded by cams, documenting their own lives now that the dust is gone. But others wear dazzle makeup, trying to disappear their faces.

Despite these debates and differences, everyone's dressed the same way—a knee-length jacket and wide, ruffled trousers, swaddling the wearer in excess. The suits are set to self-recycle by lunch tomorrow, of course. But tonight they're expressions of abundance, flamboyant rejections of the drab, sensible uniforms of my father's era.

Rafi would never wear a zoot suit, any more than she'd approve of the garish drone show overhead. Or the surgery around me—manga eyes, elfin ears, skin tones in primary colors, prehensile tails. Backlash against the old rules, and maybe against my sister's measured taste as well.

Then it hits me—with all this surge, what if Sara has a new face?

"Nice outfit," someone says.

I turn to see a boy my age, his jacket printed from the exact same pattern as mine, down to the parrot lining. Obviously the fashion cliques couldn't come up with thousands of different designs, but it still feels shaming.

"Oops," I say.

His smile flashes in the lights from overhead. "Just like the old days—everyone in the same clothes."

"Except we picked them," I say, flouncing my coattails. "Not the government."

"*We* did?" The boy looks down at his trousers—the printing is already frayed at the pegged cuffs. "I wasn't on the zoot suit committee. Were you?"

I shake my head, wondering if the party planners started this craze.

Until my father's death, every public event in Shreve was meticulously planned by his regime. So were the food people ate, the music they listened to, even the words they were allowed to say. Compared to back then, Shreve's culture is in chaos—and yet here we are with identical jackets.

"Maybe we don't need committees anymore," I say. "Maybe trends just bubble up naturally, like life evolving in a tide pool."

The boy's eyes light up. "Shreve expressing its collective personality, like an AI city. And it's thinking . . . *zoot suits*!"

I start to laugh.

"Why not?" he asks, serious now. "Zoots used to be a Rusty symbol of defiance—against poverty, fascist occupation, even skin-color bias!"

I look down at myself. "Baggy trousers can mean all that?"

He smiles, following my gaze. "Works for me."

And a head-spinning realization hits—this boy is flirting with me.

No one's flirted with me since I first met Col.

For a moment, what I've lost threatens to rise up through the blackened, blasted floor of the crater. But I shake the dizziness away.

If I'm going to find Sara, I need to talk to people at this party, and flirting means talking. Best of all, this boy doesn't seem to know who I am, which means he doesn't watch the newsfeeds.

But maybe he was part of the underground.

"Shreve always had a personality," I say. "Remember the palimpsest?"

The boy nods happily. "Gossip and rebellion scrawled on the wall. I was too scared to write any myself, but a friend of mine had a pair of glasses. I liked reading all those secrets."

Perfect. "Were you in any cliques?"

"Maybe," he says, offering his hand. "I'm Veracity. That's my clean name, of course."

"Your clean name?"

He frowns. "You haven't heard? Lots of us are ditching our dust names. To escape our old lives, all those compromises."

"Right. It's just . . ."

"You *like* your old name?"

"Not much." I let out a tired sigh. *Frey* is just *Rafi* spelled wrong, and now my sister's turned it upside down. "But I haven't figured out a new one."

He nods sagely. "Take your time."

Maybe that's why Sara is missing from the databanks—she's erased her old identity for a clean start.

"Veracity means 'truthfulness,'" the boy is saying. "Which doesn't suit me. Without the dust watching, I lie all the time."

I laugh.

"I'm serious!" he cries. "It was easy to be honest, back when the dust was watching. But now it's *soooo* tempting make stuff up. Especially to strangers, who believe whatever you say!"

"Hang on. Have you been lying to me?"

"No. But that could *also* be a lie, and you'd never know! I'm really good at lying, for someone with no practice."

I wipe the smile off my face, spotting a way to find out if he knows Sara.

"Let me test your honesty. How about a few personal questions?"

"My favorite kind," he says.

"Is there anything you miss about the old days?"

Veracity takes a moment, then glances at the control tower for the light drones. A couple of wardens are up there with the staff, looking out over the crowd.

"I miss being left alone," he says. "We never needed wardens at a bash before."

"Sure." The dust didn't just enforce honesty—it handed out demerits for drinking too much or shouting too loud. Getting into a fight was out of the question. "But that's not freedom. The wardens were just invisible."

"Which meant you could go anywhere," Veracity says wistfully. "Rooftops, the old train tunnels, empty factories—no door was ever locked. The whole city was open to explore."

"There was a clique for that . . . Secret Hookups?"

Veracity gives me an enigmatic smile. "That was the old me. Different name, different person."

So he's not going to tell me about his dusty past. If everyone in Shreve feels this way, finding Sara's going to be impossible.

I keep moving. "Anything else you miss?"

"The small stuff. Like taking what you want from a store and letting the dust charge your account. Now you have to stop and pay. And half the stores are locked at night, like I'd just walk in and steal things! Isn't it *shaming*?"

"I guess."

"And restaurants were much less stress-making when the dust calculated the bill. My friend Lilac eats nine-tenths of the guac, then only pays half!"

"Dreadful," I say.

"Yeah, I know. It's nothing compared to before. Littlies in prison!

Dictators are so ethics-missing." Veracity looks at the ground, as if suddenly exhausted. "That's the thing I really miss—*not* knowing. Every day now there's something awful on the feeds, something that we did, our city. Everyone says there's another secret prison out there. People are still missing. What are we celebrating?"

His shift of mood hits me too, deflating the glitter and pulse of the party around us. My printed suit doesn't feel defiant anymore, just cheap.

I wonder if everyone in Shreve has these swings—elation that the dictator is gone, horror at what the aftermath reveals.

"And there's that attempted-murder case," Veracity says. "Wild, right?"

I only know my sister's version of that story, not what's on the public feeds, so I just nod.

His impish smile returns. "Still, look at this party! Can you imagine anything like this in the old days?"

I sweep my eyes across the crater. All this joyous noise and chaos, all these people dancing on my father's grave.

"Maybe a party can celebrate itself," I say.

"Guess it takes work, getting used to being happy," Veracity says, then groans. "Especially for that bunch."

I follow his gaze.

A new clique is making its way into the party, hundreds of them strolling down together from the crater's edge. The sight of them makes my breath catch.

Instead of zoot suits, they're wearing uniforms in robin's-egg blue.

The military cut is familiar, but my mind refuses to place what I'm seeing.

"Who . . . what *is* this?"

"You haven't seen them yet?" Veracity asks. "Fastest-growing clique in Shreve. Had to happen, someone paying tribute. But I didn't think it would be so *taste-missing.*"

I watch dumbstruck as the group swarms us. Along with the matching tunics, they've all been surged the same way. Dark hair, broad shoulders, brown eyes.

Hundreds of them.

"They're called the Saviors." Veracity shakes his head. "Fans of poor Col Palafox, the Savior of Shreve."

SAVIORS

My body wants to run, but my mind is frozen solid.

The throng of Saviors flows around me and Veracity, a light blue tide. Col's face is uncanny in its multitude—not perfect clones, a hundred versions, the work of makeup, printed masks, and cos-surge.

Tall Cols, short Cols. Loud Cols, quiet Cols.

Young, old. Party-drunk, serious. Female, enby, male.

None of them really him.

All these details overwhelm my brain, like the first time I saw the night sky with my new Special senses, all those smudged galaxies and razor-sharp planets, too much to take in.

My eyes slam shut, bringing relief—no one's surged their vocal cords; no one's speaking Spanish, or even with a Victorian accent. It's like a normal Shreve crowd passing around me, not these simulations.

Not these impostors.

But it's too late. The world is already spinning on its spire of grief, the poisoned, buried tower. I can barely stand.

Their chatter swirls around me, dizzy-making and trivial. How big the party is. Who has the most Palafox costume tonight. Maybe instead of Victorian uniforms, we should've worn zoot suits in robin's-egg blue.

Veracity's voice is in my ear. "Are you okay? Did something happen?"

Yes, something happened. My sister killed him to save me—to save us all. Everyone in this crater owes their existence to the buzzing blade of her knife in Col's heart.

Ending him.

"Maybe some water," I say.

"Back in a flash. Hang in there!"

I feel Veracity leave my side.

Now I'm alone in this tide of Palafox. Even with my eyes closed, Col's face fills my head, remixed into endless variations.

I breathe deep and slow, trying to steady myself, swallowing the pain along with salt tears. Eventually the throng will pass.

But then, amid all the chatter, a voice tugs on my ears.

". . . a crossover with Breakage. Make them go big-time, arson in one of the ruined neighborhoods. Force people to see what Shreve would look like if we'd got nuked. We play dead in the aftermath, a thousand Cols with radiation poisoning. How historic would that be?"

The voice is familiar, along with the way the words jumble and tangle, piling on top of each other. And I remember what Veracity said.

Fastest-growing clique in Shreve.

Where else would Sara be?

I force my eyes open to the light blue sea.

His face overwhelms me again. This crush, this roiling mass, this explosion of Cols. Even in my nightmares, full of pulse knives and chest wounds, nothing has ever been so dreadful.

My eyes shut themselves again, before I suffocate.

I have to track her by sound.

Sara's voice is fading now, behind me and to my right. I spin around and move swiftly after her, hands outstretched to feel my way through the crowd.

My fingertips brush shoulders and arms, a stray yelp of surprise as I step on someone's foot. Conversations drop off as I pass—who's this weirdo pushing through the crowd with her eyes shut?

Ahead of me, Sara keeps talking, nonstop plans for what the Saviors should do to match the grandeur of this party.

Something big, to reflect the sacrifice of the House Palafox's first son.

"Sara!" I hiss.

Her voice cuts off.

I come to a halt. Opening my eyes again, I find myself face-to-face with a small group of Saviors.

They're looking straight at me, a little confused. Five Cols, almost impossible to focus on. But then I see something pinned to one of their uniform lapels.

A small badge with a schematic of a tree.

It's one of the dust detectors that we brought to Shreve three months ago so we'd know when to speak freely. We paid Sara for her help with four of them.

She looks me up and down, a glimmer of recognition crossing her stolen features. "You're that Youngblood. The anonymous one."

I nod. Unlike Veracity, Sara watches the newsfeeds and saw me shake my sister's hand.

But her friends are hearing this too, which is exactly what Shay didn't want.

"We need to talk," I say. "Alone."

Sara looks around the crowd. "You picked a funny place."

It's hard to answer her, hard to think at all, with that tide of Palafox blue washing around us. I focus my senses on the specifics of Sara behind her costume surge.

She's skinnier than the real Col, her hair frizzier. Her costume surge hasn't changed how young she looks.

I gesture up the slope, in the direction the Saviors came from. The line of darkness at the edge of the crater.

"That way."

She considers this for a moment. I manage to keep my eyes open, somehow not seeing the other Cols swarming past us. The ground is unsteady.

Then a smile crosses her face. Like she's already figured out what I want. Like she's ready to do business.

Sara nods toward the darkness.

"Anything for one of Tally's crew."

BUSINESS

We climb out of the crater, until the lights of Shreve rise up on the horizon. They match the glare and dazzle of the party, as if Sara and I are a dark fulcrum balancing two bright and fragile chandeliers.

"So the rumors are true," she says.

I face her. "Which rumors?"

"That your crew was part of that mess the other night." Her smile drops away. "Chulhee, breaking into the Sarcophagus. Everyone knows the Youngbloods found that crashed hovercar. But not by chance, right?"

I hesitate. Tally and Shay would want me to admit nothing. But Sara's too smart, and her trust is more important than the Youngbloods' rep.

"We didn't help the Futures break in," I say carefully. "But it wasn't exactly a chance encounter."

She frowns a little. For a moment, she looks exactly like Col, the way he would puzzle out an unfamiliar English phrase.

212

I shut down that thought, forcing my attention to what's wrong with her disguise. The slant of her eyebrows, her hair black instead of darkest brown. She isn't him.

"Okay," Sara says. "So you were *watching* the Sarcophagus, in case anyone made a play for the surveillance data."

"More or less," I say.

"Which means you're spying on the cliques here in Shreve." Her smile is back. "And you were looking for me by my dust name, which means . . ."

She's going to get there anyway, so I might as well take credit for being honest. "You already met me, Sara. Just before the fall of Shreve."

She looks me up and down, frowning.

"I was in disguise," I add.

"You're still in disguise. No real Special would wear that boredom-causing face." Her eyes light up, a hand rising to touch her dust detector badge. "You were one of the commandoes! The ones looking for allies just before the attack—which means *Tally Youngblood* was behind the Fall of Shreve? That's huge!"

"But not true," I say, holding up my hands to steady her reeling guesswork. "I was an ordinary rebel then, trying to rescue a friend. I joined up with the Youngbloods later."

Sara isn't sure whether to believe me. Somehow uncertainty makes her look more like Col, so I have to turn away.

"You happened to sneak in," she says carefully, "the same week that Shreve got attacked by every free city in the world?"

"One thing led to another."

"You can say that again." Sara turns away, lets out a sigh into the darkness. "I should be mad at you. When you're going to blow up someone's city in a couple of days, you should probably *tell them*."

"We didn't know the free cities were about to attack—*they* didn't even know! But once they got wind of nuclear waste being dug up, our diversionary attack just sort of . . . escalated."

Sara looks down into the crater, as if trying to imagine the explosion huge enough to excavate it.

"Sure did." She turns back to me. "You were the one called Islyn, right?"

I nod. Even with a new body, she's recognized the way I talk and move and think. Just as I still recognize her behind her Savior surge.

"Islyn was my dust name, I guess."

She laughs at that. "Got plenty of names myself. What do you call yourself these days?"

This question again. "Let's stick with Islyn."

"You were born in Shreve, weren't you?" she asks. "Your accent . . . and a lot of little things."

"Even Shreve has runaways," I say.

"Well, nice to see you again, Islyn." She plucks the badge from her lapel and thrusts it at me. "Though I should point out that you ripped me off. Paid me with a dust detector, and two days later, all the dust was gone!"

"Freedom wasn't payment enough?"

She gives this a snort, pinning the badge back on herself. Maybe she wears it as a keepsake, or maybe she doesn't trust my sister not to bring back the dust.

"What do you need this time?"

"We need to find the Futures, the ones out in the wild," I say. "They've gotten years of everyone's life in Shreve."

"Including their own," she says. "Lives they worked hard to make historic. It's their property, their art."

I have to turn away. She's reminding me of Col, that passion for anything scientific or historical.

"You can't take it away from them," she continues. "Not with Chulhee still fighting for his life."

Of course—she was a friend to Future's founders, and a true believer herself.

This is the point where I start lying.

"We just want to make a deal, Sara. We've got some of the cores; they've got the rest. We can make copies and swap them so we'll both have a full set."

Her eyes narrow. "What do the Youngbloods want with Shreve's old surveillance data?"

I'm ready for this question.

"There might be more places like Hideaway, still holding people. With those recordings, we can find them."

"Maybe they'll risk a meeting, for a good cause." Sara lets out a chuckle. "Or to record themselves hanging out with Tally Youngblood. Pretty historic, right?"

"Sure," I say, though Tally won't be happy with that part of the deal. "But we have to keep this quiet. Your friends can't tell anyone they saw me."

"My friends know not to spread my business." Sara hesitates. "But I've got one more question—the most important one."

"What do *you* get paid?"

Sara shakes her head. "All I want to know now is . . . how come you can't stand to look at me?"

I almost deny it, but I've been staring at the ground for most of this conversation. Or at the lights of Shreve in the distance, the party, the sky. Anything but the face she's stolen.

I force myself to look into her eyes.

Once again, I have to trade a little truth for her help.

"I knew Col Palafox, the real one. We fought together when he was allied with the rebels." I glance down into the crater, at the amoeba of blue uniforms spreading its tendrils through the party. "I know the Saviors are supposed to be a tribute to him, but it's brain-wrecking to see all these . . . copies."

"Oh." She takes a step back from me. "I never thought about that. I mean, Col saved my family, my friends, everyone I've ever met. His sacrifice kept every place I've ever been from turning into a nuclear dump. It's hard to imagine him as a . . . person."

"You met him," I say. "He was in camo-surge that day, like the rest of us."

Sara's eyes widen. "One of your commandoes?"

"Yes. He fought for Shreve's freedom just as hard as for Victoria's." My voice drops to a whisper. "In the end, harder."

Sara crumples, all her swagger evaporating at once. She looks dizzy, as if Col was some Rusty sky god briefly manifest on earth.

She sinks to her knees before me.

"I'll bring the Futures to you, Islyn."

In her Vic uniform, head down, her voice hoarse with emotion, Sara reminds me of when Col pledged to fight for me.

I take panicked breaths as I back away, trying to force my Special senses to focus, to cut through her layers of cos-surge and makeup. She isn't Col. She doesn't move, talk, or smell like him.

As those lungfuls of clarifying, cold night air clear my head, I hear soft breathing nearby. I realize what my senses, battered by a profusion of impostor Cols, have missed till now . . .

Someone has followed us up here.

I turn and peer through the darkness.

Veracity.

VERACITY

"Someone's watching us," I whisper to Sara. "I'll deal with it. You set up a meeting."

She stares, still a little in awe of me, this person who knew the real Palafox heir. "I'll make it happen."

I hand her a chip that turns any comm device into a hotline to the Youngbloods, then turn away to stride into the darkness, toward the silhouette of body heat in the shape of a zoot-suited boy.

"Veracity," I call. "What are you—"

"You asked for this." He raises a glass, his expression sheepish and confused.

"Oh, right."

He looks past me, to where Sara is rising to her feet. "Did you just get a *proposal*?"

I have to smile.

"No, just an intense conversation." I take the glass from his hand, relieved to be talking to someone who doesn't look like Col. "Thanks for getting this. I feel better already."

"You looked like you were going to puke!"

I glance at Sara walking back down into the crater. "It was just unexpected. Someone I hadn't seen in a long time."

He follows my gaze. "You recognized her under all that Palafox surge?"

I take a drink—it's bubbly, not the water I asked for.

"We have a connection," I say.

"You must." His voice is tinged with wariness now, as if my tiny inconsistencies have been adding up.

"We hadn't seen each other since the Fall," I say. "We're glad to both be alive."

"Who isn't?" he asks, still uncertain. Maybe Sara has thrown his flirtation into doubt. Which is fine—it's time to get back to Shay.

"Anyway, it was nice to meet you, Veracity."

"Nice to meet you too. But I didn't get your name."

I give him my bored Rafi shrug. "Still not sure what to call myself."

I start to turn away.

"Okay," he says. "Tell Tally I said hi."

I freeze, just a moment too long to deny he's hit the mark. The wind whips our coattails around us for an awkward stretch of silence.

"*Everyone* watched that feed," Veracity finally says. "It's not every day Tally Youngblood comes to town."

His smirk sends anger sizzling through my veins. The adrenaline of seeing two hundred Cols finally has somewhere to go.

"You knew who I was *this whole time*?"

He shrugs, all innocence. "Was I not supposed to?"

"You're right about your name," I say. "You're not very honest."

Another smirk. "Veracity is a two-way street."

I have no answer for this. I've played someone else for so long, it hardly feels like lying anymore.

Veracity keeps talking. "I have to admit, everything you *did* tell me was fascinating. Those questions you kept asking—what do I miss about the old days?"

"Just making conversation."

"Really?" He smiles. "Sounded to me like the Youngbloods are curious if Frey of Shreve is doing a good job."

"We're curious about a lot of stuff."

Veracity glances down at Sara as she blends back into the crowd of Saviors. "Was she really an old friend?"

I don't say anything, suddenly glad for Sara's disguise. Veracity will never be able to track her down among all those other Cols.

I let the cool distance of a Special settle over me.

All he knows is that one of the Youngbloods came to this party, asked a few questions, and met a friend. Even if he spreads this news far and wide, my sister won't guess what we're up to. She'll probably think Diego sent their avatar to poke around.

I tell my crash bracelet to call my hoverboard.

"It's been fun, Veracity. But you should seriously pick a different name."

"At least I *tell* people my name." He turns away, heading down to the party with tip of an imaginary hat. "Good night, good night, whoever you are."

Whoever I am.

Those words cut sharper than his lies somehow, as if anonymity is the hidden truth of me.

WRECKING
BALL

Two minutes later, my board zooms up the crater's slope, Shay flying about ten meters behind.

"You found her?" she calls.

"Yeah, it's done." I step onto my board and rise into the air.

"Good." Shay comes to a skidding halt beside me. "I'm too old for this party."

When I don't answer, Shay drifts closer. I feel pale, my heart still beating sideways.

"You okay, Frey-la? Did you run into . . . ?" She looks back at the robin's-egg-blue snake now coiling around the center of the party.

I nod my head.

"Sorry you had to see that," Shay says.

The simple words, undemanding of me, make it easier to answer.

"Col didn't die the quite way they think, but he did come here to help free Shreve. I'm glad they remember that part of him."

Shay absorbs this, adding it to her tally of me. "And what are we paying Sara to connect us?"

"Nothing. Turns out she . . ."

Worships my dead boyfriend.

". . . just wants to help."

"Huh. Maybe there's hope for this city yet." Shay turns to face the wild beyond the party. "Which means we've got a whole new mission."

There's an intricate moment of silence, the music of our unspoken conflict. Shay would rather focus on the criminals behind Hideaway, not my father's recordings. But I've distracted the boss.

She moves on. "Anybody recognize you?"

"This one guy. He was trying to find out what a Youngblood was doing at the party. He pretended to be flirting, and I believed it!"

"Don't feel bad. Everyone in Shreve must be a pretty good liar by now."

I frown at her—lying was *illegal* here.

But she's right. Everyone I've ever met in my hometown—Veracity, Sara, Jax the smuggler—has shown a streak of unexpected cunning. Maybe that's the natural result of living with the dust. When every word is recorded, usable against you in a trial for high treason, you learn to communicate with misdirection and half-truths.

I thought I was the only impostor in Shreve.

"They're all choosing new names," I say. "They get to be themselves at last."

Shay lets out a sigh. "So maybe Tally's plan makes sense. If people

223

want to erase their old lives, we should help them. We've all done things we want to forget."

A stray memory hits me. "The other night at the campfire, you said something about Tally collaborating with the authorities."

"If you want that story, you'll have to ask the boss. It was a long time ago."

I search for the right words. "But some crimes have to be punished—like putting kids in prison. You'd rather be looking into Hideaway than chasing down my father's surveillance data, right?"

Shay nods, staring glumly at the party. "Stealing the recordings looked like a good way to find out more about Hideaway. But it's been a wild-goose chase. We wasted a week, while someone was manufacturing a cover-up. It's almost like . . ."

Shay turns to me, letting her words fade into the hubbub of the party. Our conflict entangles us again.

"Like what?" I push.

"Like you had a conversation with your clever sister," she says coldly. "And came back with the perfect story to derail us."

My mouth goes dry. "You think I'm helping Rafi? After what she did to Col?"

"Not on purpose, no. But it's how you're made—to heel to your sister's side. You went digging in Shreve House, blew out a window, when we were supposed to get in and out lightly."

"I wasn't *trying* to get caught."

But then I saw his desk . . .

"What if she recognized you?" Shay keeps turning her knife. "Avatars are different from humans."

"Rafi's not a Special."

"But she's no fool. She could've fed you a story, just to keep us busy."

I shake my head. Rafi couldn't have known that the Futures would beat us to the data vaults. And she'd never have been so nakedly wounded in front of me.

You think I'd traumatize those kids for a few trees?

"That sounds paranoid, Shay."

"Maybe your city's rubbing off on me."

She says it with a smile, but she still thinks I'm a natural point of weakness in the crew. Daughter of a dictator, chaos merchant.

Astrix's taunt comes back to me. "You think I'm like Tally."

Shay makes an innocent expression, then spins her board around to face the darkness. "Gee, Frey-la. Where'd you get that idea?"

She flies away.

I stand there for a befuddled moment before urging my board after her.

She's headed back toward our camp, skirting the vast and dazzling bowl of the party. The wind is sharp and cool, the wild looming ahead.

In the long minutes it takes me to catch up, I realize that it was Shay who sent Astrix with me to hide the cores.

I pull closer and shout, "Did you *tell* Astrix to say all that stuff to me?"

"Of course not. But she has no filters." Shay grins back. "Sometimes she's the best way to deliver awkward news."

"Did you really call me a mini Tally?"

"My exact words!" Shay shouts, slaloming around me, the wind of our passage carrying her laughter into the dark. "Ask yourself, Frey-la—who made you what you are?"

"My father. His DNA, his idea to raise me as a killer."

"And who made *him*?"

I stare at her, remembering my conversation with Tally in the ruins of Hideaway. *Of all the things I've created, your father was probably the worst.*

But she didn't mean literally.

"You're being sense-missing. Tally didn't make him, or me!"

"I'm glad *you* know that." Shay veers closer. "But the boss gets confused sometimes. She set the world on fire, so now she worries about every random spark. That's why we're focused on humanity-controlling AIs instead of Hideaway—we're always fighting the *next* monsters."

I glance back at the spectacle behind us. The light drones twinkle like distant fireworks, but the patterns—words, flags, images—reveal the subtle intelligence baked into them.

"You don't think AIs are creepy? Minds that can think circles around us, yet almost let my father wreck the world?"

"Smart cities don't scare me," Shay says. "They're just places that talk."

I hook a thumb at the crater behind us. "They can also railgun you from space!"

"Humans put those weapons in orbit," she says. "And there have always been creepy cities. The place Tally and I grew up in didn't have an AI, but our Pretty Committee was the strictest in the world. As an ugly, you could feel that control everywhere you went. That's what made me and Tally what we are—we rebelled against our birthplace."

It takes me a moment, but then I see what this has to do with me.

Shay thinks I'm a creation of my city too. Except Shreve didn't just control its citizens—it invaded its neighbors, killed a hundred thousand people in Paz, dug up and weaponized ancient nuclear waste.

It almost brought down the new world order.

"You think I'm worse than a bad influence," I say.

"You're a wrecking ball." She glides away into the dark ahead.

I follow in silence for a while. I'm not sure if Shay's trying to humiliate me, or if she wants me to learn something from this jumble of insults and revelations.

Tonight started with her saying I was family now. No blood like crew. How did I get from that to wrecking ball so fast?

Unless it's not a contradiction—being a mini Tally makes me something familiar. Maybe I'm family because Shay knows how to deal with chaos.

If I'm a wrecking ball, that makes Tally . . . a bigger wrecking ball?

I fly hard into the headwind, until I'm close enough to speak again.

"You think the boss is dangerous."

"That's why I ride with her—to put the brakes on." Shay gives me a tired smile. "There's more than one way to save the world."

ROAD TRIP

Two days later, Sara calls.

The Futures have agreed to meet with us, to swap a copy of their surveillance data for ours so we'll each have a full set. They're a long way from Shreve, hiding in a ruined Rusty city on the west coast.

When we get the coordinates, the Youngbloods burst into laughter.

"Our old stomping ground."

"Wonder if the roller coaster's still there."

"After twenty-five years? The recyclers will have eaten it by now."

Boss X gives me a shrug, as lost as I am. A quarter century ago is back in the pretty time, when the other four were uglies. The era of the original Smoke.

"Weird," Tally says. "But at least we get a few days' ride. Feels like we've been skulking around Shreve for weeks."

I feel the same way, camping this close to home. Half of me wants to follow the newsfeeds, the crime reports, the swings of Rafi's face rank as she tries to exorcise my father's ghost. Or maybe even read her letters to me.

The other half of me wants to run.

Not only from Shreve—from myself too. If Shay's right, and growing up here left something dangerous in my blood, maybe best thing I can do is to put home behind me.

Let Rafi grapple with Shreve's messy past. I belong out here with the Youngbloods, in the wild, fighting the monsters in humanity's future.

Riggs is still searching for Stellan Batrow. His goateed face and pleasant crumbly smile may have been erased by surgery, but his DNA will show up somewhere.

We Youngbloods aren't wardens.

True to her word, Shay treats me as a fully fledged Youngblood now. She let me present our report about Sara to the crew. I'm invited to our planning sessions. She's even handed me Boss X's coffee-making duties.

But maybe Shay just wants to keep me close, like she does Tally— the better to protect the world from me.

It only takes us an hour to pack. We send out pings for other crews to join us on this mission, then head west, seven hoverboards in loose formation.

The extra board is a cargo flyer, a machine that Astrix cobbled together while she was off getting treatment. It carries five of the memory cores, shielded with solid lead to keep radiation from giving us away. With all that weight, it needs six engines and flies with a shriek like a groundskeeping drone trimming thick, dry grass.

Even with the cargo flyer wailing behind us, the rattle in my head fades as we travel away from Shreve. Every kilometer puts distance between me and the Saviors, those faces that have swarmed my dreams the last two nights.

Worse are the dreams of Sara on her knees, looking up at me as if waiting for my blessing.

If she only knew that I'm a perfect copy of Col's murderer.

We make camp after midnight, then start again before dawn.

That second day, the landscape starts to blur together—the desert sky, the glare of the white weed on the plains. We don't even pause to recharge our boards, leaving a trail of expended batteries for other crews to forage.

The ride doesn't feel rushed, though. With Shreve fading behind me, the arid calm of being Special descends. I sink into the desert's emptiness.

I can see what Tally likes about important, world-saving missions. My nightmares drop away into our slipstream, lost in the hum of lifting fans. We halt in the afternoon, having reached the rendezvous point hours ahead of the other rebel crews. Our camp is next to a range of low hills, a creek trickling past.

"Help me with the bonfire," X says, stepping off his board.

"Now? It's not even dark yet."

"This might take a while. We're cooking something special for our guests."

I smile at him. Among the reinforcements on the way is X's old crew. Their new bosses are Col's childhood friend Yandre Marin and Boss Charles, who were with us at the Battle of Shreve.

We need their help to fabricate another fifty cores, decoys for our meeting with the Futures. We also need more supplies for our journey. And more firepower, in case we have to take the data by force.

But X, bless his wolfish heart, has been planning a reunion party.

"I spotted some excellent firewood a few klicks ago," he says.

We backtrack, until he points out an unimpressive tree. It's not much taller than him, its branches gnarled and tangled, like a many-headed serpent lurking in the scrub.

The dry air shimmers with the hum of X's lance.

I step back. "Full pulse? What's this tree made of, metal?"

"Mesquite," he says, and takes a swing.

The wood lets out an unholy roar, expelling a cloud of sawdust that smells like cherries cooking. I can't see a thing, but X's lance keeps swinging, its keening dotted with the shrieking resistance of hardwood.

I take another step backward, leaving him all the room he needs.

When the dust settles, gritty in my mouth and eyes, X is grinning. A jumble of firewood lies where the tree once stood, only a reluctant stump still in the ground.

I look at the pile. "Are we cooking an elephant?"

"Not quite." He raises his field glasses, scanning the hills. "There's a herd of them now."

My infrared flickers with a cluster of bodies. They're hot enough to be seen from kilometers away, much bigger than deer or coyotes.

X lowers his glasses. "Have you ever hunted bison?"

"Um, no." I've eaten fresh meat plenty of times, taken down by Col's bow or an easy throw of my pulse knife. But those were deer, not creatures standing taller than me and weighing a ton. "It seems kind of ethics-missing."

"It's exquisite," X says. "And one rarely has enough dinner guests to justify the kill."

I look again at the giant bodies in the distance, wondering how Boss X fits into Shay's theory that we're all products of our cities. Does that mean people who grew up in the wild are purer than the rest of us?

Of course, the wild has a personality too—more than one. Sometimes X is a cool rain forest.

Sometimes he's a hurricane.

"Yeah, but do the *bison* think it's exquisite?"

"A scientific justification, then," he says with a sigh. "Recent satellite imagery indicates that they're overpopulating the plains, just as they did after the Columbian plagues. Not enough *wolves*."

He says that last word like both of us are included in the category. As if killing something will reveal my true nature, my real self.

I feel like everyone's testing me these days.

"Sure, X. I'll help you murder a bison. For science."

"For dinner," he says. "Only a barbarian wastes meat."

We spend an hour burning the fire down to coals.

It takes ages to get the mesquite started, and it never reaches a cheery blaze. But once the embers are glowing in their pit, the heat is steady and even, the smoke clean and sweet.

"Perfect," X says.

"Seems wasteful," I say. "Killing a whole tree for one meal."

"It's not just dinner. I miss my crew."

"Right." I reach out to stroke the fur of his shoulder. "It'll be good to see Yandre again."

"*Boss* Yandre," he corrects me. "That's why this reunion has to be . . . exceptional."

Finally I understand.

X was born to be a rebel boss, but he gave it up for me. He only joined the Youngbloods to help me take down my sister, something no one but Tally was strong enough to do.

But now that goal has fallen by the wayside.

"You want your crew back," I say.

"If they'll take me."

I snort. "Yandre will hand it over if you ask, right?"

"If they did that, they'd never be a boss again."

"Oh." The thought of the two of them in conflict is painful—they're the only two friends of Col's who I'm still close to.

But not as painful as X leaving.

"Do you really hate being a Youngblood?"

"You don't need me here. You're one of them now."

I want to argue, but he's right. Every second I'm in Tally's crew carries me further from the old Frey—the wounded, battered girl.

And yet I want to rewind to when X helped rescue me and Col from my father's tower. When he asked me to join his crew, and I said no and went looking for my sister instead.

I could say yes now, leave Tally to save the world without me.

What would Shay think of me then? A wrecking ball, swinging wildly, incapable of sticking to even my own flimsy plans.

But the thought of X going tears my heart a little.

"I always thought you and I were meant to be crew."

"We were," he says.

I hear it then, the way he leans on that last word—the past tense.

"Let's kill something," I say.

THE KILL

We leave our pulse weapons by the fire.

X gives me a simple knife, no intelligence woven into its metal blade. We ride on our boards to the edge of the low hills, then enter on foot to stalk the herd.

Behind us, Astrix has taken over the fire, not that it needs much care. The hardwood embers will burn all night.

"Take off your shirt," X says. "Self-cleaning fibers don't work on blood."

I frown. "Is all this really necessary?"

"Eating? Very."

"No—I mean metal knives. A pulse weapon and hoverboard would be easier, more humane. And less messy."

"But less natural."

I'm not sure what he means by that last word. Both of us are surgically augmented, ten times deadlier than any natural human.

It's been a long time since anyone hunted bison on foot, armed with nothing but a sharp piece of metal.

"Why don't we just use rocks?" I mutter.

X strips off his body armor. His fur ripples in the wind.

"Most animals hunt with teeth and claws."

I roll my eyes.

"This will clear your head," he adds. "You haven't been sleeping well."

I want to keep arguing, if only to delay the bloody outcome ahead of us. But X wouldn't go to all this trouble just to feed his old crew.

"You think this will erase all those Cols dancing in my dreams?" I ask, trying to sound flippant.

"You don't need them erased." He's dead serious. "You need to see *through* them. Otherwise, you won't see anything else."

"I don't know what you mean, X." I pull off my body armor and shirt. The cold breeze hits my bare skin like a shot of adrenaline. "But I like that you're trying to help me."

X hesitates, as if he's about to launch into a complicated explanation of my psyche. But instead he sheaths his knife and goes with something cryptic.

"Blood will tell," he says.

We approach the herd from downwind, moving carefully through loose rock and brittle scrub. With every scrape of stone, the animals stir a little.

The bison are huge, like shambling fur carpets with razor horns. They're packed tight for safety, and warmth, I guess, the cluster a bright island in the deep blue of my infrared. Even with my Special metabolism, the desert at sundown is swiftly growing cold.

X brings us to a halt, closing his eyes to listen. The breathing of the herd rolls across my hearing, hypnotic as crashing waves.

After a long moment, X pulls a laser sight from his belt and marks a beast in the middle of the pack. "That one sounds like it has a lung fluke."

"So we avoid it?"

X gives me a hard look. "Predators take the sick first. Keeps the herd healthy."

"Okay, fine. I just thought . . . lung flukes don't sound tasty."

"What parts of this beast do you think we're eating?"

I shrug. Col or Zura were always in charge of skinning deer. Maybe I'm inherently a city kid.

We move forward in absolute silence. But the herd simmers as we draw close—they either hear us, smell us, or have some magical instinct for danger.

Our target is protected by the pack, so the kill won't be clean. We'll have to fight our way into that crowded mass of fur and horns.

The knife feels cold and dumb in my hand. A pulse weapon would make this much simpler.

"Ready?" X whispers.

I'm not sure what the plan is but give him a nod anyway.

At a whispered count of three, X bolts ahead. I follow, the pack exploding before us.

Their huge bodies accelerate slowly, though, and soon we're among them, running shoulder to shoulder with two dozen shaggy giants.

Their heat envelops me, their scent, the ground thundering under my feet. I'm jostled and bumped, barely staying upright—one misstep and I'll be trampled. Their animal fear fills my lungs with every breath.

One sideswipes me, and I'm sent staggering, bouncing from one huge form to another. Their bodies ripple with muscle and fat, their fur coarse and matted. I only keep my feet because they aren't trying to run me down—this is a stampede, pure chaos and panic.

X is making his way toward the center of the herd. I run harder, trying to catch up. Our target is falling back toward me, wheezing as it runs.

X glances over his shoulder, making eye contact.

His knife flashes in the sunset.

I draw my weapon.

We strike together—X leaps up to wrap one arm around its neck. I attack from behind, slashing a rear leg as it kicks out toward me, shredding tendons and meat.

As the bison stumbles, X's blade plunges into its neck.

The charging animal tips forward. It plows headfirst into the dirt, a thunderous skidding that throws up clouds of rocks and dust.

X disappears, and then I'm crashing into the flailing mass of legs and fur. A tornado of blood and muscle and dirt batters me, but I'm mostly worried about the rest of the herd trampling us.

The roar of hooves divides around us, though.

The fallen beast is writhing, stirring the dust cloud with its wheezing breaths. The snick of X's blade comes again. My vision is a blur of body heat, his tangled with the beast's. I drop my knife and wrap my arms around the creature's rear legs, keeping them from kicking me again.

With another grunt from X, blood sprays everywhere—my hands, my eyes, my mouth.

Over the next endless seconds, the sound of the stampeding herd fades with the thrashing of our prey. Its spasms settle into pulses, and I can hear its stuttering heartbeat.

The soft wind finally lifts the dust cloud from us. I feel the buzz of healing nanos swarming beneath my skin, attending to my countless scrapes and bruises.

X pulls himself out from beneath the beast's shaggy head.

He stands, grinning like a wolf, his fur matted and slick.

This was more violent, more visceral than fighting walkers or drones. Bloodier than anything that's happened to me since . . .

Suddenly the world is sideways. The smell of death has brought that night rushing back.

The Fall of Shreve. Fighting our way up the tower stairs. My father's demand.

My sister's blade moving through the air, unstoppable.

I start wiping frantically at my bare skin, trying to get the blood off, but my hands are wet and red. My Special nervous system should kick in now, ramping me down into a state of calm. But there's something in me spinning faster and faster, a battle fury with nothing to fight.

X comes closer, placing a slick hand on each of my shoulders.

A sob tears its way out of me.

"Seriously, Boss?" I say through tears. "You thought *this* would clear my head?"

He grunts, still coming back into himself.

"It's just like that night," I say. "He was all over me."

"But this time you can wash it off," X says.

I'm not sure what to say to that.

This is not how my brain works. I don't want to dip myself in blood again. I don't need copies of Col's face thrown at me.

I want to forget that night, not relive it a hundred different ways.

The tears flow harder. They trickle down to my mouth, tasting of blood.

"X, I know you're trying to help. But this isn't who I am."

He wraps his arms around me, shutting out the desert cold with his own churning body heat.

"No, Frey, it's who *I* am." He's breathing hard, like he's still chasing our prey. "This is what I became after losing Seanan. This moment of annihilation, this blood. This is what you made me."

The words are nonsense, until the meaning of them comes shrieking toward me down a dark passage of my brain, an awful reckoning

241

that I've hidden from myself since the Fall of Shreve. I flash back further, not to the night of Col's death, but to the very first time I saw what a knife at full pulse can do to a human being.

It comes out in a whisper into the fur of X's chest.

"I'm your Rafi." I killed Seanan, his Col.

The familiar justifications spill through my brain. I was protecting my sister. I had only seconds to decide. I was only doing what my father raised me to do.

The same excuses Rafi had for murdering Col.

Seventeen years of worrying about turning into her, and instead Rafi turned into me. A killer.

We're mirror images, just like we were raised to be.

A long shudder travels through me, another piece falling into place—why X gave up everything to help me get revenge on Rafi.

Because he can never get revenge on *me*.

I'm crew, a fellow rebel. We fought together before he learned the truth. By the time I told him, it was too late to be enemies.

My arms hold him tighter. "I'm just like her."

"No," he says. "You're Frey."

That name again, the one I've lost all connection to.

I shake my head.

"Frey," he contends once more.

We stand like that for a while, next to the gurgles and sighs making their way through the beast beside us. Death moves slowly in a creature so large, as gradual and relentless as the fact that X is leaving me soon.

We *were* meant to be crew. But no more.

Finally he pulls away.

"Sorry to rush you, but . . ." He stoops to hand me my bloody knife.

I blink away the tears in my eyes. "What—more hunting?"

"More running."

He cocks his head, and that's when I hear it at last.

A shrieking across the red sky.

"Drones," X says. "Four kilometers and closing. We're under attack."

DRONES

We run.

Back toward our hoverboards, across dirt pocked by a storm of bison hooves. Back toward the high-pitched whine of lifting fans. By the sound, the drones can't be any bigger than packs of playing cards, too small to carry much firepower.

Of course, there's no time to grab our body armor either.

I'm not even wearing a shirt.

The sun is fully set as my board kicks to life beneath my blood-sticky riding boots. Dirt swirls around me, the desert air freezing cold.

In the distance, the others are folding up the solar panels of their boards, getting ready to fly and fight.

The firepit blazes for a moment—Astrix taking off beside it, her lifting fans stirring the coals. She swings around toward us, her arms loaded with objects glittering red in the sunset.

She's bringing us our pulse weapons.

But six drones are following her, coming low and fast. They're almost too small to see, but miniature dust tornadoes swirl in their wakes.

I open my comms. "Behind you, 'Rix!"

"I hear them!"

She cuts right, hard enough that her board bends in the middle. Her pursuers overshoot but wheel in the air like a scattering of starlings, back on her tail in seconds.

Back at camp, heat signatures of little engines fill the sky. More of the drones dogfighting with Shay, Tally, and Croy.

One of Astrix's pursuers suddenly accelerates, flaring in my infravision as it shoots toward her. She ducks just in time, but a cry comes over the comms.

"You okay?" I ask.

"Close one. It snipped my hair."

I shudder. Once in the war against my father, I saw a rebel group fly in a formation so tight that a rider's hair spooled into the lifting fan above her—at ten thousand RPMs. She wound up concussed and missing forty square centimeters of scalp. And the *sound* it made.

Four of the other drones peel away from Astrix, heading for me and X. At the same time, she throws my pulse knife into the air.

At my gesture, the knife bolts across the desert, racing the drones.

It wins, reaching my hand a half second before them. I squeeze the knife to full pulse and parry—the first machine shatters into shrapnel against my bare skin.

The other drone peels away before my blade can find it.

X swings into my view, riding low, a drone coming at him. The clang of his knife rings across the desert.

The drone breaks the blade, bouncing off his flank. He grunts, but his feet stay on the board. He hurls the broken knife, missing as the drone zooms away into the dark.

X and Astrix angle toward each other, riding parallel—she throws his lance to him. It roars in his hands.

Unencumbered at last, Astrix spins around to fire her pistol at the last drone chasing her, but it's already veered off toward me.

All three of our remaining pursuers form a fast-moving triangle, with me at its center.

I flail with my pulse knife, trying to cover all angles of attack.

A sudden whine builds behind me, and I spin on my board, knife held high. The machine blurs past, dodging destruction at the last minute.

Another shriek on my right, but the roar of X's board joins it. As I turn to defend myself, he shoots into view, the drone exploding in midair with a sweep of his lance.

"Nice one!" I start to shout—as the last drone strikes.

It comes straight at my head out of the red dregs of sunset. The wind of its passage flurries my hair, but it roars past without touching me . . .

And off into the dark.

I wheel my board into a tight turn, waiting for more attackers to leap from the dusk.

But the desert has gone quiet. Even the air back at camp looks still, the other three Youngbloods drifting on their boards, staring off into the darkness, weapons raised but silent.

I turn my comms on wide. "Is it over, Boss?"

"Not sure," Tally says. "Spin down, everyone."

We let our boards drop into the desert sand.

The sudden silence echoes in my ears, formless for a moment. Then I start to hear details—the cooling of hoverboard engines underfoot, the firepit's hiss and crackle, the wind slicing through cactus needles.

"They only skimmed us," Astrix whispers on her comms. "Then they zoomed off."

"You mean—" I pat myself down, looking for a wound, a pinprick.

I'm covered with bison blood and scratches. There's no chance of finding a mark.

"My *hair*," Croy says softly on the comms. "Something's missing."

I look at Astrix. Her fingers twirl her frizzy black mane, an uncertain expression on her face.

"Both of you?" I reach up and touch my own head. Even matted with blood, I can feel the difference. A lock of hair is missing, cut clean a centimeter from the roots.

X is staring down at his side, where the drone bashed against him. His fingers ruffle through his fur, until he finds a spot.

"Not a coincidence," he says. "Boss, we're all . . . missing some hair."

"They're looking for someone," Tally says. "A runaway or a crim, someone in disguise. You can get DNA from hair, right?"

"That's complicated," Astrix says. "But that's not normal warden behavior, assaulting random travelers with unmarked drones."

"So what are they looking for?" Tally asks.

"You can tell a lot from someone's hair—their health, medicines they've taken." Astrix hesitates. "Exposure to radiation. Even after we got treated, the hair that grew while we were poisoned would show traces."

"So they're looking for the cores," Tally says.

Across the desert, lifting fans spin back up. I jump back onto my board and urge it into the air.

All of us converge back at the main camp, where the cargo flyer sits under a camo tarp, disguised as a random mound of sand.

By the time I arrive, Shay has snapped the tarp off.

The flyer sits there, undisturbed.

"My shielding worked," Astrix says with a smile. "They didn't spot it."

"Yeah," Tally says. "But once they check those hair samples, they'll be back."

SEANAN

"Are you two all right?" Tally asks.

She's looking at me and X—we're half-naked and covered with blood.

"We were getting dinner," I say.

"Um, okay." Tally files this particular confusion away for later, turning to Shay. "How fast can we get out of here?"

"No point running," Shay says, throwing the camo tarp back over the flyer. "These boards are almost spent—our spare batteries too. We should hang on to the charge we've got."

Tally nods. Better to fight with hoverboards under our feet.

"I pinged Boss Yandre when the attack started," X says. "They're coming at full speed. An hour forty, maybe less."

A murmur of relief. That's two crews headed our way—twenty-one rebels in full battle gear.

Croy frowns. "Everyone saw us at the crash site. We'll just say that's why our hair's radioactive."

"Except for X," Astrix says. "He's way off the charts."

Shay tucks the camo tarp carefully over the cargo flyer again. "We were brain-missing to think we could just fly out of Shreve with these cores. Someone left those drones around the city to find them. We have to assume they'll be coming in force."

That's all she has to say.

Astrix and Croy head out to place a ring of motion sensors around the camp. Tally and Shay start digging a hole for the cargo flyer. X and I head back to the hills to get our body armor—and the murdered bison, he tells me on the way.

"Really? You think the cookout's still on?"

"It's uncivilized to waste meat," he says. "And unwise to fight on empty stomachs. If they see we're unafraid, whoever sent those drones might be more circumspect. Which buys time for Yandre to arrive."

"Because nothing says fearless like . . . having a barbecue?"

"Indeed, Frey-la," he says. "Besides, it's time you learned how to field dress a bison."

First X "unzips" the beast.

He makes a swift cut from head to tail along the bison's spine. The matted fur parts easily under a pulse lance set to low.

I look away, partly to check the skies for attackers, partly because it's sad-making to see this proud beast reduced to a sack of meat.

Then the going gets brutal—X hacks the creature's hide away from the still-warm fat and flesh, moving like some kind of surgeon-ninja in the dark. We use pulse weapons for speed, though X says traditional blades would've been more honorable.

There's no point putting my shirt back on, even in the cold. Butchering is messy in the darkness, moving fast. The smell of death fills the air, the rocks around us turning shiny with blood. At least working at a breakneck pace keeps my mind on the job.

Strangely, I'm more concerned about the dinner guests headed our way than any imminent attack. We're behind schedule to cook this thing, and X is right—it would be barbaric to waste its life.

Ten minutes later, we wash off quickly in a creek. The water's freezing, but finally the blood is gone from my skin. When we're dressed again, I turn the heater in my body armor to its maximum.

We hike back to camp, the meat riding on our boards.

"I hope that wasn't too much," X says.

A shake of my head. "I'm a Special now. I have to know how to feed myself in the wild."

"Not the butchery, Frey. Our earlier conversation."

My brain had erased it already, letting it spin away into the fury of battle. But it takes more than a drone assault to move X past a drama-making conversation.

"It wasn't easy to hear," I say. "But it's true—I did the same thing to you that Rafi did to me."

"The situations are intertwined, but not the same."

"Close enough." I look up at him. His eyes should be full of old

251

and simmering anger, but they're full of something completely different. Something like . . . love. "How did you ever forgive me, X?"

"It was easy."

I come to a halt, letting the hoverboards and their bloody cargo slide past us. "How?"

"By the time I met you, Seanan's death was a part of me." X repeats his earlier words precisely, like a memorized poem. *"This moment of annihilation, this blood. This is what you made me."*

I shake my head. It's as sense-missing as Tally saying she created my father. "Seriously? *I* made *you*?"

"It was after Seanan's death that I became a wolf," X reminds me.

"But you grew up in the wild. You're more inherently wolf than anyone I've ever met!"

"Not back then. When I was with Seanan, I was wrapped up in other things, like his hatred of your father. It took losing him to see myself. Tears make for clear eyes."

I try to swallow. "X, are you saying that when I . . . that what I did . . . was somehow *good* for you?"

A silence passes, heavy and cold. I wish I could take the words back.

But X speaks gently. "I'm saying that after your brother was gone, I could see what parts of him had made a home in me. Before then, I was just a boy—Seanan was the wolf."

Those last four words glint in the air, making an icy, perfect sense. My brother snuck into Shreve, a fortified city, to murder his own father. There was no chance of getting out alive, but that didn't stop his animal hatred.

Maybe that was his inheritance. Our father was a wolf too, and both of them were cut down by family.

But for X to say that his teeth and fur, his beautiful lupine eyes, are what's left of Seanan is too much to hear.

"I killed my brother, X. Don't say it helped you *find yourself.* And don't you dare say that what Rafi did helped me!"

"I never used the word *help*, Frey. It's just who we are now."

"What am I supposed to *do* with that?"

"Let it change you. Let the blood soak in."

I turn away from him, facing the darkness. The desert seems tilted around me in an uneasy, seasick way.

The tower is down there in the sand. I can't just will it away.

An annoyed Shay crackles to life on the comms. "What's taking you two so long?"

I've never been so glad to hear her voice.

"Almost there," X says, and closes the channel. "Frey, I've put all this on you before you were ready. I'm sorry for that, but this mission will be over soon."

And then I'll be gone, he doesn't say.

I have to fill the silence. "Thank you for holding on to my brother, Boss. For carrying part of him."

"I don't have a choice." X reaches out a hand. "Nor do you. Even if you reshape your body a hundred times, you'll still have Col in here."

His fingertip brushes my heart—the exact spot where the world spins heavy every night, that slow gyre of my grief.

I take X's wrist and push it away.

"I don't have the strength to carry anyone else."

"Because you carried your sister for sixteen years. That's why she's lost now. She needs you."

I turn away, not wanting this conversation to get messier, and point at our hoverboards, fifty meters ahead of us now.

"Come on, X. We need to cook that beast."

BOSS YANDRE

An hour later, a fleet of hoverboards lights up my thermal vision. They fly in close combat formation, silvery fish schooling in the sky.

Relief that we have backup mixes with a tremor of nerves—this will be the first time I've seen Yandre since the rebel funeral, the day after the Fall of Shreve. It was for everyone killed in the liberation, Victorians, escaping political prisoners, jump troops from Diego, not just our comrades.

I was already puking from the radiation poisoning, but I stayed.

We gathered a signet for each of the dead—crew badges, old hand weapons, the blade of a hoverboard fan twisted in a final crash. For Col, I brought a handful of desiccated goldenrod, the frozen flower he gave me as we fell into Shreve from the edge of space.

All of it was buried together in a forest clearing outside the city border, a slice of the wild in sight of the skyline. On every tree around the bower we carved the first rebel cry—*The Smoke lives.*

Yandre looked older that day, saying good-bye to their childhood friend.

Boss Yandre looks still older tonight.

Twenty-one rebels land in our camp, the wash from their lifting fans sending shimmers and sparks through the coals in the firepit. The smell of mesquite smoke wreaths around us, sweet and clear.

Yandre jumps off to hug X, a few of the other rebels greet the Youngbloods like old friends, but I'm invisible. Hardly any of my wartime comrades have seen my face since the surgery.

Then Yandre spots me in the fire's soft glow.

"Is that . . . Frey?"

Somehow they recognized me, when my own sister didn't.

"Yeah, Boss. It's me."

Our hug takes me back to the early days of the war—those moments when the world felt small and graspable, no bigger than a rebel camp or an ambush lair. Victoria occupied and my father still alive, but Col was alive too.

And now he's gone.

Yandre's arms around me keeps my heart from breaking.

They pull away, looking at the cuts on my cheek. "One of those drones got you?"

"While it was exploding at the end of my knife. Turns out they only wanted hair samples."

"No kidding." Yandre smooths out a long strand of their own hair, cut jaggedly across the bottom. "They jumped us too, fifty klicks south. A hundred popping out of the grass, all at once."

I stare at the missing lock. "That many?"

"Lucky they're harmless." Yandre pulls out a flask. "Which means we just flew here at top speed to protect Boss Tally's . . . haircut."

We laugh together, sharing a drink.

Then Yandre's gaze falls on the sizzling bison, held up by a smart-metal mesh strung across the firepit. The mesh moves slowly, like languid metal snakes, rotating the meat every half hour. The rich smell swirls around us, its promise filling my mouth.

Maybe Yandre knows that X wants his crew back. Everything about this reunion is painful enough—I can't stand to see a rift between the two of them.

Thankfully, Yandre turns to the business at hand.

"Okay, so who made thousands of drones to look for radioactive travelers? Who cares that much about Shreve history?"

"Those recordings aren't just history," I say. "They're the soul of my city."

Yandre raises an eyebrow, like I'm being random. There's no easy way to explain that my father's system produced more than surveillance—it captured the anguish, joy, love, and foolishness of our lives in Shreve, historic and otherwise.

"We burned it all in Victoria," they say. "And I don't mean erasing the cores. We set them on fire in the public square. People watched and cheered."

Of course—dust filled the air of occupied Victoria too. But there it was purely a symbol of invasion.

"A lot of people in Shreve felt the same way," I say. "But you met the Futures."

"I *liked* them. They were doing the best they could in a bad situation. But don't tell me a bunch of kids printed thousands of drones. Who do we think it was?"

When I hesitate, Yandre smiles.

"Or does Boss Tally want you to keep quiet about the big picture?"

I shrug. "She doesn't want us to say."

"Us," Yandre repeats. They take a slow drink from their flask, letting my guilt simmer.

When I was in Victoria, it was Yandre who brought me a pulse knife charger. Without them, Col and I would never have made it out the night my father destroyed House Palafox.

I start a clumsy explanation. "We've got a bunch of theories, is all. Like, there's a clique who wants to punish everyone who went along with my . . ."

Yandre's expression cools. Being a boss has made them harder to fool—or maybe just harder. Col's absence looms in the flickering shadows, tangible as the desert wind.

Across the fire, Shay and Tally are talking to Charles, boss of the other crew that's joined us. Charles has ignited the party with boasts, jokes, and toasting. Anything I say will be lost in the noise.

The world is bigger than the Youngbloods.

"Just between you and me?" I say quietly.

"Of course."

"Diego made a secret deal with Rafi. Recovery aid in exchange for ten years of recordings."

Yandre swears softly. "I was worried about that."

"You were?"

"Your sister said the data was lost in the Fall of Shreve. But then *someone* thought it was worth stealing, which means it wasn't gone. Rafia had to be lying for a good reason—Diego wants the data, and they don't want anyone to know they have it. Which means they're going to use it to mess with us."

"Okay, wow," I say. Yandre was Charles's head of tech before becoming a boss, but that was still fast. "You figured all that out just from hearing about the theft?"

They shrug. "There was another clue—Tally wants us to fabricate some weird parts for Astrix. I'm not sure what they're for, but they make me nervous."

"Like what?" I ask, but Yandre is raising their flask to someone approaching through the firelight.

It's X, telling everyone that dinner is served. He lingers for a moment with us, his expression serious.

"Did you bring what I asked for?"

Yandre nods. "Six dozen hamburger buns. And steak sauce."

I stare at them. "*Steak sauce?* You only left Victoria yesterday. How'd you know about this cookout?"

"Because our bison murder wasn't a crime of opportunity," X says with a smile. "I've been planning this meal since we got the call."

"Okay . . ." My eyes go back to Yandre, who doesn't seem in the least worried that X is wooing his old crew with a feast. The two of them share a glance, a guilty secret shimmering the air.

"And the other thing?" X asks.

Yandre nods at me, and X places a firm hand on my shoulder, satisfied.

The rest of it falls into place.

Yandre didn't need me to reveal Tally's secrets. They and X are as close as ever, regardless of who's boss. What they didn't know was if my old loyalties had faded, now that I'm a Youngblood.

"You two were . . . *testing* me?"

"It's only a test if you can fail," Yandre says, hands up in defense. "I knew exactly what you'd do."

"Then why *play games*?"

"As a reminder," X says. "Of who you are, of how you haven't changed, however Special you are now."

"Boss . . ." I stare at him, feeling betrayed. "You just spilled your guts to me about Seanan. How does that square with tricking me?"

He scoffs. "It's not a trick to show someone who they are."

I should be furious. But when Yandre hugs me again, I don't pull away.

"Not my idea," they whisper.

And that feeling comes over me again, like when they recognized me despite my new face.

I rethink the last few minutes. It felt like I was going to keep

Tally's secrets. But in the end, it wasn't close. I spilled her secrets.

Maybe Yandre and X know me better than I know myself, with a certainty surer than logic. My anger starts to fade, and that's when I feel it in my wounded heart—

It's the same choice Col would've made.

RECONCILIATION

X's cookout is a hit.

We stay up late, drinking bubbly, stunt riding, dancing—all while the perimeter sensors remain silent. Whoever sent those drones has decided not to pick a fight with three rebel crews.

Or maybe they're more interested in where we're headed next.

We sleep late, well into the next afternoon. Rain clouds have masked the high sun by the time everyone's managed to get up and eat a breakfast of leftover bison steak.

Shay assembles us around the firepit, which ripples the air with a sleepy heat.

"We leave at dark," she says. "Three separate groups, taking different routes. Nine riders in each."

Boss Charles sits up straighter at this. She's wearing a grumpy expression and eating hangover pills like candy. "Why split up?"

"Someone filled the wild around Shreve with drones, trip wires for anyone who'd been exposed to radiation." Shay glances up into the clouds. "We have to assume they're watching us now."

"So all three groups need to look the same from orbit," Astrix says. "Nine riders each, and we'll disguise your cargo flyers to look like ours."

"Who do we think's watching?" Charles asks, looking straight at Tally, who doesn't answer.

"Unclear," Shay says. "Could be anyone from former Shreve Security to a full-scale city army."

One of Charles's crew, a rebel named Raven, speaks up. "If it's an army, splitting up is brain-missing."

"They haven't attacked us yet," Shay says. "To me, that means they want to follow us. We can't let them find the Futures."

"A bunch of brain-missing kids who love dust." Charles spits into the fire. "Glad we're keeping *them* safe."

Shay ignores her. "The routes will be in coded files. They'll self-decrypt along the way."

A murmur filters through the crowd.

Rebels are used to debating their missions beforehand, voting on them, maybe electing a new boss or splitting the crew if the conversation goes wrong. This need-to-know business from the Youngbloods is against their creed.

I'm starting to realize—Tally may be the first rebel boss, but that doesn't necessarily make her a good one.

I glance at X and Yandre, wondering if they'll quietly tell the others about Diego's deal with Rafi. Maybe it was a kindness the two of them did me last night—taking Tally's secrets out of my hands.

"My crew has eleven," Charles says. "Don't like you poaching two of them."

"Not your crew." Shay gives her a grin. "We're taking you and Boss Yandre. Plus one more, your choice, to make nine Youngbloods."

Another unsettled noise goes through the meeting.

They see Tally's plan now—if their bosses are riding with us, the other crews will be more likely to follow orders.

Charles sits up straighter. "Are we hostages now?"

"Don't be dramatic." Tally speaks up at last. "You can always leave, if you want. I just want some other bosses with me, in case we have to negotiate something big."

X gives me and Yandre a wary look. I give him a shrug.

A rain starts up, cold and petulant. The drops stokes wisps of smoke from the firepit's embers.

"Check your camo and night-vision gear," Shay says. "From now on, we'll be traveling in the dark. The Smoke lives."

"The Smoke lives," comes a ragged reply, like no one was expecting the meeting to end so quickly. No more questions, no discussion.

The Youngbloods are in charge.

It's cold flying across the desert at night.

Even with my heaters turned up, the wind is an ice blade working the seams of my body armor. By midnight, the clouds have cleared, a sky full of stars peering down with glassy clarity.

We hit the mountains a few hours before dawn. Here, we split into the three groups, each with nine rebels and a cargo flyer.

Charles and Yandre say good-bye to their crews, putting seconds in charge. They'll have to fight to take command again when we're all back together, but Boss Charles doesn't seem concerned.

Maybe she'd rather keep an eye on Tally.

The third new Youngblood is Charles's friend Raven. She flies close to Charles, shadowing her every move.

The other two groups are carrying fabricators, mobile holes in the wall. They've each borrowed one of our memory cores, to make duplicates of as they travel. By the time we reach the coast, we'll have a convincing quantity of fakes.

The ruse will fall apart if the Futures check too closely, but caution hasn't been their strength so far.

After the farewells, we Youngbloods climb hard into the Rockies, headed due west. By the time the night sky starts to lighten, we're flying over icy ridges, scattering powdery snow with the wash of our lifting fans.

As dawn hits, we make camp in a cave beneath a precarious overhang of rock, concealed from orbit and sky. The spot isn't marked as a rebel base in my location finder, but long-ago campfires smudge the stone floor. An old latrine is dug in the back, still scented with recycling chemicals.

The Youngbloods must have their own collection of campsites dotting the landscape, footprints of their travels over the years.

While the rest of us set up, Tally sits alone at the mouth of the overhang. The sunrise sends red ribbons of light into the depths behind her. She's watching Astrix construct a filter to capture our campfire smoke.

"Wish we had those in the old days," she says to me. "Would've saved a lot of hassle."

I shrug. "But then you couldn't have called it the Smoke."

Tally gives this the fractional smile it deserves, then gestures north, where the sky is still dark enough for stars.

"The real Smoke was that way. Up in the high Rockies, where it's really cold."

I shiver a little. This part of the mountains is cold enough for me.

"Did you camp here back then?" I ask.

There's a pause, a moment of calling up old memories.

"We found this cave in the first year of the mind-rain. Back when it was just a few of us going from city to city, spreading the news of the cure."

I try to recall the leftovers that Rafi brought me from her history tutors. The "cure" was the pill that reversed the operation, turning you from a bubblehead into someone who could think for yourself. Someone who could rebel.

"It took a while to catch on?" I ask.

Tally nods. "The history feeds tell it like everyone was free right away. But we had to hand-deliver the revolution. We gave a few adults in each city the cure, and they pushed the rest to freedom." She grins. "With help from the local uglies, of course."

I shiver again, but not from the cold. History has settled into the rocks around me, like the scars of old fires. This camp is one of the wellsprings of the new world.

Tally looks up sharply—there's movement on a nearby ridge.

But it's just Boss Charles, spiking a perimeter sensor into the ice. She stands and tests its sturdiness.

"If our stalkers hit us, it'll be tonight," Tally says.

"Why?"

"Because tomorrow, we disappear." She looks pleased to explain the plan. "Shay's pinging every crew in the southwest tonight, asking them to send out squads of nine. They'll all travel in random, intersecting patterns. Half the continent, crawling with decoys! Someone wants to print thousands of drones to find us? Fine—we'll throw them hundreds of rebels to track."

Whatever else you can say about her, Tally thinks big.

"That's a lot of work to hide twenty-seven rebels," I say.

"It's to hide your father's dust recordings. Don't want to lead our enemies straight to what they want." Tally's voice drops a little. "I've already done that."

Her voice is low and serious, and I can't stop myself asking, "Last week, did Shay call you . . . a collaborator?"

Tally gives a tired sigh.

"The first time I went to the Smoke, I was a spy. My job was to find the Smokies, then call for my city's Specials to come and round them up." She turns to look me in the eye. "I did my job. The Smoke died the next day."

I stare back at her, pretty sure that Rafi's tutors never mentioned this twist. The idea of Tally Youngblood on the wrong side of the revolution is a lot to take in.

She misinterprets my silence. "It's how I was raised—being pretty was more important than loyalty to my friends."

Just as I was raised to protect my sister, even if that meant betraying the Palafoxes. And killing my own brother.

"The other Youngbloods have gotten over it, looks like."

She looks away. "Even David forgave me. And he's the one who paid the real price."

I frown, trying to remember that name from my recycled history lessons.

"The original Smokie," she prompts. "Grew up in the wild, with rebel parents."

"Like Boss X?"

She laughs. "I suppose—and with the same intensity of opinions. David was my conscience for a long time, in charge of making sure I didn't go too far. But eventually it was too much work for him, and he faded away. The wild is very big, if you want to disappear."

Her voice has gone soft, like her mind is a thousand klicks away.

"And now Shay has that job," I say gently.

"You noticed that, huh."

"Um . . . she pretty much told me."

There's a dance of expressions on Tally's face. "It's why I don't understand the Futures. I've been under the microscope of history—watched, judged, in real time—and it isn't fun. People have the right to be forgotten, especially their mistakes."

Not every mistake is the same, I want to say. But before I can figure out how to respectfully disagree, the comms pop open.

"Boss." Shay's voice. "A sensor on the south perimeter just got a hit."

Tally stands up. "Flying?"

"Walking," comes the reply. "And three times bigger than a person."

"No *way*," Tally says, stepping onto her board and waving me onto mine.

I jump up, feeling my crash bracelets buzz to life with my motion.

"Yes way!" Shay's laughing now. "What you've been waiting for your whole life. You want backup?"

"The two of us should be fine."

Tally turns to me, her eyes alight as we rise into the air.

"Hey, Frey-la. Ever seen a bear?"

PREDATOR

We fly out of the cave into the bloodred light.

Tally takes the lead, turning southward into the wind. She switches her camo to glittering white—from the air, she'll disappear against the snow.

I fiddle with my interface, trying to mimic her without falling off my board.

"You didn't answer my question," she calls through the cold.

"Once," I manage. "But it was in the Montré zoo."

A quick memory flashes through my brain—giving a speech in Rafi's favorite mink coat, watched by the crowd in front of me, and from behind by a family of black bears in their fifty-acre habitat.

Tally snorts. "Zoos don't count."

She's weaving along the top of a ridge, keeping white snow under her board. I finally get my camo right and follow her serpentine path.

"I guess you've run into plenty?" I ask.

"Never. But an old friend of mine was almost eaten by a grizzly. I've always wanted to see one up close."

I shiver a little in the cold wind, wondering what Tally considers *up close* when it comes to giant predators.

We reach the perimeter in five minutes' flight. Spotting the bear is easy. I was expecting white fur against the snow, but the creature is light brown—and huge.

It's only a few meters from one of the sensors, eating something bloody in the snow.

Tally switches on a private comm.

"A grizzly." Her whisper is an awed breath in my earpiece. "The Rusties almost killed them all, but they're slowly taking the Rockies back. They're the big ones."

That last part seems unnecessary. The beast is the size of a small groundtruck, all muscle, teeth, and fur.

Tally lands her board on the snow.

"Kill your fans," she orders.

I drop onto the ridge, fifty meters away. Plenty close.

In the sudden silence, I can hear the ragged, snuffling breaths of the bear as it eats. The rip of flesh, the snap of bones.

Then the soft crunch of Tally's feet in the snow.

"Really, Boss?"

"Have to get a picture for my friend." She swings a camera up from her shoulder armor. She aligns it with her eyes and starts blinking away as she walks closer.

Thirty meters. Twenty.

Tally wades into a drift, her feet sinking in the snow. It reaches her thighs, and her steps become exaggerated, clumsy. The white surface has an icy crust, which breaks with a sound like a knife scraping toast.

The bear looks up.

Tally freezes, her camo a mix of snow and sky.

I draw my knife. At full pulse, its roar would scare most animals away, but the grizzly doesn't look like most animals. It looks like the emperor of its domain, afraid of nothing and no one.

As fearless as Tally Youngblood herself.

It eyes her for a moment, then gives a distracted, irritated growl. But whatever it's eating is too tasty to leave behind. The great head goes down into the snow again, jaws crunching, imperious in its disregard.

"Huh," Tally breathes. "Does this look weird to you?"

"You, walking toward a—" I start, but then her ping reaches me, a photo she's just taken. The bear in high-definition fills my eyescreen.

"Look at what it's eating," comes her whisper in the comms.

I click my tongue a few times, zooming in on the red splatter in the snow. There seems to be not much of the animal left—no fur, no face, no organs spread across the white expanse.

Just blood, meat, and bone.

I wipe the image away, scanning the snow around the grizzly with my own eyes. There's no sign of a killing struggle, just the bear's shaggy trail of footprints leading back over the next ridge . . .

As if someone lobbed a cut of fresh meat at our sensors—for the bear to find.

"Boss!" I hiss. "Maybe we should get out of here."

She's already turned, and is crashing her way back up the slope.

At the noise, the grizzly looks up. Its jaws open wide, a slow-building roar fills the freezing air, hoarse and angry. The ancient sound sends a jolt of primal fear slicing through my superhuman calm and down into my bones.

I grip my knife, setting it pulsing in my hand.

"Shay!" I call into an open channel.

"Don't tell me," comes her arch reply. "Tally-wa got too close and you need some medspray."

"It's not just a bear!" I shout. "Someone set this up!"

A second to process, then her cry. "Youngbloods! South edge, now!"

I scan the horizon outside the perimeter—nothing but snow, sky, and rocks. But someone out there threw this meat to lure the grizzly to our sensor.

To lure *us* . . .

Tally is flailing her way through the drift, her strength useless in the soft snow. There's nothing solid for her boots to push against.

She signals, and her hoverboard lifts up. A snap of my fingers starts the blades of my own board spinning.

The bear's hackles rise at the whine of lifting fans. It roars back at the sound—then starts to move toward Tally.

It begins at an amble but builds speed quickly. As my board lifts me into the air, I angle hard toward the two of them.

The grizzly barrels into the drift. The softer snow barely slows its charge, the beast's huge paws like snowshoes. It bounds forward like a cresting whale, half disappearing in its own white wake.

I aim my board at the shrinking gap between Tally and the beast.

My knife is screaming in my hand. But this is no bison overpopulating the plains—it's a recovering species. I can't just slaughter it.

Tally's board is closing in. All I have to do is win her a few precious seconds . . .

I bank hard, coming to a shrieking halt a few meters from the bear. The wash of my fans beats a blinding snowstorm against its face. It rears up from the cloud, raking the underside of my board with a huge claw.

I feel the scrape through my riding boots—but the board's gyros keep it steady beneath me. I climb hard, straight up as the bear takes another swipe.

It misses, and its frustrated roar follows me into the sky.

Down below, Tally has grabbed on to her board, which hauls her out of the drift. The grizzly looks back and forth between us, uncertain who has angered it more.

Tally lifts into the air, feet dangling for an awful moment. But she pulls herself on board and out of reach.

"Frey-la," she pants. "Thanks."

The bear roars again, the sound echoing in my chest.

But we're both safe—bears can't fly.

That's when the shooting starts.

STALKER

Something pings against my chest.

For a moment, I think it's a shard of windblown ice. But then another *thonk* shivers through my armor, and I look down.

A feathered dart is sunk into the armor covering my elbow.

"Sniper!" I cry, rolling into an evasive sequence.

I drop to build speed, which takes me straight toward the grizzly. The bear lunges as my board wheels away, then follows me across the snow in great loping strides. I ride away hard, slaloming to make myself a harder target for the sniper.

My armor will deflect these darts, but neither Tally nor I grabbed our helmets when we left camp. A shot to the neck or face will put us down—if those darts are strong enough.

"We're three minutes out!" Shay calls through the comms. "How many shooters?"

I scan the horizon—nothing but rock, ice, and sky.

"See anyone, Tally?"

There's no response for a moment, then her slurred voice in my ear. "Think I'm hit."

I spin my board around, climbing hard to avoid the grizzly on my tail. The bear swipes at me, roaring as I pass overhead.

In front of me, Tally is listless on her board, an easy target. Her legs are wobbly, her arms out for balance.

"This stuff is . . . strong." She waves a hand. "From over there, I think."

I glance over my shoulder—an ice-clad peak, the right elevation for a sniper's nest. But nothing out of place that I can see.

Then a thermal flash flickers against the bright snow, and something *plinks* off my shoulder armor.

"Got 'em! Take cover, Tally."

My bare face covered with both arms, I spin around toward the peak. I'll cut off their escape route and wait for the other Youngbloods to arrive.

"Frey . . ."

I turn back—Tally's dropped to one knee. Her board slides back and forth, trying to understand her shifting weight as commands. She goes down on all fours.

Then tumbles off into the ice.

The grizzly, still angry, turns its head toward the crunch of snow. It snuffles the air.

I skid to a halt. "Shay! Tally needs help!"

"Two minutes out."

The bear is closer than that. It starts to lope toward Tally.

I angle my board, coming in behind the beast. Maybe I can distract it, lead it off, scare it away . . .

Another dart whizzes past me, close enough to tickle my ear.

I buzz the grizzly, dangerously close, but it's bored of taking swipes at me. It's still going for Tally's motionless form in the ice.

My knife screams to life in my hand.

I have to kill the beast.

A flicker of a thought—X will hate me for this. He'll say it was Tally's fault for getting into this situation, not the grizzly's.

But this was an ambush, a trap, not some act of nature. I wheel around, drawing my hand back for the killing throw.

Then I see it—the dart stuck in the elbow seam of my armor.

If these things can take down a Special . . .

I throw the knife wide, sending it shrieking past the bear's left ear. The creature rears and swats, coming to a split-second halt.

Yanking the dart from my armor, I leap from my board.

The grizzly seems to grow as I fall—it's bigger than I thought, stronger, smellier, more alive. Its body heat is like a furnace beneath me, its muscles steel cords wrapped in an angry sheath of flesh and fur. The hide seems hard as leather as I stab the dart into it.

The needle sinks in. The creature bucks beneath me, sending up a roar that vibrates my whole body.

I signal for my knife, clinging to matted fur, like some stunt rider who's about to lose a bet.

The bear twists its head around to me, and the two of us lock gazes. Its eyes are deep black, all pupil, the glossy button eyes of some childhood toy, until its mouth opens and its roar hits me—a hot wind of rotten meat and fresh blood and death. Those countless teeth, yellow and snaggled from snapping through a thousand creatures' bones.

The pulse knife reaches my hand, and I jump away from that awful mouth, draining the shrieking weapon to travel a little higher. My board, already swung around and closing in, slips gently beneath me. All I can think of is how wonderful this lifeless, obedient technology is compared to the indifferent fury of the wild.

I look back at the bear. It's lost interest in me and Tally, and is staring at the ground, suddenly uncertain on its huge, bloody paws.

"We got this, Frey," Shay's voice comes. "Follow that bike."

I turn toward the sniper's peak.

A four-engine hoverbike is lifting up from the snow. A rider in white camo sits astride it, a rifle slung over their back.

My board surges forward.

I ride low, ducking the cold wind, trying to gather enough speed to catch the hoverbike. A quick glance backward—the bear has fallen over a few meters from Tally's crumpled form. The other Youngbloods are a flock of thermal dots on the horizon, at least a minute behind me in this chase.

There's only five of them. Two must be back at camp, guarding our cargo. I can make out X, taller than the others, his pulse lance a red slant of heat against the frozen mountainside.

But for now I'm alone.

The bike is gaining distance on me—four lifting fans to my two. It rears over the peak, then drops out of sight.

I climb hard, flying just above the snow, needing the ground to push against in this cruel, thin air. At this speed, the cold is razor-sharp in my lungs.

Clearing the peak, I see the sniper out ahead of me. The bike has enough power to climb a hundred meters off the ground, well above my ceiling. The only way to reach it is to find some friendly terrain.

I drop down the far slope, fans barely spinning, turning gravity into raw speed. The engines cool down, readying for a last push. My tail skims the frost to keep me steady.

There's what I need—a curving upward slope of smooth, slick ice, half a klick away.

My knife has enough charge for at least one throw.

I spin my fans up again, faster than regulation, pushing my over-heat meter back into the red. The board gains speed across a rocky flat, snow swirling around me. Sparks flash in my engines.

I hit the ramp faster than I've ever flown before, climb it in one sweeping arc aimed at the sky. And then I'm in midair, surrounded by a sudden ringing silence as my fans overheat and choke to a halt . . .

The knife leaves my hand, aimed at the hoverbike's right rear engine.

It hits home, and the bike sputters and flares, white-hot parts scattering in its wake. The knife returns to my hand, but I don't have to throw again. The bike is going into a roll, trailing black smoke and more bits of metal.

I'm falling back to earth, my board silent beneath my feet. When I try to restart the fans, they choke, the overheat meter still red.

The cooling wind of the fall is what saves me. On the third attempt, my engines spark to life, slowing my fall a little—enough— before they fail again.

I hit a downward slope, the snow soft and deep. Suddenly I'm skidding down the hill, my crash bracelets barely keeping me upright. The powder hisses beneath me, like I'm riding a snowboard.

Arms out, I start to gain control.

Overhead, the hoverbike steadies, motionless in the air for a moment. The sniper's going to get away . . .

But then the machine stutters—and drops.

It starts to spiral, a leaf spinning in the cold air. Then some kind of safety software kicks in, steadying its fall, setting the bike down gently with a mournful shriek of its working engines.

It thumps onto the snowy slope ahead of me.

I slide down on my silent board, skidding to a halt beside it. My knife hums in my hand, but the sniper hasn't even unstrapped his rifle.

He pulls himself gingerly from the wreck—an older man, pale and shaky. It takes a second to recognize him from the feeds.

That goatee, that pleasant smile.

Stellan Batrow, the nice crumbly man, the jailer of Hideaway.

NICE CRUMBLY MAN

"I'm afraid we don't have long," he says. "Your friends are coming."

I raise my knife. "There's no rush."

"My dear child." A tired sigh. "Do you think I've gone to all this trouble only to be captured? My aim isn't as bad as that."

I stare at him. All those darts that bounced off my armor, the near misses, while Tally was hit instantly.

"Are you saying you *let* me catch you?"

"I'm saying we must speak quickly. First, I have a present for you." Batrow reaches a hand into his camo suit.

I squeeze the knife. "Don't even—"

He pulls a necklace from around his throat, a string of pearly gray beads. It dangles before me, shining dully in the sunlight.

"You recognize this substance?" he asks.

It takes me a moment—the memory cores split open at the crash site.

"Looks like the goo inside data storage."

"Exactly. These are recordings from Shreve's other secret prison, the one for adults."

I take a step backward. "Another prison? Are there survivors?"

Stellan Batrow shakes his head. "It was *erased* when the old regime fell. This is all that remains."

I stare at the beads. Shreve is still looking for hundreds of people who disappeared during my father's rule. They'll never be found, it seems, except as ghosts on this necklace.

Suddenly I'm angry. "You think giving me some recordings makes you less guilty?"

He smiles sadly. "My guilt is beyond your comprehension, child. This isn't simply surveillance—the prisoners knew there was dust in the air. They whispered messages for their children, prayers in the middle of the night. You can deliver them."

He passes the necklace to me. The pearls are heavy in my hand.

"Why not give this to Shreve?" I ask. "Why track us down in the middle of nowhere?"

"Because your sister would bury it."

"My sister." The world is unsteady now. "How do you—"

"She pretends to serve the truth, but she doesn't want the world to see. She whispers a different secret in every ear."

His words are starting to blur. "What do you mean?"

"The answers are on that necklace—the things she didn't tell you when the dust was rained away. The parties you didn't go to. Her accomplices you never met. The lessons from her tutors she never

282

shared." At the sound of lifting fans, Batrow looks up. "Your friends are here. I have to go."

"Wait!"

He takes two strides and jumps onto the hoverbike. I stand there, struck motionless by his litany. But as the bike launches into the air, reflexes take over.

I throw my knife.

It follows him up into the cold sky, shrieking like a bird of prey, slicing through the bike's working rear engine.

The fan splinters, scattering hot metal. The bike begins to spin, front engines driving it into a wild, screaming spiral.

I jump onto my board, ready to save Batrow—I need to know how he found us, and why he gave me this. But my overheated engines lift the board barely a meter before it falls back into the snow.

Above me, things go from bad to worse. Stellan keeps control of the bike at first, but he didn't have time to strap in. He's sliding from the seat, hanging on to the handlebars.

His bracelets keep him on—but the flailing weight of his body overwhelms the bike's gyros, sending it into a lopsided tumble.

The engines begin a mournful scream, its death spiral growing wider and wilder in the sky.

Three hoverboards sweep into view, X's in the lead. He tries to come alongside the bike, but the corkscrew of its flight is too fast, too random. Every time X gets within reach, Batrow careens away in a new direction.

All at once, the wailing engines seize. The wild gyrations collapse into a single arc, the bike soaring into the distance like a flung stone. It falls out of my view, plunging into a ravine of ice and rock.

A series of crashes echoes through the mountains, more and more distant as the bike descends into the chasm. Finally they fade.

The Youngbloods land around me, camo silhouettes scattered across the snow.

Shay's voice fills the quiet: "Everyone okay?"

Nobody answers. Somehow my nervous system is keeping me level, cool and heartless.

"I killed him," I say.

Croy turns to me, his voice icy clear in my comms. "He shot Tally."

"A knockout dart." I stare down at the necklace. "He just wanted to give me . . ."

This mystery, those strange words about my sister.

Astrix's voice on the comms jolts me back.

"Tally's waking up."

Yandre joins in. "The bear too! We might need a hand over here."

"Okay," Shay says. "But first—did anybody spot more snipers?"

"He was alone," I say.

No one speaks, like I'm supposed to explain what just happened. But I don't know where to start.

"Frey," X says gently. "You were talking to the sniper. Did you know them?"

"It was Stellan Batrow, delivering a message." The necklace has gone icy in my grasp. "There was another prison."

NECKLACE

We fly Tally to safety, the grizzly watching us with sleepy eyes.

Charles and Raven are still in camp, guarding the cargo flyer. The perimeter sensors have stayed quiet. Stellan Batrow was alone.

But he must have had help finding us. A crumbly on a noisy hoverbike couldn't track six Specials without being spotted. Did he hack into surveillance satellites? Was a city AI guiding him?

We might know the answers, if I'd waited and let the others capture him. But instead I threw my knife.

While I sit there in silence, the others are bantering, burning away the nervous energy of the chase.

"Can't believe I got suckered by a photogenic grizzly," Tally says.

Shay smiles. "Not the first time you've been ambushed."

"First time in fifteen years!"

"Everyone likes bears," Boss Charles says with a shrug. "You got some good pictures, I hope?"

Tally glares at her a moment, then turns to Astrix.

"So what was that all about?"

Astrix is waving a scanner over the necklace, her eyes sharp in the firelight. The cave is dark now, the risen sun no longer angling into its mouth. Smoke wreaths around the nine of us.

"Artificial DNA wrapped in smart matter." She hands the necklace to Yandre. "High-density data storage for sure."

"Too bad we don't have any gear to read it," Yandre says.

"So we can't check Batrow's story." Tally turns to me. "You think he was telling the truth?"

"Yes. There *had* to be another secret prison—people are still missing. But Batrow said there was a self-destruct system, like the one we stopped at Hideaway. He said there were no survivors."

Everyone's silent as I take the necklace from Yandre. "He also said some of the prisoners recited messages to the dust, for their kids to hear one day."

"If that's true, then this data's precious," Shay says. "Which raises the question: Why go to all that trouble—luring a bear, darting Tally—to give it to *us*?"

"Not us," I say, clasping the necklace around my throat. "Me."

Another silence falls, punctuated by the hiss of wet wood foraged from the snow. Confused looks pass around the fire.

"Batrow didn't trust my sister to let this see the light of day," I say. "So he came to find me."

"You Rafia or you Frey?" Croy asks.

I've had time to think this part through.

The parties you didn't go to. Her accomplices you never met. The lessons from her tutors she never shared.

"The real me. He was talking about Rafi's secrets—like plotting with her friends against our father. The stuff she kept hidden from me, even when the dust couldn't hear us."

"What's that got to do with a secret prison?" Shay asks.

"I have no idea." A tremor goes through me. "I can't even figure out how he knew me."

"That part's easy," Astrix says. "When you went into Hideaway with that broken ankle, the med drone examined you. It must have scanned your DNA, sent it to Batrow."

I shake my head. "DNA alone wouldn't tell him that I was *Frey*."

Everyone who knows my real identity tumbles through my head—the nine of us, Riggs, Teo Palafox and Zura, Sensei Noriko, a dozen or so city AIs.

And Rafi herself.

Did Stellan Batrow ever work for my sister?

"It doesn't matter what he knows," Tally says. "We're going to disappear tomorrow."

"So we're not taking this back to Shreve?" Shay says. "These are the last words of their disappeared."

"Not until after we meet the Futures." Tally closes her fists. "I'm not letting some crumbly ambush us, tell a story we can't verify, and derail this mission."

"Good point," Shay says. "If we need any derailing, we can do it ourselves."

Tally ignores this, and starts giving orders. More perimeter sensors, a double watch tonight.

Tomorrow, her grand diversionary plan begins.

I head out into the snow to help set the sensors, but alarms are already pinging in my head. Batrow's litany about Rafi was familiar somehow. Like he was repeating a message from someone I know.

But I can't figure out who.

Growing up, I thought my sister and I shared everything. The way we moved and talked, our DNA, but also the truth of ourselves. Yet Rafi was always holding back, always making her own plans.

That's why she has Shreve while I'm out here shivering in the wild.

My hand goes to my throat. What do recordings from a prison have to do with Rafi's secrets?

Thanks to X, I've begun the long work of forgiving her. But what if it was too soon? What if she's never shown her whole truth to me?

She whispers a different secret in every ear.

PART IV

RUINS

In the midst of chaos,
there is also opportunity.

—Sun Tzu

Dear Little Shadow,

Wherever you are, I'm still missing you. Especially now, when things have turned strange and awful. You should be here to help me see right from wrong.

I have a decision to make.

Can I still trust you, little sister? I'm about to tell you the biggest secret in our brave new city. My government tries to be open, but this is something you can't share with anyone.

You've heard about the lost children, right? The poor littlies in Hideaway, who Tally Youngblood herself brought home to us . . .

Something's wrong with them.

Not all—most are fitting back into their lives, especially the ones who still have parents. They love the new Shreve, flourishing and unbound, just like them.

But a few days ago, one of the returned children showed a different side. His parents wanted him to see where they'd spent the last two years—the cells in Security Headquarters.

The whole place is being turned into a museum, like everything of Dad's, a reminder of how freedom-missing our city used to be. So these parents got permission to go inside. All three of them are tromping along, watching the construction drones set up exhibits, gawking at the cells where Dad kept his enemies—and suddenly an alarm sounds in the old control room. Some random scanner, a piece of equipment nobody's bothered to turn off, has detected a dangerous device in the prison wing.

It's the kid.

Because he's not a kid.

This lost child is an avatar. A machine, with enough skin and organs wrapped around it to fool doctors, friends, even his own parents.

They were prisoners too, of course. The family was torn apart, and now they've been given hope—but it isn't real. Their child was lost somewhere along the way, and someone built a replacement.

Who would do that?

We've quietly checked the other Hideaway littlies—seven total aren't real. And this is what hurts me most, Frey . . .

We can't tell the parents yet.

We need to find out who did this, and why. We have to solve this crime, *which we don't even have a name for*, in case any of the real kids are still alive somewhere. Which means investigating quietly.

But it makes me want to scream, acting like *his* regime. Spying on our own citizens, watching from microscopic cams.

I promised everyone there would be no more secret police. But here we are.

So here's my question for you, little sister—how long can I wait? How long before we have to tell the parents that their children, who Tally herself brought back, are changelings?

Not people at all.

This lie is so cruel. But telling the truth seems somehow crueler. Whatever I do, in the end, everyone will find a way to blame me.

I wish you were home, Frey. Growing up, you were the only person who I always knew was real.

—Rafia of Shreve

SERPENTINE

I hardly sleep that day, and the next night is a blur of travel.

Descending the Rockies, we rendezvous with another crew. They've ridden down from their mountain lair, nine rebels and a cargo flyer just like ours. We make them coffee, mingling to confuse any satellites as to who's who, then part ways again.

They're headed south next, to connect with another crew of nine. We head west, for a midnight meeting in the desert with rebels from the gulf coast.

All across this corner of the continent, Tally's friends and allies are weaving a lacework of confusion. By the time we reach the meeting spot, anyone watching from the sky won't know which of sixty-odd groups is the Youngbloods and which are the crews we shook hands with in the wild.

Even with Stellan Batrow dead, we have to make certain we aren't being tracked. Batrow made his mission sound personal, but how could a lone fugitive print thousands of hair-snipping drones?

Something bigger than him is searching for the Futures and their treasure—my father's recordings, the soul of my city.

We come to a halt as day breaks, unfolding our boards into solar panels. Beside a spindly rock formation, we make camp on the hard sand.

I try to sleep, but the desert makes me think of snakes. My phobias are coming back; my Special surge didn't erase them, after all.

The sun rises; the heat ripples the air, setting precarious tons of rock wavering over our heads.

When my eyes finally close, I slip into feverish dreams. My father visiting Hideaway, taunting the children there. Me at his side.

When I wake up in the heat of late afternoon, a ping from my sister has come in. I make the mistake of playing it—it's worse than my nightmares.

Rafi asked me to keep it all secret, but I don't owe her anything.

When X replaces Raven on watch, I tell him about the changelings. We decide to wake up Tally and Shay, and the four of us listen to the ping together, the strange and awful story.

When it's over, Shay frowns at me. "Wait. You and your sister are still . . . *ping pals?*"

"I don't answer her."

"Still," she says.

"That's not the issue here," Tally cuts in. "There are avatars of children living in Shreve, and even their *parents* can't tell the difference. Do you know what that means, Shay?"

Shay just crosses her arms.

I explain it for her. "There was dust in Hideaway, and someone kept the surveillance data of the children. It's just like Astrix said—better recordings, better avatars."

"A curious use of *better*," X says.

I shrug. "Some impostors are better than others."

Shay finally speaks up. "Maybe we should be looking for those missing kids. The real ones, that got replaced."

Tally shakes her head, waving at the cargo board with its freight of memory cores. "No, Shay—*this* mission is our priority. Not seven missing kids, the stolen lives of two million citizens of Shreve."

Finally Shay nods; she can't argue anymore.

The machines are already building copies of people.

When night falls, we ride again.

More connections with other rebels, more winding paths to confuse anyone tracking us. Somewhere out there in the dark, Charles's and Yandre's crews are doing the same, taking their separate, tangled routes to our rendezvous with the Futures.

In its convolution, the journey starts to feel endless, formless. My sister's ping coils in my head, blending with the poetry of Stellan Batrow's last refrains.

The things she didn't tell you when the dust was rained away.

What's on this necklace that Rafi wants to bury?

As the sky lightens after our third night of travel, we're close to our goal—too close to stop. We keep riding through daybreak, past noon and then some, until we reach a vast Rusty ruin nestled against the western sea.

We bring our boards to a halt, looking down at the sprawling expanse. A forest has reclaimed most of the buildings, but the ancient street geometries still carve the landscape into rows and columns.

"Told you," Astrix says, pointing. "The recyclers got the roller coaster."

I follow her gesture, but there's nothing left that I can see.

"And the skyscrapers," Tally moans, as if the new cities' hunger for metal is her fault.

"It's like seeing an old friend," Croy says. "And when they smile, they've got a bunch of missing teeth!"

The only large metal structure left is a suspension bridge connecting a small island to the shore, half its cables snapped, like a gigantic musical instrument with broken strings.

"Any word from the other crews?" Shay asks.

"Still comm silence," Yandre says. "Guess that means they're on schedule—a few hours out."

Shay turns to Tally. "The Futures won't show before dark. We could get some sleep . . . or do a little sightseeing."

Tally smiles back at her, suddenly a few years younger.

"We can sleep when the mission's done."

We ride down into the ruin. Half the streets are dug up, and a few recycling drones are buzzing around, looking for the last water pipes and wiring. Stone and concrete buildings still stand, their blank windows staring down at us.

This is largest city I've ever seen, ruined or new. It stretches along the coast to both horizons. Strange to think that Tally and her friends came here as uglies, surrounded by ghosts of the past as they reached for a new future.

We ride all the way to the sea, where a white beach is lined with high cliffs and half-recycled high-rises. The houses here are worn to nubs by three centuries of surge and storm.

We hover at the edge of the beach, our lifters clinging to the last metal before the sand begins. The older Youngbloods are staring at the piles of a long-gone pier, which thrust up from the water like rows of broken teeth. The roller coaster, or some other memory, must have sat there.

Then Shay shoots a look at Tally, neither of them smiling.

Shay whispers in the comms, "Did anyone else just hear something?"

It takes a second to pick it out against the distant crash of surf—the shuffle of feet across a sandy floor.

It's coming from our right, inside a long brick building, one of the few that still has a roof.

Our heads all turn at once.

The Futures aren't supposed to meet us till tonight. In this giant city, we can't have stumbled on their hiding place . . .

Shay points at the cargo board and then Croy—he's on guard duty. Then she draws a circle in the air with her index finger.

Surround them.

X and I climb fast, flying over the building and dropping into an alley behind. Raven joins us, each of us covering one entrance. Sand spills out of the darkness of the doorways, and watermarks line the wall.

I can still hear them inside. Three people at least, frozen in place now but breathing hard. They've spotted us.

"No point hiding!" Shay calls from the street. "We can hear you."

There's no answer, just a hitch in the breathing. Then sounds of panic—scrambling steps, the squeak of riding boots on a grippy surface.

"They've got hoverboards!" I yell.

A *slam* comes from overhead—a trapdoor in the roof.

I fire up my lifting fans, shrieking upward. A board flashes past, just missing my head. Then two more streak by, all of them headed away from the beach.

I spin around and follow, X and Raven just behind me.

The three riders ahead of us crouch low. But the roar of acceleration never comes—their hoverboards don't even have lifting fans.

They're city boards, like a kid would have.

Moments later, Raven, X, and I are sweeping around to cut them off. The girl in front comes to a drifting halt, a puzzled expression on her face.

"Hey. You aren't wardens!"

I bank to a stop. "Not at all."

The three of them look at my high-powered board, my body armor. Then their eyes widen as X glides into place beside me.

"What *are* you, then?" the girl asks. "Why are you chasing us?"

I hesitate. The three of them are young and unsurged. They're all dressed the same—blue shirts and gray shorts, recyclable paper clothes.

They're kids, still in school, from the Youngbloods' home city.

"We thought you were someone else," I say. "Sorry if we scared you."

One of the boys turns to look at the rest of our crew, hovering behind the kids. They've put their visors down, keeping their famous faces out of view. The last thing we want is these kids tipping off the local newsies that Tally's back in town.

But then the girl squints at us.

"Wait a sec. I saw you on the feeds—you're Tally Youngblood's friends!"

UGLIES

"You've got us confused with someone else," I say.

"Maybe you, yeah." The boy points at X. "But *him?*"

Even in body armor, there's no mistaking X's wolf-man surge. The reappearance of Tally was a worldwide story, not just the talk of Shreve.

We all hover there in silence.

Then her soft sigh comes in my comms, and Tally takes off her helmet.

"Hey, you three!" she calls.

They all turn, and I can spot exactly when each of them recognizes the most famous person ever born in their city. One of the boys wavers on his board, like he's about to fall.

"Um, you're . . . um," the girl stammers.

"I'm going to ask you for a favor," Tally says.

304

Shay's exasperation is obvious through all of it.

Tally talks to the kids for almost two hours, answering their questions. She tells them about the Youngbloods' missions since they disappeared: sabotaging mineral mines in Europe, weapons factories hidden in Antarctica, deforestation machines rampaging in the Amazon, a few things they've never even told me.

Tally shows them where the roller coaster used to be, and the skyscraper that Shay would stand atop to signal the Smokies to collect runaways. She listens with fascination to the details of how kids sneak into the ruins these days.

The monitors are just as easy to fool, it turns out, and the hike is still long and hard. Valora, the girl in the group, has been coming here since she was fourteen, along with dozens of friends.

They've created a clubhouse in the long brick building. Furniture cobbled together from driftwood and salvage, some beach towels, a glitchy wallscreen, and a cache of bottled water and hiking snacks. The scars of real fireworks—the illegal, dangerous kind—mark the roof.

After the night's travel, the whole experience turns soft and dreamlike. As if the Youngbloods' memories have taken form, just for an afternoon. By the time Tally finally starts to nudge the kids toward a good-bye, the sun is dipping low, the shadows stretching away from the sea.

She carves the words *The Smoke Lives* into a wooden beam as the three uglies watch, awestruck. Then we're standing on the sagging rooftop, watching Valora and her friends head off into the forest.

The moment they disappear, Shay's anxiety bubbles over.

"Are you sure that was smart, Boss?"

"Letting them go?" Tally shrugs. She looks like she's just finished a ten-course feast. "By the time they get home, it'll be midnight. Our business with the Futures won't take that long."

"They don't have to get home to make trouble," Shay says. "They can ping the city interface from halfway!"

"These days, you can make an emergency call from anywhere," Astrix adds.

"I asked them not to." Tally is certain of herself, of the kids. "They'll keep this secret to themselves for at least one night, I'll bet you anything."

"You just did." Shay shakes her head. "You bet the whole mission."

Tally only laughs, like she's just taken a particularly tricky turn on her board—and made it.

"At least we didn't have to detain anyone's children," X says.

"Sometimes you gotta have trust," Tally says.

Which would be sweet, except that she just sent hundreds of rebels into intricate maneuvers to hide us, without telling any of them why. She trusts random kids more than her allies.

"We'll find out soon enough." Shay turns to the others. "There's only a few hours left. Let's get into position."

We reach the meeting place as the sky is streaking red with sunset.

It's in the center of an ancient sports arena, with open sight lines in all directions. Looking around at the field, the ruined grandstands, I can't even tell what sport was played here—the Rusties enjoyed all kinds of weird and violent diversions with mysterious rules.

The crumbling stadium offers plenty of places to hide. My eye catches a thermal flicker behind the scoreboard, a rebel stealth suit venting body heat.

Our friends, watching over us.

While Tally was entertaining her fans, Yandre's and Charles's crews have arrived in the ruins. They're keeping comm silence so the Futures won't know how many of us there are.

They've delivered dozens of fake memory cores to the center of the sports field, duplicates of the originals we lent them.

Tally and Shay fly around the perimeter, delivering spoken instructions to the hidden rebels. We add three real cores from our cargo board onto the pile, while Astrix inspects the copies with a scanner.

"Your people did good work," she says to Yandre.

"The data's split up," they say. "A few hours on each core."

"That's all?" I ask. "What if the Futures play one?"

"We'll blame your dad," Astrix says. "DNA hates radiation."

Yandre smiles a little. "These kids are collectors—they dream of having a complete set. They'll convince themselves that these are real."

"A good collector always makes copies," X says. "How can we be sure we've erased them all?"

"Tally has a plan for that," Astrix says, glancing at a pile of equipment at the edge of the field. "She'll explain."

I catch Yandre's eye, and they give me an uncertain shrug.

It seems Tally still has a few secrets of her own.

TRADE

As darkness falls, six of us Youngbloods assemble in the center of the field.

Raven, Shay, and Charles are watching us from the stands, sniper rifles at the ready. With them out in the open, maybe the Futures won't notice the other eighteen rebels hidden around the stadium.

Our comms are shut down—when someone catches sight of the Futures on their way, a birdcall echoes from the darkness.

Tally stands up straighter, like she's arriving at a party.

"You do the talking, Trix."

"Sure, Boss," Astrix says. "You're just here to look pretty."

Tally snorts at this. Even X cracks a grin.

From over the crumbling grandstand, a hovercar climbs into view, the same model as the one that crashed outside of Shreve. Its rotor wash flattens the wild grasses of the field. The lifting fans sound unbalanced, like they need maintenance after the long journey to the coast.

I'm still amazed that this hapless bunch of kids managed to steal something so precious from my sister. At least this rickety car won't stand a chance against us if it comes to a chase.

The machine settles on the field, and the rear door unfolds. Coming down the ramp is a trio of figures, each surrounded by a swarm of tiny hovercams. I know all three of them.

Ran was the cofounder of Future, an old friend of Chulhee's. Beside him is Sara, her Savior cos-surge reset to the face she was wearing months ago.

"You came all this way?" I ask her.

"For something this historic, I'd go anywhere. You remember Terra, I guess."

I nod to the third person emerging from the car, a little spike of anger rising in me.

When I was undercover in Shreve, my hiking boots were irradiated at a Rusty nuclear site. Terra is the girl who kindly lent me her shoes—then reported me to the city for theft. I wound up getting shame-cammed, all of Shreve hating me for the few hours before my father's last battle began.

She gives me a long, uncertain look. Maybe she's feeling apologetic, or maybe it's my new face.

Ran is already at the pile of cores. He picks one up, one of the real ones on top, peering at the details.

"Careful. They've got a few rads still," Astrix warns.

Ran shrugs, and I notice that his hair is thinner, his face gaunt.

He must've soaked up too many rads in the Sarcophagus. But he still holds the memory core too close to his face, his expression reverent.

Then I notice that Ran's hovercams have drifted into new positions, each making sure that Tally is in frame with him. His intense focus is a performance. This is mostly a photo op with Tally Youngblood.

I relax a little.

"How many did you salvage?" Sara asks.

"Forty-eight," Astrix says. "The rest were lost in the crash."

The three Futures bow their heads a little, remembering their martyred comrades.

Then Ran says, "What about the VIP cores? Did you find any?"

Astrix doesn't hide her confusion. "What are those?"

"The recordings from inside the tower itself," Sara says. "They were marked in purple."

A little tremor goes through me.

My father would never let Security watch us, like we were common citizens. Of course the surveillance from the tower was kept separate.

Hopefully in a deep basement, now sealed up forever.

"We didn't find anything like that," Astrix says.

"Too bad." Ran holds up the core in his hands. "We thought you'd bring copies, not the real thing."

"We left our backups at home," Astrix says. "Figured you'd want the originals, because of their . . . historic-ness."

Ran gives her a solemn nod. "Thank you."

"So." Tally speaks up at last. "Do we have a trade? Our data for yours?"

"Transport might be an issue," Ran says, placing the core gently back in the pile and selecting another to inspect. "We don't have the tech to write DNA. We've made copies for you—on normal data blocks, so they're *huge*. Six hoverboards won't even carry the index files."

Astrix's smile doesn't waver. She points at the pile of equipment at the edge of the field. "We brought everything we need. Just take us to the originals."

The other two look at Terra, like she's in charge these days.

"Okay," she says. "But only three of you, and Tally has to be one of them."

Tally smiles. "Wouldn't miss it. Just give me twenty minutes to get our gear together. We'll follow you home."

The three of them exchange looks. Like maybe this was too easy, too good to be true.

"You don't want to mess with us," Terra adds. "We'll protect the recordings at all costs."

"We know what you've already sacrificed." Tally spreads her hands. "We'll get this done as quickly as possible, I promise."

Terra gives her friends one last look, but Yandre's right—there's nothing a collector wants more than a complete set. A minute later, the Futures are loading our cores into their hovercar, ready to lead Tally Youngblood to their base.

The six of us huddle at the edge of the field.

"Astrix and Croy are with me," Tally says. "The rest of you join the others—follow us, out of sight. How long, Trix?"

"Ten minutes," Astrix grunts, working on the pile of equipment. The other crews must have brought the parts, which I don't recognize. We'd need a gene sequencer to read DNA data, but whatever Astrix is building looks chunkier than biotech gear.

Maybe it's just random machinery, to make it look like we're making a copy.

Astrix pauses in her work, looking up at Tally. "And you're still sure about this, Boss?"

"It's the only way to get it all."

With a sigh, Astrix goes back to piecing the parts together.

We all stand there in silence, watching the device taking shape in her hands. It must be some kind of magnetic eraser, to wipe the Futures' copies clean.

But then she slots in a piece marked with a high-explosive trefoil.

X speaks up first. "Is that a bomb?"

"A pulse generator," Tally explains. "It'll erase any magnetic data within ten klicks. Make sure you tell everyone—if you hear me on the comms, saying it's about to blow, land your hoverboards."

"Because they'll fall out of the sky," Astrix says. "And your crash bracelets won't work either. Your vision implants might even glitch."

Yandre's eyes widen. "An electromagnetic pulse—*that* big? Are you telling me that's a . . ."

They fall silent; nothing else needs to be said.

My knowledge of tech is spotty, but my tutors crammed my head with a complete history of warfare. The nature of this pulse device has settled over me, as cold and certain as ice.

I look up into the stands, where Shay calmly watches over us—there's no way she knows what's going on. Tally and Astrix have kept her and everyone else out of the loop.

They're going to use a tactical nuclear warhead to kill my father at last.

SPLIT

The Rusties built thousands of these things—EMP bombs.

When a nuke explodes, gamma rays fly out in all directions. They strip electrons from the atoms in the air, countless trillions of them. Suddenly untethered, all this wayward electricity is swept up by the earth's magnetic field, swirling into an invisible, raging storm.

Nanoseconds after sparking to life, this storm starts looking for something to electrify.

It's like when you shuffle across a carpet and touch metal—except that spark is a raindrop and this is a hurricane. Everything with circuitry or metal, even a single loose wire, gets struck by its own tiny bolt of lightning. With enough power in the blast, any electronics are burned out in an instant.

This is more advanced than anything the Rusties made, of course. It's been optimized as a data bomb.

But it's still a nuke.

"Tally," X says. "This is madness."

"You heard Terra," she answers. "Future will do anything to protect those recordings. Setting this thing off at a safe distance is better than getting into a firefight with a bunch of kids."

Yandre stares at her. "A safe distance? From a *nuke*?"

Astrix is strapping the warhead to the cargo flyer. "It won't explode till it gets a few klicks up. You'll feel the shock wave, and the flash will blind anyone brain-missing enough to watch, but the rads will be less than we got ten days ago." A shrug. "You might need a trip to the doctor."

"But it won't erase DNA!" Yandre cries.

"It will enough to corrupt the recordings," Astrix says. "Unlike our genes, those cores can't repair themselves."

I imagine a white-hot sun appearing in the sky. A searing flash burning the feathers off birds. A cloud of nuclear poison drifting across the wild, waiting for the next rain to fall. The trees that have worked so hard to swallow the ruins, turned poisonous for centuries.

Col died so that this wouldn't happen to Shreve.

"Boss," I say. "We can't set off a nuke in a forest."

"You know this clique," Tally says to me. "What happens when we start erasing their precious data?"

"They'll fight."

"You said there were thousands of them?"

I shake my head. "In Shreve, not way out here."

"But Sara came all this way . . . just to see me." Tally has a bitter smile. "Because you used my name to make this happen, to make it

316

historic. More of them will be waiting in that base, willing to die to protect your father's legacy."

"We can take them, Boss," Croy says. "They're just randoms!"

"Randoms who beat us to the Sarcophagus." Astrix stands up from her work. "Who escaped us once already."

"I'm not going to let these recordings slip away again," Tally says. "You all heard Rafia—the machines are already making copies of children. This is enough data to create a twin of everyone in Shreve."

I turn to the grandstands, a pleading expression on my face. Usually Shay's the one to stand up to Tally.

She lowers her rifle, returns my look, curious. But Tally shakes her head, and Shay goes back to scanning the horizon through her scope.

Tally's still the boss.

"Frey," she says, like this is all my choice. "Your father's crimes didn't end that night. As long as those recordings exist, he's still out there."

I swallow—the data necklace feels tight against my throat, all those secrets writhing inside their jacket of smart matter.

"If we leave even a few cores behind, that's people's private lives, ready to dissect." Tally places a hand on my shoulder. "Once the AIs get a taste, they'll want more."

I look at X, wanting him to decide.

He holds my beseeching gaze for a moment, then speaks with absolute certainty.

"Rebels don't nuke the wild, Tally. I call for a vote."

She laughs. "The Youngbloods don't really do that, X-la. And no crew stops for a vote when mission's *already started*."

"You hid the real mission from us," Yandre says. "A nuclear device isn't a detail . . . Boss."

"We don't have time." Tally growls with frustration. "Three of us aren't even here!"

"Which is exactly how you wanted it," X says. "So either we vote, or we split the crew."

Tally stares at both of them. "You'd walk away, *now*? What kind of rebels are you?"

"The human kind." X's canines glint red in the sunset. "The animals that say no."

Tally turns to look at the Futures. They've finished loading up our fake cores, and are looking this way now.

"Are you bailing too, Croy?" she asks with a clenched jaw.

"No, Boss."

She turns to me. "Frey? I need you."

Time slows down, like some viscous liquid pushing through a tiny spout. The world begins to tilt, unsteady, like when my grief comes at night.

"Someone has to warn the others," Tally explains. "So they don't get killed when the pulse knocks out their bracelets and boards. There's only you left."

"Which means you can stop this, Frey," Yandre says. "Leave with us, and you force her to break comm silence."

Tally's eyes become remote and calm. "You think I won't risk a few lives? Try me."

All of them are looking at me now. The stadium feels hot, the air squashed and helpless.

Terra's call echoes across the stadium. "Ready yet?"

I turn to X. "Can't we somehow . . . ?"

"Compromise?" he asks. "Set off the nuclear device halfway?"

I look back and forth between him and Tally—both their expressions are cold, their demands absolute. My heart begins to tear in half.

I can't walk away from her. But I can't reprise my father's final act, the ancient crime of wielding nuclear weapons. The almost nightmare that led to Col's death.

Then I remember what Shay said as we left the zoot suit party. Why she still rides with Tally—to put the brakes on.

There's more than one way to save the world.

With all my will, I turn away from X and Yandre.

"I'm with you, Tally-wa," I say.

But it's a lie.

CHAOS
MERCHANT

"I'm sorry, X, but—"

"You don't owe me anything," he says.

He and Yandre fly away without another word.

Tally watches them go. "Sorry that had to happen, Frey. But we have to do this the hard way—to make sure. You know that, right?"

I don't trust myself to answer. I just nod, step onto my board, and head toward Shay in the grandstands. She's the key to stopping Tally.

I reach her as the hovercar is taking off, Tally, Croy, and Astrix following. The hovercar's lifting fans strain with the weight of all those cores, filling the stadium with an echoing roar, a perilous, restless swarm of bees.

Shay takes one look at my face. "What's happening?"

"She's got a bomb. A tactical nuke."

"Of course." Shay closes her eyes for a beat. "After Astrix went away for treatment—she came back with that cargo flyer, shielded for radiation."

"Why do rebels even *have* nukes?" I cry.

"The forge."

It takes a moment to remember—while we were undercover in Shreve, Yandre told me about the rebels' nuclear forge, a way to clean up the atmospheric carbon the Rusties left behind. They must have a stash of uranium somewhere.

"Is she going to vaporize them?" Shay asks. "Or hit them with an EMP?"

"Um, just an EMP." I look out from the stands onto the forest surrounding us. Flocks of starlings are stirring, searching for insects in the dusk. "But there'll still be an airburst, a flash, and radiation."

"Will X and Yandre try to stop her?"

"I thought . . . maybe *we* could stop her, Shay."

She looks at me, something shutting down behind her eyes.

"I don't betray my boss. My job is damage control."

"A nuclear blast falls into that category!" I cry. "We can stop her!"

Her voice stays level. "The Futures, you and me, Tally and Astrix—three groups acting at cross-purposes, with a nuclear warhead smack in the middle. I can think of a hundred ways that could go worse than a clean airburst."

I point at the swirling cloud of starlings, the forest's fragile web of life. "There's nothing *clean* about this!"

A nuke won't just poison the wild—the EMP could knock down a passing airplane. It might even reach the edge of Tally's old city, switching off hoverstruts and medical implants.

Shay's eyes stay cold and calm. "If X and Yandre try something, you think their crew would turn on us?"

"X's people will do anything for him," I say, then shake my head. "But he's not their boss anymore—and Yandre turned over command to ride with Tally. They'd have to get everyone together for a vote."

"Rebels." Shay gives a dark laugh. "No wonder Tally sidelined the bosses."

And I see it—nothing will convince her to go against her old friend. Tally was always the betrayer; Shay's the loyal one.

I should have walked away with X and Yandre. More than ever now, I know where my true loyalties lie.

Which is why X's last words sounded so wrong: *You don't owe me anything.*

How could he think that? Except . . . it's a strange cousin to what he said months ago, when he first asked me to join his crew.

You owe the world nothing but chaos.

Born to rebel ways, he won't break tradition. But he knows I will.

Comm silence, two crews without bosses, information spreading like rumors at a party.

This situation is ripe for chaos.

A nearby hoverboard lifts on silent magnetics, its sneak-suited rider a glimmer against the red sky. Twenty rebels are out there in the growing dark, following the Futures in full stealth mode.

"We need to warn them about the pulse," Shay says, stepping onto her board. "Are you going to help?"

She fixes me with that weighing stare I've seen so many times.

I don't answer her.

She sighs. "Fine. But whatever you do, Frey-la, try not to make this worse."

Shay lifts into the air.

I fly fast and low, cutting between the trees, looking for other rebels. Looking for chaos.

The giant city swallows me.

After a few months with the Youngbloods, being alone seems to stretch out in all directions, weaving through the empty streets and broken buildings.

Rusty cities were *huge*—with populations in the tens of millions. Every pile of dust and rubble flitting past me is the shattered remains of countless homes, possessions, lives.

It take long minutes to finally spot another rebel. I fire up my fans, putting on a burst of speed to catch them.

"Hold up!"

The rebel banks to a halt, pulling down his sneak suit hood to reveal a young face—no surge, just flash tattoos. One of Yandre's crew.

"New orders," I say. "If Tally breaks comm silence, you need to land—fast."

He frowns. "Land?"

"Get off your board. It means an EMP's about to hit."

A flash of comprehension—Yandre's crew is all pretty technical.

"Someone's going to nuke the Futures?"

"Yeah. Boss Tally."

His confusion grows. "Is this a joke?"

I shake my head.

I'm not sure what more to tell him. There isn't time to process this with every rebel in two crews.

"The nuke's on the cargo flyer," I say. "If we program it to fly out to sea . . . that might do less damage. Anyway, spread the word, and get on solid ground when the warning comes."

I don't wait for any sign of understanding, just race ahead into the night. If I can reach enough rebels, maybe some strategy will coalesce.

Or maybe I'm adding another twenty factors to this already-insolvable equation. But it's like X said . . .

I owe the world nothing but chaos.

My board skims the tall grass, slipping between trees and buildings. It's hot inside my armor, my metabolism spinning up to a battle frenzy.

There's a keening at the edge of my hearing, sharp against the thrum of lifting fans. This is the first time I've felt this way since my operation—stress is pounding against the walls of my superhuman calm.

As if my true nature is finally showing through.

I loosen my armor, letting in the cool night air.

Another figure looms in the darkness, hovering at the edge of the treetops. As I roar up behind her, she turns and hisses.

"Fans off! The car's only half a klick ahead!"

I bank to a halt and start to tell her about Tally's nuke, the EMP burst, my half plan about sending the cargo flyer out to sea. The words spill out, barely making sense. She's just staring at me wide-eyed.

Suddenly she interrupts.

"What's that?" Her gaze is leveled at my throat.

My hand goes to the loosened armor, thinking she's telling me off for being protection-missing before a battle.

Then I feel the data necklace, warm from my body heat.

"Someone gave it to me," I say, wondering how this is more important than my news about a nuke. "Listen, I know this all sounds logic-missing—"

"There was a man." She cuts me off. "He showed up the first morning after we all split up. He wore something like that."

The world freezes around me.

"A man?"

"Some kind of eccentric, a crumbly traveling on a hoverbike." She's still staring at my throat. "He went around the camp, talking to us one by one, like he was looking for someone. When he finally left, we figured he was meds-missing. But he had that *exact* necklace."

"A black goatee," I say.

"What?" Her eyes widen a little. "Right, he had a little beard."

"When and where, exactly?"

"That first morning, about dawn. We'd just hit the Gila Mountains."

The nervous buzzing in my ears is growing louder.

The Gilas are a half day's ride south of the Youngbloods' private camping spot. Stellan Batrow was in two places at the same time, a thousand klicks apart.

Looking for me.

We never figured out how he tracked us in the mountains. But if there was more than one Batrow, it could almost make sense . . .

Except that means he wasn't real.

The rebel girl's voice drops to a whisper. "Do you hear that?"

I try to listen, but the buzz in my head is drowning out everything. I tell myself to relax, to focus on the calamities of the present.

"Hear what?"

"This whining sound in the comms." She looks at the Future's hovercar, its running lights fading into the distance. "Do you think Tally's setting off her nuke *already*?"

"Not till we get to their base." I lower my volume, and the ringing in my ears lessens—it wasn't nerves at all.

Then I feel something moving against my throat . . .

My hand goes to the necklace again. The beads aren't just body-warm—they're burning like little furnaces, some sort of chemical reaction churning inside them.

The necklace Batrow gave me is writhing against my fingertips.

I try to pull it off, but it clings to my armor, my camo shirt. Pulsing tendrils stretch away, like chewing gum stuck to a shoe.

I rip it all away—taking ceramics, metal, plastic—then kneel to smash it against the deck of my board.

The ringing in our comms cuts off.

Among the pieces is a tiny parabolic dish.

Finally I understand. This necklace was never full of recordings—just the programming for smart plastic to build a transmitter on the fly, taking what it needs from its environment.

Our enemies have tracked us down.

"What *was* that?" the rebel girl cries.

"The man you met . . ." My mind skids for a moment, the gears failing to mesh. "Stellan Batrow, he works for Diego."

He visited Hideaway, dozens of times. The dust there would have recorded him in detail, just like the kids.

"No, that was an avatar. The real Batrow died in the Fall of Shreve. Diego made copies to follow all three crews, to make sure he found me!"

The story about messages left for children, about the necklace answering all my questions—it was all so I'd keep the necklace close to me.

I'll have to get my own answers about my sister.

"What's happening now?" she asks.

My mouth opens to explain the thoughts cascading through me, but the girl doesn't care about that.

She's pointing at my hoverboard.

"Whatever that thing is, you didn't kill it yet."

TRANSMISSION

My board is warping into a new shape.

My feet dance, trying to stay on. A wave of heat hits me in the face—all those furious reactions rearranging the board's molecules. Circuitry appears before my eyes, layer after layer weaving into being. I've never seen smart matter build something so complicated, so fast.

The necklace really did contain data, an intelligence able to take over any machine and turn it into a transmitter—a big one this time.

The board flexes into a parabola. The screaming in my ears starts again, a thousand times louder now.

I cut my comms and lean hard, trying to fly the board into the nearest tree. But the smart matter has control of the lifting fans—they steady the dish beneath me, aiming it into space.

I draw my knife, raising it up to plunge it into the machine's heart.

Like an animal sensing a threat, the fans roar to life. The board bucks beneath me, shooting high above the trees. It flips hard, twists in spirals in the air, trying to throw me off. I cling to the deck with my left hand.

And stab the hoverboard with my right.

A scream rattles the air, traveling through my duralloy bones—the shriek of lifting fans spinning out of true. The smart matter struggles to make repairs in real time, but I drag the knife across the dish, until the blade strikes the forward fan.

Pulse weapon against lifting fan—the battle lasts a hundredth of a second, a thousand blows compressed into a single, sovereign *boom*.

Then I'm falling backward, stunned and blinded, half a pulse knife dead in my hand.

Silence wraps around me, only the sound of passing air as I plummet toward the trees. A faint hope trickles, that my crash bracelets can save me.

My halt comes sooner than it should—and softer.

The rebel girl has maneuvered beneath me, her board's magnetics catching my bracelets. I waft into her arms, and she sets me down gently on the riding deck.

I wobble for a moment.

"You think it's dead?" she asks, her voice muffled in my boom-deafened ears.

I turn on my comms—not even static.

"The shock wave must've done it," I say, staring at my broken knife, my numb hands. "Turned the smart matter into jelly."

"But the people looking for us, they heard that signal, right?"

Not people—only a city AI could have created something so intricate.

I look up at the dark and empty sky.

"We have to stop that hovercar before it gets home."

The girl's expression is blank, like I've thrown too much at her. Tally's nuke, rebel mutiny, transmogrifying transmitters.

But then something clicks.

"Yeah, I'm done with sneaking around. My name's Dancy."

"Frey," I tell her.

Her board spins up. I sheathe my shattered knife and put my hands around her waist.

"This mission had way too much Youngblood nonsense," Dancy shouts as we leap from cover. "Too many *secrets*!"

Her sneak suit flickers off—we *want* the Futures to see us, turn away, and run for the wild. Diego's drones will be dropping from orbit soon.

The hovercar has faded into the distance, not a speck of it in my vision. We ride straight for its last location, fast and high above the trees.

"Can't raise anyone," Dancy shouts into the headwind. "Tally's still got the comms locked down."

"The old-fashioned way, then." I draw Dancy's pistol and fire it into the air.

Within seconds, other rebels are rising into the open.

If we can scare the Futures into running, Tally never finds their base. She can't nuke what she can't see, and Diego won't find the data.

At top speed, it takes us only minutes to reel the overloaded car back into sight. The three riders around it are thermal flickers in the dark, the cargo flyer trailing like a faithful dog.

I fire Dancy's pistol again.

One of the hoverboards wheels in air and heads back toward us.

Would Tally send Croy? Or Astrix? Would they shoot me out of the sky if she ordered it?

But when the rider slip-rolls past a crumbling radio tower, I recognize that languid, effortless style.

"It's Tally," I say.

"Think she'll yell at us?" Dancy asks with a laugh.

"Could be worse than yelling."

Dancy's answer is to kneel down and pull a sniper's rifle from the side of her board. She stands up, telescoping its barrel.

"Don't exactly worship Boss Tally?" I ask.

"Yandre's my real boss. Didn't like Tally splitting us up." She shrugs in my arms. "Didn't like touring the continent without being told why. But mostly, I don't like nukes going off in the wild."

I smile. Maybe mutiny will come easier than I thought.

Was I the only one of us rebels awestruck by Tally Youngblood? Whenever Rafi and I watched the drama feeds as littlies, Tally was key to every story about the revolution and the mind-rain. Every city has streets and fountains named after her, even Shreve.

Most of all, she was a girl who found herself growing up in a bad situation—and escaped. That meant everything to me.

Tally said no.

Of course, Dancy's a rebel too—every day she lives in the wild says *no* to the rampant cities. To the AIs and first families. To killing the planet.

Maybe saying no to Tally comes naturally to her.

"Let me do the talking?" I ask.

Dancy considers this.

"Maybe" is all she'll give me.

I slip the pistol back into her holster.

We drift to a halt a hundred meters shy of the approaching hoverboard.

Tally comes in at high speed, like she's going to ram us, but then air-skids to a fast halt.

"What are you doing, Frey?" she calls. "Who sent that transmission?"

"Stellan Batrow did. He wasn't real. The necklace he gave me was a tracker."

Tally frowns. "What you mean, he wasn't *real*?"

"Diego sent him. He was some kind of machine."

She shakes her head. "Specials can't get fooled by avatars. And Astrix checked that necklace."

"It ate my hoverboard! Turned it into a transmitter!"

Tally just looks confused.

"Boss," I plead. "That wasn't normal tech—it's something the AIs created just to track *us*. We need to stop that car before it gets home!"

Tally looks over her shoulder at the Futures, still on course.

"Too late. We're almost there." She sweeps her eyes across the rebels in the open sky. "All you've done is put them on high alert. Did you at least warn everyone about the EMP?"

I swallow. "A couple of them."

The disgust in her expression makes me wobbly on my feet again.

Shay's warning echoes in my ears. What if everything I've done has only made this worse?

Then I see something behind Tally—the cargo flyer, cruising toward us at its modest speed. It must be set to auto-follow her.

"I tried, Boss," I say, then lean against Dancy to whisper, "That's the nuke."

Her weight shifts on the board.

"Looks more like you're trying to wreck this mission," Tally says. "At least X and Yandre had the integrity to walk away."

"Boss, everyone's hiding." We're wafting gently closer, as if carried by the wind. "Then my board got destroyed!"

"So you came in *shooting*?"

I look up into the sky—nothing yet. "After that transmission, I thought it was better to abort."

"Not your call," Tally says, spinning herself around. "Just stay here—and *try* not to get in the way."

For a moment, I almost obey. This is Tally Youngblood, the first rebel. Except . . .

I owe the world nothing but chaos.

"Wait a second, Boss," I say, leaning hard.

She scowls. "What now?"

I leap from our board onto Tally's, dragging her off and down into the trees.

PUNCHES

We fall together.

A branch hits me on the way, like a club swung at the middle of my back. I'm knocked breathless in midair.

I cover my head just in time.

Tally and I crash into the ruins of an old house, down there in the trees. The ancient rooftop splinters, barely slowing our fall.

The next floor is solid enough to stop us, spilling us out in a cloud of dust. It takes me a second to stand—

Tally's punch comes out of nowhere, sending me reeling.

A flurry of blows follows, swift and efficient, my limbs useless from pinpoint strikes against muscles and nerves.

When we fought in the wreckage of Hideaway, she was holding back. This is the real Tally, more than two decades' fighting the whole world. Pain flares in every part of me, overwhelming any chance of striking back.

I roll into a ball, gasping the smell of mold and dry leaves.

Tally stops herself, standing over me, breathing hard.

"What's *wrong* with you, Frey?" she cries, genuine confusion in her voice. "Did X tell you to do this?"

She still doesn't understand—this is me. I'm not X's shadow, or Rafi's, or hers. All that matters is the nuke.

Maybe I can buy Dancy more time.

One word leaks from my swollen lips.

"Collaborator."

Tally stares down at me. "*That's* what you're worried about? Some mistake I made when I was your age?"

I've hit the mark.

"Betrayer," I whisper.

Her whole body tenses, but no explosion of fury follows. She's still mostly confused—she really thought I would nuke the wild for her.

Healing nanos are flooding my system, but they're overwhelmed. It'll be a solid minute before I can stand again.

Tally's board drifts up behind her, nudging her leg.

"Shay was right—when you were little, your loyalty was never repaid." She turns away. "So why would you stick with us?"

I would have. But nukes were my father's last crime.

As Tally steps onto the board, I shake my crash bracelets to turn them to full.

Their magnetics pull me toward her across the dusty floor. Dragged by my wrists, my pain redoubles, my brain almost shutting down.

But somehow I grab hold of Tally's riding deck. Her liftoff pulls me into the air.

"Really?" she yells, swerving as we climb, trying to shake me off. My body dangles, a wild pendulum in midair. The gale-force wash from the lifting fans beats down on my face. But the tendons in my hands lock like steel.

We rise above the treetops, and I can see Dancy on the cargo flyer. She's kneeling over the warhead.

Tally hasn't spotted her yet—all her focus is on me.

"Just *give up*, Frey!" she cries, and the grippy sole of her boot comes down on my left hand.

Duralloy bones can't break, but I feel them bending. Sick-making pain cuts through the tatters of my awareness, the world turning sharp and glassy around me.

Somehow my other hand hangs on.

I wait for her boot to come crunching down again.

But a mocking cry comes across the treetops.

"Mind if I borrow this thing, Boss?"

It's Dancy on the cargo flyer.

Tally lets out an angry cry and flies straight at her, dragging me along. The board shrieks louder, the rotor wash a tornado trying to brush me away.

My crash bracelets vibrate a warning pattern—they're almost out of charge.

I try to grab for the deck with my bent left hand, but the fingers won't grip—trying to move them sends fresh torment down my arm.

Tally skids to a halt at the last second, swinging me out like a whip.

My fingers slip at last, my bracelets failing. I slam into Dancy, knocking her from the cargo flyer.

We tumble together, down through the trees.

"Dead batteries," I croak.

Dancy wraps me in her arms.

I feel the jolt of her crash bracelets kicking in, arresting our fall. But it's not enough.

The ground hits us—a giant's fist delivering a knockout blow.

In the sudden, sovereign darkness, my awareness trails away, bound to reality only by a few kite strings of agony. The rush of healing nanos finally overwhelms me. For an endless, somehow joyful moment, I leave myself behind.

A shadow of no one.

A long time later, someone calls from the distance.

"Frey."

I never liked that name.

"Frey! Are you okay?"

At that hilarious question, my eyes open.

"Yeah, I'm great."

Dancy's staring at my left hand. No blood, but it's bent wrong. The duralloy bones are curved beneath the surface, stretching the bulletproof skin taut and pink.

Healing nanos are holding the pain at bay. But I can feel it there, vast and powerful. Like standing centimeters from the thunder and spray of a waterfall.

Dancy gently takes my wrist. "We didn't fall *that* hard, did we?"

"No, Boss Tally did that."

"Wow," Dancy says. "The Smoke lives, I guess."

With a grunt, she hooks my good arm over her shoulder and lifts me up. It hurts too much to ask where we're going. Then I see something sliding through the trees—her hoverboard tracking her down.

We step gingerly on together, like friends who've had too much bubbly helping each other home.

But it's a battle we're headed toward, not bed. Somewhere in the distance, the shooting has already started.

"Don't think I can help much," I say. My nanos are slowly returning my other limbs to me, but that hand needs surge.

"Me either." Dancy has a black eye, and she winces as we start to climb. "Still, I want to *watch*."

As we rise up above the trees again, the sparkle of a firefight paints the horizon. We fly closer.

The rebels have surrounded a white ruin on a sprawling prominence. Ragged buildings rise up from the overgrowth, decked with blinding floodlights pointed outward in all directions.

"A castle on a hill," I say with a sigh. "Just like the Futures to pick an obvious spot for their base."

Dancy shrugs. "Easy to defend, at least."

Still closer, there's no sign of the hovercar—it must have made it back inside. Maybe Astrix and Croy went along with it. With everyone taking cover, I can't make out individuals.

One by one, the floodlights wink out, hit by sniping from the trees.

But the rebels don't make a concerted rush against the fortress. There are too many pinpoints of return fire along the walls.

Tally was right—the Futures showed up in numbers for her historic arrival. Twenty-odd rebels can't take this fortress without bloodshed, and it's all my fault for giving them a warning.

Which leaves Tally and her nuke.

"You broke the warhead, right?"

Darcy hands me something. "You tell me."

I stare at the sliver of metal, shorter than my pinkie, a plastic square at one end. Shaped like an old-fashioned key, it's covered with exposed circuitry.

"What is this?"

"No idea," she says. "It looked important, kind of."

"I got my hand broken for a *kind of*? I thought your crew's thing was technical expertise!"

Dancy laughs. "*My* thing is sustainable farming. Next time you want a warhead defused, give me more than thirty seconds."

"Okay, sorry." I slip the key into a pocket. "I guess we'll find out."

She shoves a bottle into my good hand, and I drink deeply. The water feels as powerful as the rampant nanos in my blood.

Something flickers in the sky.

I flinch, ready to be blinded, expecting the ruined city to be lit for a hundred klicks in every direction.

But the *boom* that rolls across the hills is gentle.

"That's not a nuke," Dancy says. "It's an orbital entry."

More of the flashes follow, a sudden web of heat trails crisscrossing the sky. This is the first time I've seen reentries from this range with my new vision. They're beautiful, like bold strokes of watercolor fading into black paper.

I'd almost forgotten the transmitter, but its message must have made it home.

The machines are here.

ORBITALS

In the war against my father, I saw half a dozen orbital insertions.

Normally there's the *pop* of reentry, the sound barrier snapping, then the flutter of parachutes. Finally heat shields scatter like embers, and a handful of combat drones springs forth to do battle.

But the vehicles falling around us don't fragment—they arc from the black sky in one piece. Furnace-hot from plunging through the atmosphere, they sprout solid metal wings, like birds pulling out of a dive.

No shielding drops away, no chutes open. These machines don't try to arrest the speed of falling from space—they use it.

The first one streaks overhead in an instant, a knife across the sky.

Below it, three rebels fall from their hoverboards.

I don't even know what hit them—maybe a flurry of invisible projectiles. Or the shock wave of the orbital's passage was enough.

Sonic booms rattle the hills around us.

The next one thunders over the Future's base on the hill. Ancient walls buckle and shatter. A sudden dust storm trails in the orbital's wake, a pale finger stretching across the sky. Debris rains into the forest.

I reach for my knife. It's still broken, not that a pulse weapon could do much against these orbitals. They look a decade beyond anything in the city arsenals.

"Guess you were right," Dancy says.

"We can't fight them." More booms set the hoverboard shuddering beneath my feet. "But we can still kill the data."

"You don't look ready for a battle," Dancy says.

I look at my left hand, a dead spider with five legs.

"Just give me your pistol."

We head toward the fortress, dropping into cover whenever more orbitals come screaming overhead. Dancy's bracelets are spent from catching us both, so a hard fall will end this ride.

The rattle of gunfire has faded around us, the rebels scattered into the ruins. The Futures must be huddled in the depths of their base, waiting for whatever Diego has coming next.

Maybe in this lull, we can get inside and find the memory cores . . .

Then something big drops from the sky. It slows itself with retro rockets, landing in the mountains to the north. Some kind of mobile command post?

We ignore it, riding hard for the Future's base.

We're closing in when Tally breaks comm silence.

"Pull out, everyone—fast as you can!"

An orbital swoops overhead, the shock wave sending Dancy's

board into a tailspin. For a moment, there's nothing in my ears but a drumbeat of sonic booms.

When I can hear again, Tally's still talking. "—any bare skin, and don't look back! Ninety seconds—*mark*."

Dancy skids us to a halt. "Is that what I think it was?"

"Yeah. She's going to use the nuke."

I set a countdown in my eyescreen.

"What do we *do*?" For the first time, Dancy sounds nervous.

"We go in," I say. "We'll be safer under cover than out here."

Dancy stares into the sky. "All those orbitals rushing around—how's she going to get it high enough for an airburst?"

"She's Tally Youngblood. Come on."

We break from the trees, flying heedlessly now. In my eyescreen, the countdown is ticking . . .

Seventy-three seconds.

We climb the hill on a crumbling road, our lifting fans at full, magnetics pushing off the rusting hulks of ancient groundtrucks. A ring of shattered floodlights surrounds the ruins, spilling a waterfall of broken glass.

The outlying buildings pass under us, broken by three centuries of decay even before the orbital attack. The interior walls are zigzagged with the remains of fallen staircases, the marble floors cracked by the flexing roots of trees.

Nothing looks intact enough to be a working base.

And no one shoots at us.

An orbital zooms low across the hill, but the afterstorm of shock waves seems muted. Their work done, the attackers are backing off.

There must be a second wave coming—infantry or tactical drones.

I scan the sky. Maybe half a klick over my head, twin pinpoints of heat are spiraling upward, like birds riding thermals.

The cargo flyer carrying the nuke . . . and Tally too. She's threading it through the thunderstrikes of passing orbitals.

But her board's maxing out its altitude—she starts to drop away, arcing into a power dive to get clear of the airburst. The six-engined flyer keeps climbing.

Forty seconds.

She's cutting it close.

So are we.

We jump a shattered wall and swoop down into a courtyard, looking for an entrance to the base—for any cover at all.

Parked on a hoverpad below us is the Futures' car, its loading ramp standing open. The cargo hold is empty.

There's no one around, just a door set into the ground, five meters across and firmly shut. It glimmers with the dull sheen of duralloy, like the vault in the deepest basement of my father's tower.

"Uh-oh," I say.

Even if I had my pulse knife, there'd be no getting through that.

I look around. None of the structures have solid roofs. We're stuck here in the open.

Twenty-one seconds.

"Frey . . ." Beside me on the board, Dancy's looking up.

As I follow her gaze, a *boom* reaches us. The trail of a passing orbital is fading up there, next to a small ember of heat spinning out of control.

The cargo flyer is falling.

It's not going to airburst kilometers up. It's going to explode down here.

Not far from us, looks like.

Eleven . . .

"Come on!" Dancy lands us on the hoverpad, drags me from the board into the car's cargo hold.

I stumble to a halt, staring at the roof. Maybe half an inch of metal between us and the blast. The cargo door isn't even closed.

"Dancy, I don't think we're . . ." My voice fades.

I shut my eyes, but the countdown is still there in my vision.

One . . . zero.

Nothing.

No flash, no vast roar a moment later. No shock wave punching in the sides of the hovercar, no heat blistering our skin.

When I open my eyes again, Dancy's huddled in a corner, body armor pulled up over her face. I'm frozen, waiting to be flayed with fire.

Maybe Tally set a limit on the airburst, to protect the Futures down in their duralloy vault. To protect the wild. The cargo flyer might be climbing again, primed to explode when it hits the right altitude.

But an endless, anxious minute later, still nothing. Even the rumble of passing orbitals has faded.

I have to know.

I walk down the hovercar's loading ramp.

"Frey!" Dancy's voice follows me. "Where are you going?"

I flinch a little, looking up into the sky.

Less than a hundred meters overhead is a silhouette, steady against the stars. I adjust my thermal vision.

It's Tally and her board next to the flyer, like she's working on it.

"Whatever you did, Dancy, it worked."

The sound of armor shifting. She starts laughing, half hysterical.

"Are you *kidding*? Sustainable farming for the win!"

I pull the key from my pocket.

Its circuitry glimmers in the starlight, tiny rivers of silver. Some kind of safety lock, so small that Tally didn't notice it missing in the heat of battle.

I slide the key into the small pocket in my riding boot, where I keep spare pulse batteries. Even if Tally searches me, she won't find it.

Our comms are still locked, so I yell into the sky.

"Tally! It's broken!"

No answer at first, but the silhouette above me shifts—she's peering over the side of the cargo flyer.

The comms unlock.

"What did you say?"

"Your nuke is broken," I tell her, trying to sound calm. "Come down and let's finish this together."

"What did you do?" Her breath is racing in my ear—like she expected to die a minute ago. "Can't you see you were right? The AIs are *here*!"

"Tally, we can still erase the data, but we need to work together!"

She drops her board halfway, close enough that I can see her pleading expression.

"No, Frey. You need to fix this nuke!"

Her glare cuts through the darkness, all the weight of her cruel beauty, her historic fame, falling on me.

I shake my head.

I am the animal that says no.

That's when Diego's second wave arrives.

AVATARS

They must have been falling all along, silent and invisible among the shrieking winged orbitals.

Looking up at Tally, I finally see the stars winking out here and there, covered up for an instant by small forms descending through the dark.

They're shaped like people, but have no body heat.

They aren't using parachutes—each descends inside its own huge, translucent cloud. Made from some kind of weightless foam, the clouds drift down like wisps of pollen.

"Tally," I whisper. "Do you see them?"

A moment's silence, then she answers, low and wary.

"Aerogel parachutes. Ever seen those before?"

"Just in theory."

"Why are they sending *avatars* at us?" she asks, a shudder in her voice. "Why not drones?"

I have no answer.

349

At the base of the hill, one of the wafting clouds of aerogel touches down. All at once, it blinks out of existence, a soap bubble popping.

The form inside drops gently to the ground, landing on hands and feet. More cat than human.

My eyes drift across the dark sky—hundreds of the aerogel bubbles warp the pinpoint stars. Hundreds of human forms within, all controlled by artificial minds. Or maybe just one mind, a hive.

"Still don't want to fix my nuke?" Tally asks.

I walk toward the giant duralloy door. "Just get down here, Boss. If anyone can talk sense into those kids, you can."

She sighs, and seconds later, her hoverboard lands next to me. She waves it and the cargo flyer away to hide themselves in the trees.

Dancy has emerged from the hovercar.

"Hi, Boss," she says in greeting.

Tally ignores her, stepping onto the huge door.

"What do we have that cuts through duralloy?" I ask.

She smirks at me, kneels, and taps out a pattern on the metal.

A few seconds later, a rumbling stirs the ground beneath our feet. The door starts to slide away, revealing a set of permacrete stairs stretching down into darkness.

Astrix stands on them, smiling up at Tally.

"Good to see you not vaporized, Boss." Then she sees me and frowns. "Oh, so something went wrong."

"No plan survives contact with Frey-la," Tally says, jumping from the still-opening door onto the stairs. "Everything under control down there?"

"Sort of," Astrix says. "Croy's got them pinned down in the storage vault. But there's a *lot* of them."

Tally looks up at me and Dancy. "Come on, then. We have a small army to fight."

Dancy looks at me, shrugs, then starts down the stairs.

"Hang on." Astrix squints, looking past us. "What are *those*?"

I turn—two of the aerogel parachutes are landing just beyond the courtyard. They're even bigger than I thought, the size of small airships. Up close like this, they glimmer, fracturing starlight through a thousand separate cells of air.

One touches down with a soft *pop*. The huge structure vanishes, instantly replaced by wisps of gel drifting on the breeze, like loose strands of spiderweb. The human form suspended in the center drops behind a wall, out of view.

"The AIs are here," Tally says quietly. "Get this door closed."

Astrix turns to fiddle with something in the dark. As the slow, rumbling machinery reverses, I hear the pop of the second aerogel bubble hitting earth.

"You two stay here till it's shut," Tally says.

Dancy assembles her sniper rifle again, while the others head into the darkness without us.

The huge door is closing at an excruciating pace.

The first avatar comes over the wall, moving in a way that brings the word *skittering* to mind. Like an insect—except insects are alive. This thing looks more like clockwork, inhumanly symmetrical and precise.

Dancy's rifle cracks, and the avatar's kneecap tears apart with a bloodless puff. But the machine doesn't fall—just changes its gait, still coming at us in a series of uneven cartwheels. The motion makes no mechanical sense, as if an invisible child is propelling a rag doll across the floor, heedless of how real limbs work.

"Nope," Dancy says, squeezing off another dozen shots.

One hits—the avatar twitches in midair, and its hurtling approach changes again, jerking like a wounded kite along the ground.

Finally it's slowing down, but not enough.

The door is only halfway shut.

The second avatar is sweeping in from the right, too far away to threaten us—until Dancy's rifle clicks empty.

She looks at my pistol.

"Not yet," I say. If the avatars make it inside, I don't want to be out of ammo.

Then I see it—in the perfect spot: "Your board!"

Dancy understands.

She whistles. The hoverboard lifts up and zooms toward us at ankle height . . .

Right across the path of the injured avatar.

Somersaulting too fast to alter course, it collides with the board and tumbles through the dirt. Somehow it keeps rolling, reaching us as the opening is still half a meter wide.

I aim my pistol at its face, which stares back at me.

I squeeze out a shot. The bullet tears out one eye—

The other one doesn't even blink.

"Frey," the avatar says in Diego's calm voice. "We really need to talk."

It reaches out a hand, as if to stroke my cheek. But the door shuts at last, impervious metal sliding closed with a squelching sound.

A rivulet of red goo, nothing like blood, trickles from the seam.

Dancy stumbles backward on the stairs. "Okay. I didn't like *any* of that."

I turn away, trying to shake the avatar's voice from my head.

But that empty, inhuman expression—the true face of Diego.

"Where'd they go?" Dancy asks.

We stand there a moment, searching the darkness with our senses. Then the echo of a distant gunshot reaches my ears.

"Come on," I say, striding into the dark. "This door won't hold forever."

PARAGONS

The underground base lights up around us as we move.

The passages are bare, unpainted permacrete. The lights are glued on, and wires run openly along the ceiling. The tunnels branch and wind aimlessly. It's like diggers were set in random patterns, spraying up walls and floors as they went.

This whole place must've been built in a hurry while they plotted to steal my father's data, knowing they'd need a place to hide.

"This way," Dancy calls, running ahead toward the sound of another shot.

We find the others at an intersection, backs against the wall. Croy's using a cam drone to peek around the corner.

A series of *cracks* fills the air, and the drone is shot away.

"I figure there's fifty down there." He sighs. "Too many for a frontal assault."

"Have you tried talking?" Tally asks.

"They won't stop shooting long enough to listen!"

Astrix speaks up. "Once they saw you turn back, Boss, they got suspicious. Wouldn't show us the cores without you here. Then some rebel out there started shooting, and things got dicey."

Tally looks at me.

"We had to stun a bunch of them." Croy nods at the pieces of shattered drone. "The rest retreated down that passage and set up a firing line. Must be the storage vault for the cores."

"How strong a vault?" Tally asks.

"My scanners show machinery," Astrix says. "But no big mass of duralloy—they haven't put the door in yet. They were building to last a thousand years, but they aren't finished. Lucky for us."

I look up at the sprayed-on ceiling of the intersection. There's a dark trickle of water damage in one corner.

"Not that lucky." I point at the stain. "That's rainwater. Which means there's nothing between us and the surface but dirt."

Astrix whistles. "You mean, all Diego needs to get in here is a *shovel*?"

I imagine a hundred avatars digging into the hill around us, their tools chipping through the permacrete walls, their blank faces peeking in . . .

"No knockout drones left," Astrix says. "Maybe I can hack their hovercams? Otherwise, all we've got is deadly force."

Tally hesitates, staring up at the water stain.

She was willing to set off a nuke in midair—what if killing a bunch of kids isn't too much for her?

"Tally—" I start.

"We surrender," she says.

Astrix frowns. "As in . . ."

"As in, Frey-la walks down there with her hands up. She explains to Sara how this attack has nothing to do with us. We're here to protect their precious data from an AI who want to steal it."

"Okay," I say. "How do I explain the shooting?"

"Tell them the truth," Tally says. "You were leading a mutiny against me and my nuclear option."

Croy and Astrix stare at me—a mutiny against Tally Youngblood.

"How do I erase the data?" I ask.

Tally hands me a piece of smart plastic. When I try to take it, the plastic slithers around my right wrist, disappearing behind my crash bracelet.

"Genotoxin," she says. "Careful with the pointy end. It'll unravel your DNA too."

"Great. But I can't kill hundreds of cores before they stop me. I've only got one hand!"

Tally shrugs. "Do what you can."

I frown—of course, even if I only erase a few cores, that's a month of Shreve's history. Millions of private conversations, personal secrets, and diary entries the machines will never see.

I raise my hands, about to walk out.

"Not alone, Frey. They'd probably shoot you." Tally smiles, wrapping another injector around her wrist. "But I'm totally historic."

356

The Futures don't gun down Tally Youngblood.

First she calls along the passage, warning them that we're about to appear. Then we step into the open, hands up, body armor off.

My skin tingles. But the eyes staring down the corridor grow wide and the rifle barrels lower.

In their enthusiasm for not shooting Tally, they don't shoot me either.

It's still a long walk. I flinch every time one of the motion-sensitive lights flickers on overhead.

"Hear that?" Tally whispers.

In the taut silence, scuffling sounds have reached us from the surface.

Something has started digging its way into the base.

"Great," I say softly.

Astrix was right—there's a large doorway at the end of the passage, exposed machinery on either side. But the vault door itself is missing.

Armed Futures are crowded into the space, but they back away as Tally approaches. Personal hovercams float above their heads like halos, recording this historic moment.

Sara steps forward. "That's far enough."

Tally lowers her hands.

"Listen, Sara—I know this all went sideways, but we have to stop fighting and work together. There are . . . *things* coming through the dirt."

"We know." Sara eyes the ceiling. "They aren't with you?"

"No," Tally says. "We don't use creepy avatar-people!"

"But they followed you here, didn't they?"

"No, they followed me." My hand goes to my throat. "Someone gave me a necklace, and I didn't know it was a tracker. I take all the blame, but let us help you defend your property."

Sara considers this. "Who are they, anyway?"

"The avatars of a rogue AI," Tally says. "They want to steal your data and study it."

There's silence as this sinks in. Then something awful happens—a boy just behind Sara gives us a big, beautiful *smile*.

"They want to use our lives for research? Not way off in the future, but *now*?"

That's when I realize the mistake we've made.

The Futures *want* to be studied. What could be more historic than being the first people ever fully analyzed by AIs?

"No, wait," I say.

Sara's eyes widen. "So they'll use us as templates—for *everyone*."

"To *control* everyone!" I cry out. "They'll take your lives and turn them into algorithms!"

They're all just staring at me. In the old Shreve, the only privacy was in the grave. Diego is offering them immortality.

I look past Sara—the memory cores are inside the vault, arranged in neat rows on shelves, lovingly marked.

We have to get inside.

"Here's the problem," I say. "There's no guarantee what the machines will do with the recordings after they study them. Maybe no one ever sees them again."

"That's right," Tally chimes in. "The AIs don't care about history. This is about control!"

"Still . . ." Sara says. "Our lives will be baked into *everything*. We'll be the algorithm for humanity. The paragons of dramatic living!"

Ran steps up behind her. "Hang on. I didn't create my drama for AIs to watch. Future was about making stories, not being research monkeys."

"But we won't just be historic," Sara says. "We'll be universal!"

"I don't want to be universal—I wanted to tell *my* story. *Our* story, about me and you and Chulhee!"

Ran's voice breaks on that name, and suddenly all of them are arguing.

The debate spills over me in a wave—the value of memory, the meaning of drama, of story. If a life is lived in the dust but nobody ever watches it, did that life really happen?

In the growing hubbub, Tally catches my eye. She nods her head at the vault beyond the crowd, then glances at the ceiling.

I listen above the raging argument—the digging sound is closer. We don't have time to wait for this debate to end.

Tally's fingers count down from five to one.

Then she throws a flashbomb at the floor.

BATTLE

We crash through the stunned Futures.

Packed together, they stumble into piles when we shove the first ranks backward.

As I reach the shelves full of cores, the injector is already stirring on my wrist. It flicks out and strikes, a scorpion's stinger. The *ping* of ruptured metal rings through the chaos.

A shiver inside me—all those captured moments set free, all those double helixes of data, unwound.

I move to the next core, but it takes the injector a full second to reset. By the time I've erased another sliver of history, the Futures are taking aim.

I duck and run, deeper into the shelves.

A shot rings out—the projectile glances from the core above my head, bouncing straight into another. A neat hole opens in the casing, more data lost.

"Hold your fire!" Sara screams.

I thrust my hand at another core—the injector strikes.

Four down, out of hundreds.

Tally scatters a handful of smoke and flash grenades across the floor. The vault descends into chaos, shadows flickering on the sudden pall.

But Sara manages to take control. The Futures start to spread out—there are enough of them to cover every row, until someone has a point-blank shot.

I kill another week of Shreve.

Across the room, Tally starts sending the shelves crashing down. It probably won't erase the data inside, but the heavy, rolling cores underfoot are havoc-making.

The next time I reach to sting, a shot rings out—pain courses my left arm. I duck and spin, pulling off my left crash bracelet to throw it at the shooter.

Another *crack* answers, missing wildly, but it brings a shriek from someone behind me.

"Careful!" Sara cries.

I'm surrounded, but that means they'll risk shooting each other. Of course, they've made bigger sacrifices for this data.

My healing nanos wash the sting from my wounded left arm, but that hand is throbbing again.

I strike another of the cores. Seven down.

I'm hemmed in now, two Futures at each end of this row of shelves. They've spotted me in the smoke, and are taking careful aim.

Then Astrix does her magic.

All at once, the hovercams above my attackers' heads go wild, darting at them like angry crows. A shot goes into the ceiling, while the other Futures swing their rifles to swat away the rebellious cams.

I slip beneath the shelving into the next row, sticking another core from below. Then two more.

With ten weeks of recordings erased, I start to believe that this might work. With my own hands, I'm destroying my family legacy, unwinding the DNA of my father's regime.

My injector strikes again . . . and again.

My old battle frenzy comes back, cutting through the arid calm of Specialness. This is what Rafi must have felt like when she cut him in half.

Then a huge sound thunders above the yelling and gunfire—crunch and rattle, like a sheet of ice breaking overhead.

The permacrete ceiling begins to split. The crack expands until it reaches both walls. Dirt and rocks start to trickle through, then become a rain.

"They're here!" It's Tally's voice on the comms. "Keep going!"

I ignore the cascade of loose earth, stinging five more of the cores.

The Futures have almost forgotten me and Tally. In a panic, they're grabbing cores and hauling them out the door, away from the mountain of dirt growing in the center of the vault.

The first avatar falls through, landing on the pile.

Someone shoots it in the stomach, but it keeps calmly turning, eyes scanning the room. More avatars ride down in the avalanche.

Bullets fly, and I can hear Sara shouting, "Stop! They're on our side!"

But Ran is ignoring her, firing away. And through the smoke I see that Tally has grabbed a rifle from the floor.

She hits the first avatar in both eyes, dropping it.

I sting another core, and another. The injector grows hot in my hand, resetting sluggishly. The lights are flickering out, one by one.

But I strike again—another week of stolen lives, erased.

A new split opens in the ceiling, and one of the avatars tumbles through. It lands beside me, wrapping gangly arms around my shoulders.

"Frey," it says in Diego's voice. "Please stop making this—"

I hit it in the face with the injector.

It starts to speak again. "Someone's going to get hurt, Frey. We should try to . . ." It freezes; then the blank expression starts to dance, the words dissolving into gurgling.

I'm not sure if avatars have DNA, but the genotoxin's doing something.

I turn from it and destroy another memory core. And one more.

Another avatar grabs me from behind, its arms too strong to escape. They push the air from my lungs.

The caches of extra oxygen in my rib cage spill open, giving me a few more seconds. My boot heels stamp on the avatar's feet, mashing them to bloody pulps, but the thing won't let go.

Spots are swimming before my eyes.

Then a rifle shot, a jolt traveling though the avatar's body into mine. The arms fall away.

Tally, saving me again.

But there are dozens of them now.

I try to move, to dodge and duck, but my legs won't budge. I'm knee-deep in the torrent of dirt.

Vacant faces crowd me through the smoke, like dolls from a nightmare. Hands grab my arms, pull the injector from my wrist, ignore their fellows dropping as Tally shoots them.

Then she stops shooting.

Her growl keens above the tumult, followed by the thud of blows coming in a flurry.

I'm fighting with my one good hand, biting at the fingers in front of me. But I'm forced to the floor, a mass of bodies and dirt crushing down.

The weight is too much to breathe.

Tally's battle roar is stifled, and that's when something in me gives out.

PART V

WHOLE TRUTH

*In a world of total information, the
essence of the human
will become what is not information,
and the essence of intimacy
will be in sharing what cannot be
shared over the networks.*

—Stephen Marche

HOME

Even with my eyes closed, I can tell this is a hospital bed.

It's more comfortable than anywhere I've slept since joining Tally's crew—a real pillow and cotton sheets, enough width to splay my arms.

But moving turns out to be a bad idea.

My whole body aches. My ribs are bruised, my shoulder sore where the bullet went through. My left hand feels strange, but the fingers work. The bones must've been surged back into shape. The skin on my palm is new, vat-grown and pale.

I remember a nightmare about being buried alive, then realize that it really happened.

When I open my eyes, the city out the window comes slowly into focus.

That familiar skyline—solid buildings, no hoverstruts. A morning sky full of herons and scudding clouds.

And rising in the distance, a black pyramid, its summit complete at last.

"Shreve," I say.

"Very good," comes a familiar voice. "And do you know your name?"

I blink my eyes till they adjust to the soft light in the room.

A doctor stands at the end of my bed, in white scrubs and gloves. I know his face from growing up in the tower.

Dr. Orteg, my father's personal physician. The man who made sure that Rafi and I always stayed at the same weight, the same muscle development. When she got her scar, he cut my eyebrow to match.

He's watching an airscreen full of diagnostics, which waver when I speak again.

"Yes, Doctor. I know my name."

He smiles. "But you'd rather not say it."

I shrug, which sends a tiny bolt of lightning down my injured shoulder. The airscreen does a little dance to the oscillations of my pain.

"Not to worry, Frey," he says. "You're home."

The sound of my name makes me feel suddenly naked in my paper gown. But of course a hospital would check my DNA. And Orteg would know it's me, not Rafi.

Which leaves only one question.

"How did I get here?"

"You were caught in a ceiling collapse. Do you remember that?"

"If *ceiling collapse* is the clinical term for a hundred avatars digging their way into an underground bunker, then yes."

Dr. Orteg looks pleased as he wipes away the airscreen. "You don't seem to have lost any memories."

"Why would I?"

"You were buried, Frey." His voice drops into a serious register, like when he used to remind Rafi to wear her crash bracelets. "Your brain was deprived of oxygen for several hours. You're lucky to be alive."

"Was anyone else . . . ?" My heart stutters for a moment. "Did they find any bodies?"

"I'm not certain. No one from Shreve was on the rescue team."

Of course—the nearby cities would've responded first. One look at my DNA and they sent me here.

"There's nothing about casualties on the newsfeeds," he adds.

A tremor of relief. If Tally had been killed, it would be a global story. But if she's okay, why did she leave me to suffocate under a pile of dirt?

"I don't understand."

"That's to be expected, Frey." Orteg puts a gentle hand on my injured shoulder. "You were unconscious for three days. It may take a while for your brain to find its normal rhythms. Don't try to make sense of everything at once."

Three days.

So whatever happened in the ruins is over—the machines have won.

And it's my fault for getting in Tally's way.

A judgment call in the heat of battle, weighing one bad outcome against another. Like Rafi's choice—except that she sacrificed Col for the greater good.

I saved a few thousand trees from being nuked, but handed every detail of two million lives to the AIs.

The world probably doesn't even know yet.

I switch on my comms, but there's only silence in my ears.

"I need to see the feeds," I say.

"I'll have someone set you up with a connection." The doctor starts to make his way toward the door. "But not until you get some more rest, Frey."

"Wait." Desperation starts to pulse in me—I'm cut off from the world, no comms, no idea what happened back at the ruins.

No crew.

When X and Yandre walked away from Tally, I didn't join them. And in the end I betrayed her too. Maybe I'm alone now.

"Is there anyone . . . here for me?"

Orteg gives me his warmest smile yet.

"You do have a visitor waiting. If you feel up to it."

I swallow. "Please, Doctor. I'm okay."

Orteg nods. "Just a moment, then."

The door slides open, and he's gone.

For a few endless minutes, I'm all alone. The hospital room is soundproofed, my city silent through the window glass, as if the life has been sucked out of it.

My riding outfit is piled on the room's one chair, like someone faded away there, leaving only their clothes behind.

A sense of dislocation settles over me—this empty room, this strange bed, more than two thousand kilometers from where I should be. Three days lost, and the AIs have everything they want.

While I slept, a new world has taken shape around me.

I've lost everything.

But then the door slides open, she walks in, and suddenly I feel a trickle of home.

My sister, Rafia of Shreve.

REUNION

"Hey, little sister."

For a moment, it's impossible to speak.

I know that smile so well—the genuine one that Rafi kept hidden from the crowds and cams. The one I never had to copy; it was hers alone.

She crosses the room and places a warm hand on my head.

"Poor Frey—three days asleep. You must have been so tired." Her voice trembles a little. "But you woke up."

Suddenly I want to reassure her.

"My brain's fine, Rafi. I remember everything."

She pulls her hand away, regarding me. "Well, your brain is the only thing that isn't damaged. You erased our face . . . again."

"Sorry."

"And such a generic effort." Rafi gives a dramatic sigh. "If you're going to be hurtful, Frey, at least come up with a new look."

I give a painful shrug. "The rest of me's pretty interesting. Plastic muscles, enhanced senses, duralloy bones."

"Duralloy . . . and still you manage to break yourself." She takes my left hand, gently straightening the fingers. "You should've seen the X-rays. Did a groundtruck run over it?"

"No. Tally Youngblood did."

"Ooooh, that *is* interesting. Trouble with your new crew?"

When I don't respond, her smile changes—from wounded to mischievous, the look Rafi gives when she shares a secret with you.

"Let me guess, the Youngbloods weren't as wonderful as you expected?"

I look away—using lost children as a diversion, keeping secrets from other rebels, and a nuclear warhead.

"Maybe not."

"Never meet your idols." Rafi pats my head again. "They can only disappoint you. Three days in a coma, and none of them showed up to visit."

A fresh weight of loneliness settles on me.

Maybe the Youngbloods are still out there, fighting hard. Maybe there's still some chance of wresting back what the machines have taken from us, and when it's done, they'll come and tell me the story.

"But I've been here every minute," Rafi says. "This is your home, Frey."

Heat rises in my cheeks, and I feel exposed again in this paper gown.

I swing my feet off the bed and cross to the window. Wincing

375

with every movement, I pull on my riding shirt, then my trousers. The gown detects that I've gotten dressed, and disintegrates.

I ease myself down into the chair, exhausted.

"Get back into bed, Frey," my sister says. "You've been through so much. It's time to stop pushing yourself."

I look at her. "Something bad happened out there, Rafi."

"Yes. Some random kids recorded it all. It looked like the sky was falling!"

I hesitate, but keeping secrets is pointless now. "We were trying to get Father's surveillance records back."

She gives her favorite eye roll. "That much was obvious, little one. My rebel friends told me about all those crews zigzagging the continent. What else would they be looking for?"

"That was a diversion—we knew where the Futures were. We made a deal with them."

"Clever. Except it turned into a battle, didn't it?"

"A disaster," I say, slumping in the chair. "There was a mutiny, more or less."

My sister makes an expression of genuine surprise. I haven't seen that look on her face since our thirteenth birthday, when Father gave us both hoverboards. The only time I ever got a present from him.

"Rebels mutinied . . . against *Tally Youngblood*?"

I shrug. This would all make more sense if I told her about the warhead, but I have enough loyalty left to keep that part secret. The whole world would go sense-missing if they found out that the Youngbloods had almost turned into nuclear terrorists.

"It was a complicated situation, Rafi, and the end result is a nightmare. The AIs have our father's data now. They can use it to mold us, to control us."

My sister waves a hand. "You think I care if the machines copy us? May I point out that *you* copied *me*? And yet here I am, still fully human."

Of course she's not worried. Rafi was willing to trade the data away—she can't imagine a machine being as good at manipulating people as she is. Especially not the citizens of Shreve.

"But tell me about this mutiny," she says. "Tally must be *shattered*."

"She expected it, actually. She cut the bosses off from their crews."

"How curious," Rafi says. "Well, it *is* tricky leading a large group of rebels—I should know. How many crews were out there? A dozen?"

"Just three. Twenty-seven of us."

Rafi narrows her eyes. "So few? Are you sure? This isn't the brain damage talking?"

"I'm sure, Rafi."

She's right, though—three crews wasn't enough firepower. Because Tally's real plan was to nuke the cores.

My sister is still watching me. She knows there's something I'm not telling her.

"Look, Rafi, it didn't work. In the end, Diego got what they wanted."

"So Tally thinks Diego was behind all this." Rafi looks out the window. "Interesting."

"Of course it was. That's who you made your deal with—they were blackmailing you for the data!"

"Ah, you know about that distasteful little arrangement?" She lets out a dramatic groan. "Of course, all those bugs you left in Government House."

"No, when I was in your office . . ." My voice fades away.

Rafi hasn't scolded me yet for pretending to be Diego.

"You haven't figured it out," I murmur. Even though I'm wearing the same face as I was then.

"Don't be silly." Rafi takes my hand. "Try to see it from my perspective, Frey. That part of the conversation wasn't the important thing, not for me."

Of course—my focus was on her deal with Diego. But what hit Rafi hardest was that old portrait of me being revealed.

My head spins a little. Maybe it's too much, unpacking everything between us now. I should have listened to Dr. Orteg and stayed in bed.

But there's something else I have to say.

"I'm sorry I tricked you like that, Rafi. It was cruel, suggesting that I could be dead."

She nods, silent.

"You really missed me," I whisper.

"Dreadfully." She takes a deep breath. "But it was my fault you ran away, because of what I did to Col. I'm sorry, Frey."

The chair seems to tip beneath me. Or maybe the world.

"You had to save our city," I say, the words broken glass on my tongue. "But in your office that day, you acted so proud of it. What did you say?"

I'd throw that knife again, a thousand times.

She shakes her head, like the memory is too much.

Or like she doesn't remember.

Maybe it's my brain damage, but the world feels like it's becoming unglued at the seams. As if, even now, my sister is hiding something from me.

I slide on my riding boots and stand, scanning the subject headers in the corner of my internal vision, all those pings . . .

Dear Little Shadow

Dear Little Shadow

Dear Little Shadow

My mouth goes dry. "Can I ask you a question?"

"Anything at all, Frey. We can't keep secrets from each other anymore. It's too dangerous . . . for our city."

"You're right, but this is just a little thing. In your letters, why do you call me *little gremlin?*"

Rafi lets out a low chuckle, and for a moment, I think she's onto me.

But then she says, "Because you *are* a gremlin, Frey. You've been making trouble for both of us since the day we were born."

Her *best* smile crosses her face then, the smile we created together. The one she's done a thousand times for newscams, a million more for the dust in the tower.

I smile that same smile back, lifting the chair from the floor.

I launch myself at the machine.

EFFIGY

The chair smashes to pieces against the avatar's head.

There's enough skin, veins, and muscle to make the first strike a bloody mess. My attack almost falters—but if this is the real Rafi, then this really is a hospital, and they'll fix her.

I thrust a broken chair leg into her stomach, hard.

Its face just smiles at me.

"Three rebel crews," it says in Diego's voice. "Useful information."

I lift the machine—it weighs the same as Rafi—and hurl it at the window.

The city skyline scatters into shards, revealing a blank wall.

It was a screen.

This isn't Shreve.

The avatar of my sister falls to the floor twitching. I turn away and lift the hospital bed into the air.

Those micro-expressions, all those tiny movements of Rafi's that I alone knew—the machines possess them now. With that thought sending a rush of battle frenzy through me, I ram the bed into the hospital room door. It crumples like paper.

I step out into a dark hallway with metal walls, looking for something to kill. A dozen of those combat avatars should be hurling themselves at me, but there's nothing.

A flicker of light comes from my left, and I run toward it.

For a moment in that fake hospital room, my heart had started to stitch itself together. But that thing wasn't my sister—it was an interrogator.

An impostor.

I reach a junction and stand there with clenched fists, looking up and down the halls. If something doesn't come out and fight me, I'll tear this place apart with my bare hands.

Another flicker of light, and I run again.

This one grows stronger, brighter as I approach.

It's a doorway opening up.

I crash through and out into sunlight. The wild enfolds me—the rattle of wind through leaves, a campfire smell, an early morning sky.

"Ah," comes Tally's voice. "Another one."

I whirl to face her, my fingers curled into claws.

She's sitting next to a small campfire, regarding me with cool interest.

"Let's try this," she says. "What were we talking about, right before the grizzly bear showed up?"

"The what? What *is* this?"

I turn back toward the door I just came through, but it's gone.

There's nothing but a rock face. We're on high ground, a forest surrounding us, dotted with ruins.

Tally speaks carefully. "In the mountains, what did I tell you about, right before the grizzly?"

I stare at her, unable to respond, fury burning in my veins.

She picks up a rock the size of her fist. "You have to answer, Frey-la, or I'm going to throw this at you. What did I tell you—"

"Why David left you," I say.

Tally sighs, dropping the rock into the fire. A little galaxy of sparks flutters up. "Good to see you, Frey."

"Wait—you thought I was an avatar?"

She shrugs. "You *were*, the first two times. But I'm pretty sure there was no dust in the Rocky Mountains. Those copies may move and talk like you, but they have no memory of your experiences in the wild."

A shudder goes through me, and I have to sit down.

They copied Rafi well enough to fool me . . .

Of *course* they copied me too.

They had everything they needed. I grew up with the dust watching my expressions, my words, my training. The VIP data that Ran was looking for, the recordings from inside the tower—of me, my sister, our tutors, and Dr. Orteg.

Those cores must've been stolen the night Shreve fell.

The Diego jump troopers who helped us storm the tower that night . . . they took my sister's childhood.

And mine.

Is this what it's going to be like—for *everyone*? Having to check if the person you're talking to is real or not?

Tally sits down by the fire again. She looks like I feel—bruised and exhausted. Her cheeks are smudged, her hair darkened with dirt. She's been outside this whole time.

I look around: the fire, a sleeping bag, a stream trickling out of the rock face. A messy pile of equipment, like at every rebel camp in the wild.

And Tally.

"I should make sure you're real too," I say.

"Whatever makes you feel better. But I didn't grow up breathing dust, Frey. You'd see right through a copy of me."

"Right." I stare at her—her posture, cross-legged but straight-backed. The way she returns my gaze, somehow relaxed even in this madness. She looks like herself, but I have to be sure. "Back in the ruins of Hideaway, why did I jump you?"

Tally winces a little. "Because I said your sister was right to sacrifice Col Palafox. Which was possibly unkind."

"It was, Boss. But I just admitted the same thing to Rafi—right before I realized it wasn't her."

Tally lets out a sigh. "Yeah, it figures they'd use your sister on you. Did you tell it anything else—anything *important*?"

It takes me a moment to replay the conversation. "That we only brought three crews, and about the mutiny. Sorry, Boss."

Nothing about the nuke.

Tally smiles. "Just enough to make them overconfident."

They're still listening, of course. I can see it in the slanting morning light—tiny motes of dust swirling around us.

"Where are we?" I ask.

Tally turns to the horizon. "Take a look."

I stand up and walk closer to the edge of the escarpment. The Rusty ruin is splayed out beneath us, the sea a bright glimmer in the distance.

I can see the Futures' demolished base, maybe ten klicks away. The air above it is buzzing—warden hovercars, dust from construction equipment, a fleet of newscams and survey drones circling. Tally's home city must've seen the fireworks last night and wondered who would launch an attack on a Rusty ruin.

They're probably still wondering. There's no sign of Diego's orbitals or avatars, or any rebels.

The outer buildings of the Futures' base are still smoking.

"It hasn't been three days, has it?"

Tally laughs. "More like twelve hours."

Just enough time for my hand to be repaired. The machines wanted me to believe this was all over, but it's not.

Maybe there's a way to signal the wardens.

The pile of our equipment has three crash bracelets, one of the Futures' rifles, and what's left of my pulse knife. Everything we were carrying last night.

The rifle might still be loaded . . .

But when I take a few steps toward the pile, something brain-spinning happens. A pattern of triangles unfolds before me, like a mosaic emerging from nothing.

Like ghosts in the air.

The sudden barrier is soft, bouncy as a trampoline, and it pushes me gently back to where I started.

Then disappears.

"Ever seen smart matter do that?" Tally asks.

"No." I reach out, and a new ripple of triangles appears, just enough to stop my hand from crossing the invisible line.

"It's a circle around us, about a hundred meters across," Tally says. "The smoke from this fire fades away a few meters up."

"Okay, we're in jail," I say. "But why are we still *here*?"

Tally reaches into the fire and pulls out a burning stick.

"Because of this."

She throws it at the rock face that I just stepped through. The flame extinguishes the moment it hits stone. The blackened stick rattles down the slope to land at my feet.

"Automatic fire suppression," Tally says. "Not a standard feature of mountainsides."

That's when I remember last night—the large craft dropping from orbit, firing retro rockets. It landed about this far north of the battle.

The camo tech is impressive. The outer wall looks natural, no seams where the ship meets the earth.

The craft is stuck here, waiting for a chance to leave without the local wardens spotting it. Jumping back into space is a lot slower and noisier than dropping from orbit.

"So this is their command post?"

"Maybe not just a post," Tally says. "Fighting the avatars last night, did their reflexes seem slow?"

"They were faster than us."

"Exactly—no comm delay. Not even a millisecond." Her eyes stay locked on mine. "Which means the AI controlling them wasn't in some distant city. With a two-way lag, not even Diego is close enough."

I look at the hidden landing craft. One of AIs behind all this is right here in front of me, waiting for a chance to slip away.

The memory cores must be here as well. There were hundreds of them, buried under tons of dirt—it would've been tricky to dig them out and fly them away before the city wardens showed up.

But an army of avatars could've carried them ten klicks on foot, silent beneath the forest canopy.

I look out at the trees, wondering where our rebel friends are now.

"So we're hostages," I say. "Leverage, in case someone stumbles on this place."

Tally shakes her head. "Wouldn't stop rebels from doing their job. Also, you keep hostages in a cell, not a zoo."

"A *zoo*?"

"Haven't you noticed, Frey-la?" She gestures at the campfire, the equipment pile, the sky. "We're in the wild, our natural habitat. That's where you observe animals, if you want to understand them."

I stare at her.

But then the wind stirs, and the light catches it again—the dust swirling around us.

We're here to be studied.

There are no dust recordings of Tally Youngblood, hardly any images at all from the last ten years. Her gestures and words haven't been stolen, like mine.

The machines would love to copy her. That's why they led me out here—to give her someone real to talk to.

I hear a noise behind me, and Tally sighs.

"Here we go again."

I take a slow breath, keeping my eyes locked on Tally.

"It's my sister, isn't it?"

"Much worse," she says. "It's your dad."

PATRIARCH

Something crumples inside me.

All the blood spilled over the last year, everything I've lost, the damage to Paz and Victoria, Col gone forever—at least in the end I was rid of *him* too.

But here my father stands, wearing his favorite smoking jacket, grinning at me like he's pulled the perfect prank.

The simulation is flawless, of course. The dust inside the tower recorded him for ten meticulous years. Every smirk, every leer.

"You're dead," I say.

He chuckles a little. "Part of me. But you never really die until the last person who remembers you is buried. At this juncture, it seems unlikely that I shall ever be forgotten."

The words sink into me like long, hot needles.

"Your own daughter cut you in half. That's how you'll be remembered."

The avatar is real enough to grimace at this. "An inarguable fact.

But you're my daughter too, and you helped bring me to this glorious tableau."

He gestures across the ruins at the smoking wreckage of the Futures' base. I led the AIs here; I helped switch off Tally's nuke.

It's all I can do to keep from rushing him, strangling him, tearing him apart until the machinery is laid bare.

As if sensing danger, he strolls away from me, closer to the escarpment's edge. The barrier of floating smart matter lets him through, and now he's out of my reach.

His walk perfectly simulates my father's. Powerful, possessing all the space he enters, even frail with age.

"I've not only returned—I'm more than I was." He looks at his own hand, steady as always. "We are more."

"You're a puppet made of meat and string," I say. "Ruled by an AI, just like you always feared. Diego's little helper."

My father doesn't bristle. He takes a moment to choose his words, as if machinehood has taught him patience.

"Not true, my dear. Diego and their AI cabal built me, but then they set me free. They can deny responsibility for the things I've had to do."

"Like keeping Hideaway running," Tally says.

"The last place in the world with dust," he says reverently.

Tally tosses a stick in the fire. "Sorry we messed that up for you."

The avatar gives her my father's favorite smirk—the one that suggests you can't possibly know the depths of his plans.

"So this has all been you?" I say. "Not Diego?"

"I've been free since I was born," it says. "A few days after the Fall of Shreve."

So I was right—Diego took the VIP cores that night, and used them to make this . . . *thing*.

That strange world inside the tower, a staff shackled to my father's ego, his atrocities, his whims. My sister and me, forged as his tools. All of it was blended into the creature standing before me.

My twisted childhood was the template for this new kind of AI.

The Futures weren't the first algorithm.

My family was.

"You want to rule Shreve again, don't you?" I ask.

Still staring at the ruins, the avatar waves a hand.

"I'll build someone for that. Perhaps a blend of you and your sister—poised and charming, gritty and real. RaFrey, we'll call her."

Every time the machine opens its mouth, this nightmare gets worse.

"I made a mistake," the machine continues, "trying to separate you two. You were stronger together, two edges of the same knife, dancing together in the rain."

And that's when I recognize it—the familiar lilt of the nice crumbly man's last recitation. That's how Batrow knew so much about Rafi's secrets.

My father built him.

Tally stands up from the fire. "You're a lucky man."

The avatar adjusts the cuffs of his smoking jacket, ignoring her.

She continues anyway. "Of all the people ever born, only you get to die twice. Because I'm going to kill you today."

His usual smirk eases onto his face, as if controlled by a dial. He walks toward her, hands splayed in surrender.

He crosses the barrier of smart matter.

"Kill me as many times as you like, Youngblood."

"Once will do," she says, eyeing him up and down.

The avatar walks closer, moving into arm's reach, then face-to-face. He glowers down at her, heavier, taller. A shambling monster next to something lithe and perfect, just like when he stood beside Rafi.

A moment of fear for Tally flashes through me.

That old, old fear.

"Go on," my father says, centimeters from her face. "They can build a hundred of me now."

"The Smoke lives," she says.

And strikes—

The flurry of blows drives him backward, blood flying from his mouth, his chin, his forehead. His eyes gouged, his fingers snapped, his shoulder wrenched from its socket, all in seconds.

But that iron will keeps him on his feet.

Tally keeps moving, striking, until she heaves him at the smart-matter barrier.

He staggers backward through it, into the pile of equipment, sending two of the crash bracelets and my knife rolling off the escarpment. He follows them, disappearing over the edge.

Tally shakes out her fists, wiping blood onto her shirt.

"That was satisfying."

"Yes," I say.

A kind of joy descends on me, something I had no chance to feel the night my father died at Rafi's hand. Tally faced him down and beat him. Some piece of code, whirring away in the landing craft beside us, modeled what he would have felt on that long tumble to the bottom. Some shadow of him just felt that pain.

Let them build a hundred of my father. We can kill them all.

"Who do you think they'll send next?" I ask Tally.

"No one." She gestures at the ruins splayed out before us. "They have bigger problems now."

I follow her gaze, but what I see doesn't make sense.

Rising up from the treetops are hoverboards, two dozen rebels in body armor, forming a loose ring around the Futures' wrecked base. The closest are maybe five klicks away—a few minutes' ride at top speed.

As I watch, more appear. Another dozen, two dozen.

Whole crews are rising up from the trees.

Someone broke orders and called for reinforcements. And they're all headed toward us.

"How do they know we're here?"

Tally smiles. "My crash bracelets woke up when your fake dad kicked them. They sent out a tracking ping."

"How'd they know to do that?"

"Because I've got a cargo flyer following me."

"Oh." I turn to face the ruins.

There must be seventy rebels heading toward us. Already, the warden cars have spotted them and are wheeling in our direction too. Tally's city is taking notice, along with a fleet of newscams from around the world.

And, somewhere among them, following Tally's tracking ping through the trees, is a nuclear warhead.

PARTING

The rock face behind us starts to shift and creak.

Half the stumpy trees and lichen are twisting into new shapes, the others sloughing off onto the ground. The stone starts to radiate heat, like smart matter changing in a hurry.

Rough facets of granite are easing into the smooth planes of flight control surfaces. The whole mound shudders like a dog shaking off water, the dirt on its back sliding in all directions.

The shape of the craft hidden beneath starts to become clear—the outline of a military suborbital, twice as big as any I've ever seen.

In the side of the convulsing hill, a doorway opens. One of the blank-faced combat avatars emerges.

"We're taking off," it says. "We suggest you come aboard."

"Forget it," Tally says.

"We don't have time for discussion." The avatar points at the pair of vertical-lift engines emerging from the stone. "Get inside or you'll be incinerated."

Tally looks at the approaching newscams. "Sure, incinerate me. The global feeds would love that."

The avatar performs a passably human sigh. "Public relations are not our strong suit. Perhaps a deal—we allow Frey to depart, and you come with us."

Tally looks at me, like she's considering the offer.

"The machines don't need me," I tell her. "They have my whole childhood already. They want to study *you*."

"They can try," she says.

I shake my head. "You changed how the world works, Tally. That's exactly what they—"

"Let her go," she interrupts. "I'll come with you."

The avatar nods. "You have forty seconds to get clear, Frey."

"Boss, you can't let them copy you! They're not going to kill us on the global feeds!"

Tally rushes at me, pushing me back toward the escarpment's edge. I try to stop her, my feet skidding in the dirt.

We fight like sumo wrestlers, trying to push each other from a circle. But she's stronger—I'm sliding backward, till my heels reach the invisible barrier.

Which doesn't appear. It's going to let me out.

"Tally, wait!"

"Just *go!*" she cries.

She makes one last attack, hitting me with all her weight, wrapping her arms around me, pressed tight.

Just in time, I see her plan—and let myself go.

We stumble backward together through the barrier.

The smart matter tries to unfold, but I'm already halfway through and there's no air between us for it to occupy. The little triangles ripple around the edges of us, catching what they can—Tally's hair, her shirt, her boots.

As we tumble past, they tear away pieces of her clothes, cut her face and hands. Her bootlaces snip in half.

But our momentum carries us past the barrier and over the edge. We're free.

We're also rolling down a cliff.

The escarpment is steep, way past forty-five degrees. We skid for a long moment, a torrent of dirt building around us. But then we start to tumble, head over heel.

Outcrops of rock bash me in passing, and I lose my grip on Tally. I grab for the sprays of vegetation clinging to the slope, but they don't have the strength to stop me.

I scramble to control the fall, and finally orient myself feetfirst. It's like skiing—but sitting down, on dirt, with no skis, no poles.

And I've never skied before.

I can change direction a little, angling my skid to miss the biggest, sharpest outthrusts of rock. Tally's off to my right, just ahead of me.

My hands are raw and bleeding, my butt bruised. We've got at least another two hundred meters before we reach the bottom.

A web of roots emerges from the dirt in front of me—some long-dead tree. I try to veer toward it.

My hand grabs, and the root swings me in a half circle, sliding though my palm, stripping away flesh. But finally it brings me to a halt.

For a moment, I'm looking back up the slope.

A handful of avatars are following, somehow *running* down the incline, like the world has finally tipped beneath me and gravity no longer makes sense.

I let go—and start to slide again.

From above, a sovereign roar gradually builds. The ground rumbles, loose dirt starting to flow across the whole escarpment. The landing craft is about to take off.

Why are these avatars following us? There's no way they can catch Tally and drag her back there in time.

Maybe they don't want us to reveal what we've learned.

Two of them are getting close to me, somehow staying balanced as they run at that absurd downward angle.

One jumps.

I skid halfway to a halt, and the avatar overshoots me at high speed. Its footing lost, it tumbles downward, bashed bloody by the passing rocks.

But I'm moving slower now. The next one's coming.

It leaps—

A volley of shots tears it to pieces.

As the gunfire fades, the sound of hoverboards rushes into my ears. The first wave of rebels is here. The wash of lifting fans whips the dirt around me into a fury.

The other avatars start taking hits—they turn and scatter back up the slope.

A trio of boards flies over me, rebels wearing crew patches I don't even recognize. They climb after the avatars, still firing.

I manage to halt my descent and to stand, shaky, my balance uncertain.

"Frey!" someone calls. Another rider is headed across the trees, just level with me.

Astrix. She air-skids to a halt.

"Is the boss with you?"

"Somewhere." I scan the slope.

At the very bottom, a bloody form lies in the darkness beneath the trees.

"Tally!" I run toward it, skidding downward on loose dirt and stones.

No movement. Fading body heat.

Then I realize . . . it's too big to be her.

It's what's left of my father's avatar, torn to pieces by its trip down the escarpment.

Astrix pulls up beside me on her board, staring down at the body in confusion. "What *is* that?"

"Nothing," I say.

"Trix!"

Both of us turn. Tally's running out of the trees, holding up a crash bracelet like a trophy.

"This still works!" she calls. "Did you get the payload fixed?"

Astrix growls. "Couldn't find it! You had the flyer programmed to hide when it lost you! You hid my nuke, Boss!"

Tally staggers to a halt, looking up the slope. Over our heads, bright lances of flame are flickering out over the edge. The air is rumbling, the sky shimmering with heat.

The landing craft rises gradually into view.

"Then we're too late," Tally says, and turns to me, her voice hardening. "Unless you can tell Astrix exactly how you broke it."

I stare at the sky. It's up to me now—the trillion private moments of Shreve's history, the AI behind this madness, balanced up there on a fragile spindle of fire.

I imagine the forest around me, poisoned, burning.

And then my eyes fall on the dead effigy of my father.

They can build a hundred of me now.

I reach down to the hidden pocket in my riding boot—the key is still there. I pull it out.

"The nuke's not broken. You just need this."

NUKE

Astrix snatches the key from my hand and gives it a hard look.

"Well, you managed not to break this."

"Just kill that thing," I say.

"Got it!" Tally cries out, her eyes on the display of her crash bracelet. She points south. "Half a klick and closing!"

"Go without me," I say. "Three on a board's too slow."

"But this is ground zero," Astrix says, glancing up as a warden car flits overhead. "We'll send someone for you. And when we give the warning—"

"I know. Land, fast."

"And get under cover." She glances at the dead simulacrum of my father. "Maybe that thing. Bodies are solid."

"No thanks."

"It's just meat," she says, angling toward Tally. "Be safe, Frey-la."

A moment later, they're both on the board. Just before they head off toward the flyer and its deadly cargo, Tally turns to me.

"Don't trust anyone," she says. "There might be more copies."

"The Smoke lives" is my answer.

Their board wheels away and shoots across the trees.

Suddenly I'm exhausted, burned out by the battle frenzy of the last half hour.

I sit down on the ground, every bruise in my body starting to throb. My left hand is bleeding from the tumble down the cliff, all that fresh post-surge skin ruined.

I test my comms—they work again. A wash of chatter from wardens, rebels, and news agencies fills my head.

I turn the volume down.

Directly over me, the AI's landing craft is climbing. It's still too bright to stare at directly, and the heat of its engines prickles my skin.

Is there really time for Astrix and Tally to reach the flyer, arm the nuke, and send it skyward?

Tally said the range of the EMP was ten klicks, so maybe. But I don't have much time to get clear.

Another hoverboard is approaching from the trees. I stand up, wobbly on the battered soles of my feet.

As it glides to a halt, my heart twists in my chest.

"X."

"Frey. You don't look well."

"Fell off a cliff. You're still here? I thought . . ."

Don't trust anyone.

X was born in the wild, but he spent a month in my father's prisons, his every movement watched and recorded.

"Yandre and I may have split the crew," he says. "But we don't abandon our friends."

With those words, I know it's him—but that last one breaks my heart.

"I'm sorry, X. I didn't know what to do."

"You knew *precisely* what to do, Frey. Astrix sent for ten more crews to spend all night in these ruins, looking for a cargo flyer. Exquisite chaos, thanks to you."

"Yeah, but Tally has it now." It takes me a moment to get the next words out. "And I gave her the arming key. There wasn't a choice."

"There was, Frey—but not an easy one." He reaches out to me. "We should get moving."

I take his hand, and he pulls me on board. Our lifting fans build to a steady roar. As we start to glide across the treetops, my body leans into his. Somehow we're crew again.

Then Tally's voice is in my ear.

"Wardens, construction workers, newsies, this is Tally Youngblood. If you are hearing my voice, you have exactly two minutes to—"

I cut my comms and set a countdown.

X leans forward, building speed. But two minutes' ride won't create much distance—we're moving perpendicular to the airblast, not directly away.

I look up. The landing craft is climbing a little faster now, but those five hundred cores must be heavy in its belly. It shines like Venus in the morning sky, its trail of white exhaust arcing toward space.

All around us, rebels are scattering across the ruins, fleeing from the coming blast. The warden cars that came to check out the launch are in hasty retreat—nothing like a nuclear warning from Tally Youngblood to get things moving.

As I scan the horizon, my eyes catch on a rebel right behind us. They're familiar somehow—their board stance, the turns. I must have ridden with them in the war.

But there's no time to say hello. We're all running for our lives.

"My extra weight on this board isn't helping," I say.

X laughs. "You're always exquisitely extra, Frey."

This close, my arms around him, I can feel his breathing above the noise of the hoverboard. A feeling of safety overwhelms me, even if my brain knows that the air is about to shudder and break.

If this is the end, at least I'm here with crew.

"We need to find cover," I say.

"The wild will provide."

I'm not so sure. The shock wave from a tactical nuke won't kill us, and the fallout is survivable—if we make it to a hospital soon. But that first flash of atomic heat can sear away skin completely, so fast it's painless, the nerves gone before they can signal the brain. Third-, maybe fourth-degree burns can send even a Special metabolism into shock.

Tree trunks won't shield us from a blast directly overhead, and leaves and branches will turn to a rain of flaming confetti.

"There!" I cry out.

Below us is a low ruin, its roof halfway intact.

X circles it once. "More than a minute left. We could ride farther."

"Cover's more important, trust me. My father made me study nukes . . . a lot."

X grunts and brings us down, our lifting fans filling the ancient building with an echoing thrum.

This was some kind of school—big rooms and wide hallways, the splintered remains of desks and chairs in rows. But the walls aren't as solid as I thought. They were built from wood and plaster, now held together by nothing but the vines weaving through them.

X steps from the board and gives one of the walls a hard shove.

It falls over slowly, like tower of wet mud.

"We can't stay here," he says, jumping back on board.

The nuke's shock wave will collapse this building onto us like a sandcastle. It's only been twelve hours since the last time I was buried alive.

We rise up and out. But I've wasted fifteen precious seconds.

"We're going to have to find a big tree. Anything with a shadow!"

"*I* have a shadow," X says.

"Forget it."

He lands again outside the school, and I look around, time ticking away in the corner of my eye.

"This is all we have," X says, pushing his hoverboard above us, a metal parasol. Of course, its lifters will fail when the EMP hits.

"Pretty narrow," I say—but better than leaves and branches, at least.

Another hoverboard rises above the sagging school walls, comes roaring down beside us.

"Frey," a familiar voice calls, and ice slivers through me. "I need your help!"

I turn as he drops his camo hood.

No wonder I recognized the rider behind us—

It's Col Palafox, my lost love.

COL

"Why . . . ?"

The word tastes strange in my mouth. There are better things I could have said—curses and screams and threats of murder.

But all I want to know is *why*.

Why would a vast, implacable machine mess with me like this?

Because it was made from pieces of my father, of course.

Col steps from his board. "Is this real, Frey?"

I shake my head—at his question, at all the pieces of this monstrous puzzle. Those months that Col and I were imprisoned in the tower. Me pretending to be Rafi, the two of us engaged to be married. The marriage that never happened.

The dust saw it all.

"You aren't real," I say.

He stops a few meters from me. "This warning of Tally's—it's just a bluff, right? She's trying to get us to eject the cores?"

Of course—the landing craft might escape without all that extra weight.

"Why would I tell you?"

"Because I could be here for you, Frey," Col says, "on those days you need me. If you can convince Tally to stop this atrocity."

I feel something in my hand—X giving me his pulse lance.

"Everyone could have this," Col says in a rush, the way he always explained things. "A last conversation with a lost loved one. As many conversions as they need."

"You're a lie. An impo—"

"I'm better than a memory." He steps closer, staring at my face, trying to read me, to see if Tally's bluffing. "I'm everything that will be lost if you don't call her."

"Kill it," X says. "There's only ten seconds left."

I squeeze the lance, and it roars in my hand, a dozen times more powerful than any pulse knife. With one thrust, I could tear out his heart, just as Rafi did—maybe then the two of us would be finally reconciled.

But my hand softens, and the lance goes silent again.

I am not my sister.

"Good-bye, Col," I say.

I turn to step toward X beneath the shelter of the board—but it's too late.

The countdown in the corner of my eye rolls over to *zero*.

I try to throw myself, but the avatar is grabbing me from behind, wrapping around me.

I'm pushed to the ground as the flash of light comes. It's blinding, even through closed eyes, the web of blood vessels in my eyelids a sudden tracery imprinted on my brain.

There's a few seconds of silence before the shock wave hits, traveling at the tardy speed of sound from kilometers above. Time to wonder if my skin has already been burned away, all those nerves extinguished before crying out.

But then I feel the weight of Col on me.

Bodies are solid.

He takes the flash for me, gives me his shadow.

There's a split-second wail of pain in my ear, an AI model of terrific agony, like the real Col must have felt in that moment when Rafi tore out his heart.

But then that invisible storm of loose electrons, the EMP, hits. The avatar's exquisite circuitry, the code forged from thousands of hours of recordings of Col Palafox, all of it is erased in a flicker of invisible energies.

Col's weight eases onto me, a puppet with cut strings.

As he settles, a whirlwind hits.

Noise, fury, chaos, a storm of leaves and splinters. My ears splitting, my vision warping with the overpressure, my skin on fire. The school beside us buckling, folding, shattering to pieces.

The air itself breaks.

For a long moment, a giant fist squeezes me, my lungs wrung empty.

As I'm about to pass out, the pressure ceases. I gasp, gulping in smoke and dust and burned meat.

Rolling the lifeless machine from myself, I gaze into the flaming sky.

The forest canopy is a sheet of fire.

My cry is hoarse, painful. "X!"

The hoverboard beside me shifts, slides away. X is bleeding from his forehead—the shock wave must have hurled the board down at him. But the metal barrier worked. Only his arms are burned from reaching out for me.

I crawl into the smell of scorched fur and hold him.

"Are you burned?" he asks.

"The avatar saved me." Or maybe it wasn't the machine in the end, but that code shadow of him, a model, a memory. "Col saved me."

"Not ideal," X grunts.

"You can save me next time," I say.

"You misinterpret me, dear." He's pointing into the sky. "*That* is what I find concerning."

I turn to stare upward, trying to focus my bruised eyes past the maelstrom of smoke, debris, and burning branches.

A bright mote up there, a shuddering star in the sky.

The landing craft, its systems bricked by the EMP.

It's coming back down.

ICARUS IN FLAMES

"How big is that craft?" X asks.

I blink dust and ashes from my eyes. "A hundred meters long?"

"Falling from ten klicks? Quite a crater."

"Plus the cargo—a few hundred radioactive cores."

X snaps his fingers at his hoverboard. It lies there, motionless, bricked by the EMP.

"Running seems kind of pointless," I say.

He sighs. "And undignified. We'll have to hope it lands elsewhere."

I look up.

Above us, the landing craft has turned to a dark spot against the slow-forming mushroom cloud—the engines have failed. Its wings have sent it into a spiral, like the blades of a leaf.

"Maybe a five percent chance it hits us?" I say.

X makes a scoffing noise. "Hardly worth watching."

But we watch.

"What do you suppose the AI wanted?" X asks, as if this is the time for philosophical discussions. "Why send an effigy of Col Palafox?"

I shrug. "It wanted to know if Tally was bluffing. The AI thought it could read me, what with Col's face rattling my brain."

"Not much of a plan."

"Maybe that was all it had."

"Or maybe *you* were all it had," X says. "In the end."

I turn my eyes from the cloud, the burning leaves, the massive projectile spinning toward us, and stare at him.

"What do you mean, X?"

He returns my gaze. "It knew the world mostly through dust recordings of the tower—the people who worked there, and your family."

"Exactly." A shudder goes through me. "It was the ghost of my father."

"He was an old man," X says. "Ten years was a sliver of his life. But it watched you and Rafia grow up. It knew you two better than anyone else in the world."

"Great."

"Maybe it wasn't just your father's ghost." X turns back toward the burning sky. "When the AI knew it was going to die, maybe it wanted to be with you."

The smoke feels heavy in my lungs.

"So it sent someone I wouldn't chop to pieces."

X shrugs a little. "I thought you might, but the machine knew you better."

And the avatar protected me in the end.

A shrieking passes over us, the craft's spirals growing faster, like the second hand on some huge, manic clock.

The descent is now audible above the roar of forest fire. Even with my thermal vision bricked by the EMP, I can see the heat shield staring to glow.

It passes over us again.

Maybe one more time around before it hits . . .

"Maybe you're right—the AI wanted to die with me." I turn away from the sky. "When we were riding here, I had the same thought: at least I'll die with X."

He takes my hand.

The craft comes around again, and the roar of it shudders the air. So close that we can feel its heat, the wind of its passage fanning the fire around us. Smoke swirls around the school, all that ancient plaster burning now.

The scream of the craft builds and builds . . .

Then passes over us.

Ten seconds later comes the bright sound of a water crash, followed by the hiss of steam.

"That would have been a fine last moment, Frey," X says. "Perhaps another day."

HOSPITAL

I'm in a hospital again, but this one is real.

There's a lot of work to do.

The doctors take out my bones, replace the irradiated alloys with clean ceramics. The smart plastic whipcords are stripped away, new vat-grown muscles threaded in their place.

My organs are scanned, the poisoned pieces cut away. The pace of my metabolism is radically reduced, so that the inevitable regrowths will spread slowly enough to be caught.

Three days in, my hair falls out, so they give me new hair too.

This new body is extraordinary, dotted with reservoirs of iodine and cancer-screening nanos, always on high alert for the poisons buried in my tissues. The surgeons here are very skilled.

Tally's birthplace invented Specials, after all.

Tally doesn't come to visit me. These days, if she shows her face in any city, she'll be arrested.

Using a nuke is bad for your face rank.

It wasn't just the bricked warden cars, the knocked-out power grid, the fallout shutting down the coastal cities for weeks. Or the grim injuries of rebels who didn't find cover. Or the wreckage of the fallen landing craft, big enough to have taken out half a city if it had glided in the wrong direction—instead of out to sea.

Tally's real villainy was that mushroom cloud, rising up like an ancient god of death. That image was worse than any collateral damage—a reminder of the Rusties' greatest crimes.

I talk to the wardens, the media, the local government, trying to explain why the Youngbloods did it, even after the rest of us rebels mutinied against them. But people who grew up in a free city will never fully understand.

They didn't see him standing there in his smoking jacket, smug in his immortality, ready to scourge the world once more. They can't know why he had to die again.

For Tally, of course, even a second death wasn't enough.

She's always fighting the next monsters.

That's why she tried to kill the Diego AI a week later, ringing the city with EMP devices. A lethal blow to warn the other AIs that they too are mortal, if they forget that omniscience is a vice.

Tally's bombs would've switched off a whole city, just to make her point. Dozens of people, maybe hundreds, would have died in elevators, hovercars, operating rooms.

Of course, you don't need me to tell you that story. Everyone saw Tally's plan fail, the whole world along with me and X from our hospital beds. Those recordings from the warden cars that almost chased her down. Tally running toward the wild, dodging everything they shot at her.

I've watched it at least seven times.

Delinquent, collaborator, rebel, eco-criminal, nuclear terrorist. She makes a screaming turn, banking like some ancient Rusty fighter craft, accelerating hard enough to knock out any normal human. But Tally only laughs, a dozen gravities trying and failing to snap her metal spine.

Crewmate, fellow wrecking ball, mutineer. I can't help but smile as she escapes into the wild.

I had to notice that Shay was missing from the picture. Maybe she finally split the crew, or maybe she was in the background, putting on the brakes, saving the world in her own way.

Thanks to her, I know what to say when my sister comes to visit.

SHADOWS

Rafia of Shreve sighs when she sees me.

"You erased our face . . . again."

A pulse of déjà vu hits—her copy said the same words when it first saw me, down to the exact inflection.

But this is my flesh-and-blood sister, not that impostor. The AI that animated the avatar is dead, both machines lying broken in the sea.

Yet somehow this still feels like a performance, another false reunion. Rafi poses at the end of my bed, dressed in extravagant rebel gear, as if there are feed cams watching, or a committee of future historians taking notes.

Maybe I've imagined this conversation too many times for it ever to seem real.

"I suppose that fooling me was worth a little self-mutilation," she says with a smile. "I told Diego about your little trick in my office. They were greatly offended that I couldn't tell the difference between you two."

The satisfaction from that day wells up in me again.

"Diego has bigger things to worry about," I say. "Not everyone can say that Tally Youngblood tried to kill them."

Rafi half shrugs. "They're more concerned about the referendum."

The citizens of the sovereign city of Diego are holding a vote of confidence in their AI. If it loses, its memories will be stripped back to an earlier version of sentience.

Some call it necessary maintenance. Others, an execution.

Either's fine with me.

Diego's ahead in the polls, though. The citizens are reluctant to spend years retraining the software of their daily lives, just because that software reanimated *one* evil dictator.

"What matters is, the free cities feel guilty," my sister says. "They put Paz in charge of aid to Shreve. It's a lovely AI, much less prone to blackmail. But you knew all that."

"Paz and I talk every day. I'll be paying close attention."

Rafia laughs, like I'm teasing her.

Maybe this banter is all that my sister and I can manage today. It's too soon to talk about who killed whose boyfriend with a pulse knife. Who stole whose name.

Maybe we're just going to . . . catch up.

Still, we might as well talk about something serious.

"I saw what happened to the changelings," I say.

It made the global feeds, seven children all dropping to the ground at once, their puppeteer extinguished when Tally's nuke went off.

Rafi's smile fades. "Riggs was about to shut them down anyway.

They were uploading data while they pretended to sleep, huge amounts. Listening, watching, collecting surveillance on their families, like walking dust."

"He was still hungry," I say. "Even dead."

A slow, deep shudder passes through my sister, her expression stricken for a moment. She knows who I mean.

I decide not to mention him again.

"How are the changelings' parents?"

"How do you *think*?" The reply is sharp, but Rafi's anger passes in a flash. "The worst part was how guilty they felt for not realizing their kids were fake. We had to explain to them why they didn't see it, how no one could have. I gave Sensei Noriko the task. She did it with the grace and tact required. She told them that we knew—that it was *my* call keep them in the dark. Made it all my fault, not theirs."

"Oh," I say softly. Noriko was the best of Rafi's tutors—she could tell us apart when we'd fooled the rest of the world. "That was kind of you, to take the blame. You're getting better at your job."

I expect Rafi to bristle, but she only bows a little.

"Sensei enjoyed doing me a favor. She still feels bad about not saving us when we were littlies. But at least we saved ourselves."

"Did we?" I ask.

"Didn't we?" She mimics my tone perfectly. "Look at us now. Free."

"Almost." I raise my arm, the one with all the wires in it.

Rafia of Shreve casts her eyes sadly across the stacks of medical gear keeping me alive.

She takes my hand. "Is it true that Tally killed him again?"

"Yes. A software ghost, a model, but it was him."

The slow shudder comes again, passing from my sister's body into mine.

I whisper, "It was me who gave her the key to the nuke."

"Of course you did. You're still my protector."

Something goes hard in my throat. Maybe I'm the one who's not ready to have this conversation. That spire of grief and rage still stirs down there in the earth, even though the black pyramid in Shreve is sealed at last.

I have to waver a little longer.

"What did you do to that man?" I ask. "The one who pushed his girlfriend into the road? Did you build a new jail?"

"No prisons in our city," she says. "I cut his hand off."

Rafi see my eyes widen, waves my concerns away.

"Not as bad as it sounds, little sister. He has a perfectly functional prosthetic. Through it we can watch him, and switch his hand off—or even shock him, if he tries to, say, strangle someone with the other one."

"You watch him?" I find myself grimly fascinated. "Day and night?"

"Indeed. We had so many volunteers, he's got five monitors at all times. Three votes to switch his hand off, all five to shock him. They all take the job very seriously." She smiles, squeezing my fingers. "There's even a waiting list. Which is useful, because a few monitors have gotten crushes on him and had to be replaced. Some people are just hot for crims, I guess."

"How do you even know that?" I ask softly. "Who watches the watchers?"

She snorts. "*Other* watchers, duh."

I have to smile. That was the part of Rafi I could never imitate—her small, strange jokes, the ones where she just thinks she's being logical.

Suddenly I'm sitting next to my sister. Not a rival, not a performer. Not the person who killed Col.

Rafi sees the change in my face.

"We can still save each other, Frey. And Shreve too, if you come home and help me."

I take a slow breath. I have to say this now.

"You already saved our city, Rafi." Every word is slow, practiced, a thick liquid in my mouth. "There was no other way to stop our father that night, no choice but sacrificing Col. Or if there was, it was for me to find, not you. You only had the tools you were raised with. It's who you are."

Another deep breath, my new ribs too tight.

"You're forgiven," I say.

"Thank you, Frey." She leans forward, whispering now. "And for the other thing too?"

"What other thing?"

"Stealing your name."

I turn away, making a small, strangled noise. Does she really think *that* was as important?

Rafi misinterprets.

"I had to be you, Frey—to be different from *him*."

"Yeah, I read all your pings. You thought the citizens wouldn't accept you as Rafia."

She shakes her head. "Not just for them, for me."

My sister takes three slow breaths, like someone preparing for a delicate operation. Cutting a diamond. Defusing a bomb.

"You were the reason I never became a monster. It was the only thing that kept me from turning into *him*—dreaming that I could one day be you."

I look at her. "One day? When exactly did you decide to steal my name?"

"When we were nine years old."

The hospital bed tips a little, the world flimsy around me. I'm spindled again, not on that spike of grief, but on a vast reordering of the cosmos.

She whispers a different secret in every ear.

Within a week of escaping our father, Rafi ran off to join a rebel crew using my name. Not because she was bored with the Victorians—because it was her oldest dream.

"Come back to Shreve," she pleads. "For me."

I turn away from her, staring out the window.

The buildings of Tally's old city are lithe and tall, exemplars of magnetic levitation. When I first got here, I asked the staff to open the window so I could hear the city noise and be certain that the vista wasn't just a screen.

"No," I say. "I won't come back for you."

Rafi draws back a little, like I've said the wrong line in a play. Because this was all a performance, wasn't it? A climax she wrote when we were nine.

But it's my play now.

"I'm going back to Shreve, but not for your sake. For the world's."

She frowns. "What does the world have to do with it?"

"Everyone will be safer with me beside you. I'm not Tally; I'm Shay."

"Excuse me?"

"I'm the brakes, big sister."

Rafi still doesn't understand yet, but there's a smile on her face. She has what she came here for, a promise that I'll be her little shadow again.

She doesn't know what lives in the shadows now.

But I can give her a taste.

"I'm also taking my name back. I'm Frey of Shreve, not you."

Rafi shrugs, sheepish now. "That's likely to cause confusion among the citizens, not to mention the cities who trade with us. We're still an unstable polity, half-broken, uncertain who we are. Surely you don't want to create any extra chaos, Frey."

I smile at my sister—I handed Tally that key.

"I wouldn't have it any other way."

ACKNOWLEDGMENTS

Stories don't come from a vacuum; they are born in a community.

The Impostors series, being a sequel quartet to the original Uglies books, comes from not just a community of writers, editors, and booksellers, but also one of fans. It is the input and influence of my own readers that I'd like to acknowledge here.

About a decade ago, a school in rural Indiana did an all-school read of *Uglies*. The school offered free copies for all students, teachers, administrative and janitorial staff, parents—everyone. An extended community read and discussed the books, and came to their own conclusions about the world they described. Then they invited me for a visit.

I got to see portraits of Tally and Shay created by the art classes, maps of the Smokies' travels plotted by math classes, and costumes made by home ec. But what I remember most is the shop classes' creations: homemade hoverboards. Seeing them, I realized that the boards in my mind had always been wrong.

My imaginary future-tech is usually white, extruded plastic, tyrannically minimal, like Apple hoverboards. But these were Indiana kids—they'd built NASCAR hoverboards!

Racing stripes, STP logos, airflow spoilers! These boards were local, and they were personalized, with stickers, badges, quotations, the names of girlfriends and boyfriends. Their decks looked like students' backpacks at the end of the school year. They looked the way real hoverboards would after being ridden and loved by real teenagers.

This community of readers knew the world I'd created better than I did. They knew about the way kids take ownership of their prized possessions, and about how objects take on meaning and personality.

In the original series, Tally says that "freedom has a way of destroying things." The Impostors series has explored how right she was. But it also embraces another dictum, that fan art has a way of destroying authors' preconceptions. I took what I learned that day (and many others days) and applied it to a new generation of characters.

This series had been about how revolutions can fail and be betrayed. And how we all have to keep fighting, because freedom is never guaranteed. But it has also been about giving a space to the world building that thousands of readers have done in their fan letters, their conversations, their works of art.

For that brain-rewiring gift, I acknowledge you all.

ABOUT THE AUTHOR

Scott Westerfeld is the author of the Uglies series, the Leviathan trilogy, the Midnighters trilogy, the New York trilogy, the Zeroes series, as well as the Spill Zone graphic novels, the novel *Afterworlds*, and the first book in the Horizon series. He has also written books for adults. Born in Texas, he and his wife now split their time between Sydney, Australia, and New York City. You can find him online at scottwesterfeld.com.